THE LOST FRÄULEIN

THE LOST FRÄULEIN

HAAS, BEN

BY [RICHARD MEADE]

RANDOM HOUSE/NEW YORK

C. 1

PART ONE: JUNE

Romance and intrigue surround an
international munitions dealer when
he becomes involved in an African revolution.

CHAPTER 1

THE HIGHWAY WEST from San Antonio was dead level, straight as an engineer's tape. Its pavement shimmered in the ferocious noonday heat in which nothing stirred except the speedy little ground birds called roadrunners. On either side, vast jungles of thorned brush—mesquite, prickly pear, cholla and yucca—spread across the overgrazed and desolate land; and the fences seemed endless. John Allison drove the rented car flat-out, eager to reach Del Rio, to have a cooling shower and a rest before he met with General Marc.

Nothing, he thought, had really changed in this part of Texas since his childhood. This was still the same raw, wild, spacious land in which he'd grown up, unaware then that someday he would travel and live in lands and circumstances unimaginably different, dealing on equal terms with prime ministers, generals, presidents, dictators—and rebel chieftains. He tried to feel some nostalgia for that bygone past; but it was difficult. The tall, muscular man edging into his forties, black hair frosted with gray, suit beautifully cut by his London tailors, was such an entirely different person from the raw, provincial ranch boy of twenty-five years ago that it was almost impossible to make a connection between them. That youth had seldom been outside his home county except for hunting trips; the president of Allison Trading Company had offices in New York, London, Bonn, Vienna, Montevideo and Beirut. The young Allison had been dirt-poor; the mature one had a personal worth of more than two million dollars. In fact, Allison thought, the only link,

3

the only continuing thread, between the boy and man was guns. The young Allison had been raised in the frontier tradition of loving fine weapons and using them expertly; the older Allison was one of the largest independent brokers of military weapons in the world, prepared to furnish to the highest bidder anything from a pistol small enough to be concealed in the palm to a bomber capable of laying nuclear eggs. No, there was simply too much distance to bridge between the child and man. Besides, the self-indulgence of nostalgia and sentiment was unprofitable: look at those damned Sherman tanks.

That, Allison thought, was one thing about driving across Texas; its very endlessness gave you almost too much opportunity to think about your problems; and while the twenty Shermans were a comparatively minor one, they had come back to haunt him on this drive. He did not like to make mistakes, especially mistakes that cost him money; and buying the Shermans had been a mistake.

It had indeed been an act of sentiment. Allison and a girl— this had been early last winter, and he could not immediately recall her name—had been driving back to New York from a long ski weekend. And when Allison had seen the old iron ghost, her squat ugliness almost obscured by snow and ice, parked in front of the National Guard Armory of a little upstate town, he had brought the car to a halt so sudden that his companion had been thrown against the seatbelt. Then, while she fumed in incomprehending impatience, Allison had got out and walked around the tank.

Over twenty feet long, more than ten high, she weighed in at better than thirty tons. On a good day in her youth she should have been able to exceed twenty-five miles an hour, and she carried two light machine guns and one heavy one in addition to her 76-mm. cannon. With all that, by modern standards she was puny, undergunned and passé—but she and her sisters had crushed Rommel at El Alamein, helped seize the Pacific bastions of the Japanese, and slashed through France and Germany. She'd fought in Korea too, but even that was ancient history, and now she'd come to the end of the line—no longer a weapon, only a souvenir, as anachronistic in this pleasant little town as a dinosaur.

Allison had, for a long time, commanded a platoon of her kind in the Armored Cavalry; and as he walked slowly around her, half-forgotten sounds and sensations returned: the hoarse thunder of powerful engines, the roar of cannons, and most of all, the exhilaration of riding, like a man on horseback, atop thirty rolling, bucking tons of steel. Almost affectionately now, he slapped the icy flank of the steel monster. The Shermans had been good weapons in their day; damned good weapons. Honest ones, well made. There was no higher tribute a man like him could pay.

But all that had been a long time ago, and the warmth of memory was devoured quickly by the bite of the wind sweeping across the Armory lawn. He'd been about to turn back to the car when he glimpsed something that made him halt.

He kept in good shape and he'd had no trouble hoisting his nearly two hundred pounds up the ice-glazed front of the old vehicle. When he attained her deck, his height added to hers enabled him to look down into the fenced motor pool behind the Armory. There, parked in neat rows, was a company of huge new M-60's, the United States Army's present Main Battle Tank. But his eyes slid quickly over them to the twenty old Shermans like the one on which he stood, guns elevated to permit closer parking and jammed into one corner of the enclosure.

The girl, he remembered, had not been happy when he left her in the car to seek entrance into the Armory. And the first sergeant who was in there alone this Sunday afternoon, trying to catch up on paper work, had been surprised to see him. But he relaxed and quickly became cordial when Allison began to speak with the expertise of an experienced tank man. It had not taken long to bring the conversation around to the Shermans or learn their status. "Well, yes, sir," the sergeant said. "They are surplus. Sort of, anyhow."

"What do you mean?" John Allison offered the man a cigarette and took one himself.

The sergeant laughed. "Well, if you've been in service, you know how screwed up things get sometimes. We haven't used Shermans in years, but we're still charged out with them. Hell, I don't know how long we've been trying to get authority to dispose of 'em, but there's some kind of mix-up at Division or Army or in Washington, and it's never come through. Finally we just gave up and shoved 'em over in a corner."

"I guess they're pretty well junk by now," Allison said casually.

The sergeant flared. "I'll be damned! Anything that's charged to this company gets proper maintenance. Batteries are dead, of course, but charge 'em up, throw in some gas, and you could take right off in any of 'em."

"I see," Allison murmured.

Larry Moore was an ex-Congressman, a weapons expert in his own right, and John Allison's permanent Washington man, with an unlimited expense account. His knowledge of the labyrinths of the State and Defense departments and even the CIA was second only to Allison's own. What Moore did not know was what went on behind closed doors in such places on certain occasions when Allison was present. Neither did Congress, and Allison had thought wryly, back in New York, as he had waited for Moore to come on the line, if it ever found out . . . Then Moore was there.

And, as Allison had expected, his order puzzled Larry. "I want you to see Nichols in the Pentagon tomorrow. Get those twenty tanks declared surplus, released, and sold to us."

Moore hesitated. Then: "Sure, Johnny. No sweat. But— M-4's? Hell, the things are so obsolete you can't give 'em away. It's a damned poor government these days that can't have at least M-47's just for the asking; and those old Shermans won't even junk for what they'd cost you. Of course, I'll do what you say, but—"

Allison had laughed a little self-consciously. "Maybe that's it, Larry. If I don't buy 'em, they'll eventually go for junk."

"So?"

Now it was Allison's turn to hesitate. Then he said, "I don't know. I trained in the damned things. I commanded a platoon of 'em. There were times when I swore I never wanted to see one of the bastards again. But—a horse soldier wouldn't let the last twenty cavalry horses go to the glue factory if he could help it, would he?"

Moore was silent for several seconds. Then he chuckled. "Well, I'll be damned. Okay, Johnny. I'll save your cavalry horses for you."

But Moore, of course, had been right, as Allison had known all along. There was no market any longer for tanks so old, lightly gunned and obsolete, and for eight months now they had sat, carefully mothballed, parked in storage. A bad investment, the result of sentiment, not judgment; and if they weren't sold soon, Allison would have to unload them for junk. Well, charge it off to experience. He wouldn't let it happen again.

He drove on swiftly, glancing automatically from time to time in the rear-view mirror. His wariness was habitual; in this business it was impossible not to raise a bountiful crop of enemies. People, countries, bought weapons because they were threatened or wanted to threaten; either way, when you made a sale you automatically made an enemy. Most men in Allison's position would have traveled with a retinue of bodyguards, but Allison contented himself with a Colt .357 Magnum Python revolver in a shoulder holster. He was thoroughly expert with it, and to date it had been enough . . .

His thoughts raced ahead to the meeting with General Marc. He imagined it would be a waste of time; he doubted that the rebels of Southern Acanara had any money. Still, perhaps it would be useful, worth the trip, to become personally acquainted with the strange and brilliant man the news media were beginning to style the "Che Guevara of Africa." Probably Marc's reputation was over-inflated; the underdog guerrilla was becoming a fashionable hero. Yet there was no doubt that few men could have done so much with so little, and when the message had reached Allison through a member of another African country's delegation to the U.N., he had elected to respond in person, as Marc had requested, rather than to send a subordinate . . .

Then his eyes flickered to the mirror again. He did not become alarmed, but he became alert. Ever since Uvalde he'd had the road virtually to himself. Now there was someone on it behind him, a mile back. That in itself was no cause for concern; but the fact that the following car was a red Ford hardtop was. Such a car had been behind Allison coming out of the San Antonio airport; he'd lost it in traffic, but he'd noticed another like it behind him on the main street of Uvalde. Now such a car was bound in the direction of Del Rio. Maybe only coincidence; but survival for Allison had more than once depended on habitual suspicion of seemingly random occurrences. He gave his own Chevrolet the last of the slack in the gas pedal.

As it moved ahead, the Ford responded, closing up, keeping its one-mile interval precisely. Then Allison slowed and the Ford dropped back. Allison frowned and increased speed again. The Ford came on, just holding its distance.

Allison's lips thinned. Whoever was tailing him was a touch obvious, seemingly a bit inexperienced. Yet, that could have come from unfamiliarity with the road, even with the car—someone willing to risk notice in order not to lose him. He'd see: he shut off the air conditioner. Freed of the extra drain, its accelerator crushed to the floor, the Chevrolet leaped ahead.

Driving flat-out, Allison looked in the mirror. The Ford had

speeded, maintaining its distance. It was handled more awkwardly, but there was no doubt that its driver meant to keep
him in sight.

All right, you bastard, Allison thought. He did not know how
his appointment with Marc had leaked; but in this business
everything leaked sooner or later, and, of course, neither the
legal government of Acanara nor the British would want him to
come together with Marc . . . Whoever was tailing him, perhaps
unfamiliar with American driving, might be waiting for an easy
chance. The road ahead had been clear so far, but let him have
to slow, come up behind traffic, and then the Ford could over-
take with ease, draw level in the other lane. Then— Well, an
automatic shotgun was the best weapon for shooting from one
speeding car to another if you wanted a sure kill.

Allison drew the Python, laid it on the seat beside him. His
foot kept the gas pedal crushed. His eyes shuttled to the terrain
rushing past on either side. He was not going to make it that
easy. But the country remained as relentlessly flat as the road:
ditch, fence, thickets, all repeated endlessly, no hills, no curves.
It was not going to be simple to lose the Ford.

Then he saw it, ahead and to his left. He never slackened
speed until he was opposite it. His hands jerked the wheel; his
foot braked, then fed gas again; the car slewed crosswise in the
road with a howl of rubber, back end swinging. Now its nose
aimed straight at the barbed-wire ranch gate that closed the
dirt track leading into the brush-grown pasture. Allison gripped
the wheel tightly, shoved the accelerator to the floor.

The gate rushed toward him, mesquite poles and wire. A
metallic twang mixed with crash of wood as the car struck it
head-on, ripped it down. Then the vehicle bounced and leaped
along a rutted road made not for cars, but for livestock, jeeps
and trucks. It took all of Allison's strength to steer as the Chevrolet hurtled down that narrow lane through high, spiked
brush.

Ahead there was a sharp turn. Allison jerked around the

bend, slammed on brakes. The car bucked to a dead halt on the blind side of the curve; he scooped the Python from the seat, sprang out, dodged into brush. Thorns raked his expensive suit, clawed his flesh, as he took cover in mesquite and cactus. The dust of the car's passage still boiled along the road like a smoke screen.

He heard, from the highway, another squeal of tires. The Ford's driver had seen him turn, was following. Allison let out a long breath; indeed, he'd not over-reacted, panicked. He heard the oncoming clash of running gear, the roar of an engine. He raised the Python. The red car hurtled around the curve; its driver saw Allison's parked vehicle, hit his own brakes.

Too late. Dust billowed, as back wheels grabbed; metal crashed as the Ford's front bumper slammed into the Chevrolet's rear. Allison's car was knocked forward on its running gear; there was the sound of glass shattering as headlights crunched. Then the cars bounced back; the Ford halted. Its door opened, the driver leaped out into swirling dust; steadying his right wrist on his left arm, Allison swung the gun—

Then lowered it, cursing savagely.

Panting, he ripped loose from the thorns. At the thought of how little pressure it would have taken to fire, his knees were watery. "You!" he yelled in fury, plunging out on the road. "Damn you, don't you ever give up? Do you know how close you came to making me kill you? Do you know—?" He sheathed the gun, seized the blonde girl by the shoulders and shook her without mercy.

Her head snapped back and forth. In the blazing light of afternoon, her hair was a windblown swirl of brightness. Her eyes, blue, enormous, were terrified, confused, suddenly streaming tears of reaction and fright. "Please!" she begged in a strangled voiee. "Let me go! *Bitte, Herr* Allison!"

Releasing her, he stepped backward a pace, his black eyes savage. She was tall, beautifully made, with full breasts, slim

waist, fine long legs. Her skin was pale; like her white summer
suit, it was coated now with reddish dust. "You little fool!"
Allison grated, still shaking with fury. "You idiot! What do you
mean, following me like this? I told you in New York and I
told you in Washington that I won't talk to you!"

She put her hands to her temples, smoothed back her hair,
and with obvious effort regained some measure of control. Her
voice, tinged with accent, was husky and trembling with reaction. "I am sorry, Herr Allison. But I promised my editors a
personal interview with you, and I shall not stop until I have
it."

Allison growled terse profanity. Two weeks ago Erika Wolf
had descended without warning on his shabby Seventh Avenue
office in New York and, by sheer luck, had caught him in.
Since then, scarcely a day had passed without her popping up
to importune him for the sort of interview he never granted,
loathing, almost frightened of, publicity as he was. A quick
check by his organization had assured him that she was what
she claimed to be—correspondent for one of those big-circula-
tion West German illustrated weeklies, and for a smaller one in
Austria.

"Well, you don't have a chance in hell of getting it," he told
her roughly. "Not only that, you damned near got yourself
killed, you made me ruin a good suit, we've both messed up
rented cars—" He broke off at the sound of another vehicle
coming up the road. "On top of that," he finished with utter
disgust, "now we've got a damned mad rancher or cowboy to
deal with . . ." He turned to face the sound.

Erika Wolf brightened a little. "Really? A cowboy? I have
never met one." Then the black Thunderbird came around the
bend, stopped short. "Oh, do cowboys drive such cars? I have
seen that one on the road behind me since I left Uvalde—"

"Get down!" roared Allison, and with a sweep of his arm he
knocked her sprawling. In the same instant, he threw himself
aside, hand clutching the holstered Python as he hit the ground.

The Thunderbird's door opened; the automatic shotgun held by the man who leaped out boomed. Allison heard the harsh, ugly rip of buckshot tearing the air where he and Erika had stood but a half-second before. Then he was rolling, the Python out; he fired and fired again. The shotgun thundered once more; Allison heard the sound of its load ripping the brush just over his head. He fired a third time, but there was no need; one of the two previous shots had gone home; the Python's heavy slug had literally picked up the man and dropped him across the car's low hood. There he lay, feet barely touching the ground, his weapon dangling from his hand, eyes staring at the brazen blue overhead. Then, as Allison watched tensely, his body oozed downward, crumpling into an awkward pile by the left front wheel.

Breathing hard, Allison got unsteadily to his feet. He was aware of a high, hysterical shrieking. He whirled toward Erika, who sat in the dust by her car. "Are you hurt?"

With face buried in her hands, she just went on screaming. Allison ran to her, eyes searching her white clothes for any stain of red, saw none, got his hands under her arms and jerked her to her feet. As she did so, the screams died away in racking sobs; she pressed against him and there was nothing he could do but hold her.

It seemed forever, but it was only a moment before he could release her. She backed away, stared at the body by the Thunderbird. Her lips moved soundlessly; then words came out. "You've killed him."

"You're God damned right," Allison said, and he turned from her and went to the body.

The man was in his early thirties, pale, overfed, with greasy black hair. One bullet had smashed straight through the breastbone and come out the back; Allison could see no mark of the other two, either on him or on the car. He dropped to his knees, quickly frisking the pockets of the bloodsodden sport shirt, the cheap, off-the-rack pants. A pack of ruined cigarettes, a bulging wallet; nothing else. There had to be a pistol somewhere, but it must be in the car. He thrust the wallet into his own coat without looking into it. When he stood up, Erika was staring at him. "I don't understand," she whispered. "I don't understand at all."

"You don't have to," Allison said. "But this is why I don't give interviews—it draws them." He appraised her; she was still trembling. "Do you think you can drive?"

She nodded mutely.

"All right, I'll move his car. When it's out of the way, you back down the road. Before you get to the highway, check to make sure it's clear, so nobody will see you leaving. Then head straight for Del Rio—it's about fifty miles. Drive carefully, not too slow, don't do anything to get stopped or excite suspicion." He examined her car and his, nose to trunk. She had smashed her headlight; the bumpers were dented; no other damage. The headlight glass was in two big pieces; that was a stroke of luck. He picked them both up, dropped them in her car. "When you reach Del Rio, register at the first motel you come to. I'll be along in a few minutes and meet you there. Don't stop anywhere this side of there for anything—understand?"

"But . . . it's *murder!*"

"Murder, hell! Not in Texas—it's self-defense! All the same, I can't afford to be mixed up in a trial, and if you're smart"— he made his voice threatening— "you won't be, either. After all, you're an alien . . ." He shoved her roughly into the Ford. "We'll talk about it later. Now, for God's sake, get going!"

She nodded, started the engine. Allison got into the Thunderbird, used his handkerchief to shift gears, back it into the brush one-handed. The keys were in it; he opened the glove compartment. It held a .25 automatic pistol and rental papers on the car. He left all that intact. Erika roared past him as he got out.

The Thunderbird was well-hidden in the brush. Allison's skin and suit sustained further damage as he got back to the road, seized the dead man, and with considerable effort dragged the body into the thicket. When he reached the road again, he cut a feathery limb of mesquite, used it to erase all the footprints he could find in the dust, looking especially for Erika's. He threw the limb far into the brush and started his own car, backed quickly down the narrow lane. Before reaching the ruined gate, he halted, as he'd instructed Erika to, and on foot, furtively surveyed the highway. A tumbleweed drifted across the pavement, propelled by a gust of hot wind. Otherwise, the road was empty. Allison hurriedly slid behind the wheel, backed the car onto pavement. Then, curbing his desire to go flat-out, he drove at an even, mile-consuming pace, toward Del Rio.

Once on the road, he calmed, could think more clearly. No doubt of the man's being a hired assassin; but Allison did not even speculate on who had paid him. Maybe Acanara; maybe the British or the oil companies; maybe the connection was with another deal entirely, although that was unlikely. Anyhow, the main thing was to get clear, not be involved. He didn't want Crider in the State Department finding out that he was down here, or why.

All he could hope, he decided, was that the German girl would keep her mouth shut and that they'd be lucky. The killer undoubtedly had a police record; when he was found and identified, that might lessen efforts of the local law to find his slayer. And nobody had seen them enter or leave the road, so far as Allison knew; probably, in this vacant, desolate country, the shots had not even been heard. If it weren't for the ruined gate, it might be some time before the body was discovered, but tampering with a gate was a cardinal sin in cattle country, and it would not go unnoticed for long.

Well, it would all depend on the girl; on her good sense and stability. Or on his ability to manipulate her, cajole or frighten her into keeping her mouth shut. He would have to learn more about her, what she was and what made her tick. That was urgent, because she had a hold over him, and he did not like that.

CHAPTER 2

SHE HAD FOLLOWED his instructions precisely; he spotted the red Ford parked at the first motel on the edge of Del Rio. He pulled in and parked beside it. As he hoped, the clerk gave him the room directly in front of his bumper, next to hers. At three in the afternoon, theirs were the only two cars here.

He carried his gear inside, the pistol under his folded, ripped coat. The little room's dimness made him blink after the brutal glare outside; it smelled of dead, conditioned air and was almost cold. He slid the gun and the assassin's wallet into a table drawer. As he did so, there was a knock on the door, and his hand clamped on the Python's butt inside the drawer. "Who is it?"

"Erika Wolf. Herr Allison?"

"Yes." Allison released the gun, went to the door. When he opened it, she stood there clean and fresh, the very model of that slender, Teutonic sort of beauty that was the hallmark of prosperous, postwar, urbanized German girls. Her hair glistened like pale, finely spun golden silk; her mouth was freshly painted, her blue eyes carefully emphasized. She wore a long-sleeved white blouse with ruffles around the wrists and a linen skirt; no sign of what she'd been through showed. She had a manila folder under her arm.

"Come in," he said, and when she did, he shut the door behind her. "Have any trouble?"

"No." Her voice was cool, steady, now. "I was very dusty, of course, but I explained that by saying I'd had a flat tire. The

15

gentleman in the office was horrified that I had changed it myself; in Texas a lady must wait for a man to come along and help. I told him I did, but none came and it was very hot. He accepted it. You? Are you all right?"

"Yes. Sure. Except that I need a drink." He unlocked his suitcase and took out a bottle of Scotch. "I imagine you could use one too."

She let out a long breath. "Indeed I can. I am still all"— she gestured helplessly— "confused. I don't know what to make of all this." She paused. "Besides, I've never seen anyone killed before. It was horrible."

Allison nodded, pouring whiskey into two glasses.

"Why did he try to shoot you?" Erika sat down, crossing her legs, the short skirt revealing excellent thighs. "And—and shouldn't we go straight to the police?"

Allison did not answer until he had gone out to the gallery, filled a bowl with ice from the dispenser there, and put some in each drink. Then, with another glance at the door to make sure it was tightly shut, he handed the girl a glass and sat down on the bed. "No," he said. "I told you. We're not going to the police. I have plenty of enemies and this man was an assassin hired by one or another of them. He tried to kill me and he tried to kill you, and I had to get him first to save both our lives. You were standing beside me until I pushed you. Do you know what kind of pattern a gun like that throws? It would have torn us both apart. And that weapon was unplugged, which meant it held five rounds, each with nine buckshot this big." He measured it on the end of his little finger. "He fired twice at me. That left him three rounds. If he'd got me, do you think he'd have sent you on your way to testify against him?"

She stared at him, and he could see the comprehension dawning in her eyes. He got up and took the wallet from the drawer. "Anyway, he was a professional killer and probably wanted by the law himself. Let's see."

The wallet contained two hundred dollars cash, three New

York state driver's licenses, each bearing a different name, and credit cards with a similar variety of aliases. In addition: a couple of obscene photographs, a return airline ticket from San Antonio to New York, and a miscellany of paper of the sort that clutters every wallet. Amid all this was a clipping from the London *Times*—a bad halftone of John Allison from a photograph taken unawares some years before.

Allison spread all this before the girl. "There you are. Everything he needed to home right in on me." Except for the money, he carried the wallet's contents into the bathroom and flushed them down the commode. When he came out again he said, "Now, it may be a day or two before he's found. It'll be awhile longer before he's identified. When they do identify him, I doubt they'll strain themselves worrying about who killed a man with a record like the one he's bound to have. Meanwhile, there's nothing to tie us to the killing and we can both probably be out of Texas before they even find him. So we're in the clear. But if we—you—go to the police, we'll be tangled up in a mess that won't do either one of us any good."

Erika Wolf looked thoughtful. "Perhaps you're right."

"No perhaps about it. By the way, how did *you* follow me?"

She laughed a little, and he could see that the whiskey had relaxed her. "Men," she said, touching her pale gold hair. "They are so blind. With a black wig and dark glasses—I was on the airplane with you from Washington to San Antonio, and you did not even recognize me. I thought I'd lost you, leaving the *Flughafen,* where we both rented cars, but I picked you up again just in time."

"You'd have been better off if you hadn't. Well, the thing for you to do is to start back for San Antonio at first light tomorrow, take the next plane north, and forget this ever happened."

Erika uncrossed and recrossed her legs. "Oh, no, Mr. Allison. I can't do that without my interview."

Allison stared at her. Before he could speak, she set down the glass and picked up the folder. "I have already done the preliminary research. Listen." She began to read. "Born in Texas, 1929. Father of Scotch-Irish descent, mother second-generation German. Grew up on ranch or farm. Father died when seventeen, mother two years later. Then you went into the Army. Trained at Fort Knox, Kentucky, graduated from Officer's Candidate School. Because you spoke fluent German learned from your mother, you were sent to Vienna, the Armored Cavalry. You fell in love with Vienna and took your discharge there. Then you were recruited by a special American State Department team—"

"For God's sake!" Allison sat bolt upright, astounded.

"—whose mission was to infiltrate Iron Curtain countries, setting up propaganda networks encouraging her satellites to rebel against Russia. This was when your Secretary of State, *Herr* Dulles, promised aid to any country that would fight to free itself from Russian domination and said American policy was to roll back the Iron Curtain ... According to my information, you were given special training, taught to speak Hungarian like a native, and sent to Budapest. When the 1956 revolution broke out, you actually fought against the Russians. In fact, under your cover name of Horvay Karoly, you remain something of a legend in Budapest even today."

Allison finished his drink. "Go on," he said coldly.

"Oh, our researchers are very thorough." She turned a page. "When the revolution collapsed, you escaped to Austria. Then, there is a gap of a year; you must have been very bitter and disillusioned; obviously you believed your own promises to the rebels of American aid—which did not come. Where did you wander? What did you really feel? I should like to know ... Anyhow, you surface next in Bavaria. There you buy a stock of Luger pistols remaining from the war, which you sell to dealers in your own country. This puts you in business as an arms merchant. Your rise and success are astonishingly quick; you are evidently a fine businessman; but, more than this, it's rumored that a special relationship with your own government may have contributed somewhat. The exact facts are unknown . . ."

She turned another page. "You speak excellent German and Hungarian, fair French. Your knack for languages was one of the reasons you were chosen for the Hungarian venture; another was your skill with weapons of all kinds. In addition to the *Panzerkorps,* you served your army as small-arms instructor and as a member of its International Rifle Team, winning many prizes. You have no college degree but are considered well-educated and at home in virtually any circle. So far as is known, you have no permanent residence, but travel always, everywhere in the world, living only in hotels. Your firm is now quite large and you are quite wealthy and"— she laid down the folder and looked at Allison— "and you have never married." She picked up her glass and sipped from it. "That's strange. That intrigues me. You are a very attractive man, Mr. Allison. Why have you never married?"

Allison got up, poured more whiskey into his glass. For one moment, then, he thought of a Hungarian girl named Iren, of betrayal and disillusion. Then he said crisply, "I don't think that's any of your damned business, Fräulein Wolf." He turned. "And there's not going to be any interview."

She looked at him steadily and perhaps with even a little mockery. "Oh, isn't there?"

"No."

Erika sighed. "Then perhaps I shall have to go to the police after all. It will be inconvenient for me, as you say, but perhaps not so inconvenient as it will be for you."

Allison stood there a moment, carefully checking his temper. "Look, Erika," he said at last, using her given name for the first time, "this is only a story to you. But it's a matter of life or death to me. You saw that picture from the London *Times* in that gunman's wallet. He used it to home in on me. There are a lot of other people who would like to do that too. The more publicity there is about me, the easier it is for them. Do you want to get me killed just to have something to print in your magazines?"

She was silent for a moment. When she spoke again, her voice trembled slightly. "I do not want to get anyone killed. Not after today, what I have seen . . ." Then she uncrossed her legs, sat up straight. "Nevertheless, I have a job to do and I must do it."

Allison rubbed his face wearily. "All right," he said. "How much will you get for the stories? I'll double it to keep them out of print."

The girl laughed shortly. "Oh, a bribe? No use, Mr. Allison. I have plenty of money. I come from a good house, and my father left a very large inheritance when he died. I work because—well, my brother manages his hardware factory. Besides, I had no interest in hardware anyway. Too dull; I prefer more excitement." She stretched arms and long, perfect legs lithely, catlike. "Unfortunately, I have no desire to be a *Kirche, Küche, Kinder Hausfrau* like my mother. Not for some time yet, anyhow." Her glass was empty, she held it out. "Please, may I have another drink, Mr. Allison?"

Allison took the glass, and he thought hard while he filled it. What he was up against here was a Germanic doggedness of a kind he himself had inherited from his mother, a determination to carry out an assignment in the face of any odds. It was something he understood thoroughly and did not underrate. Neither bribery nor reason would work on this girl; she was in a position to blackmail him and might very well do it. Puzzled as to what tack to take, he turned back to her with the drink. She reached for it; the ruffled cuff of her blouse rode up; and in that instant he saw the faint scars on her right wrist.

Allison's eyes met hers. "Why did you try to kill yourself?" he asked harshly.

The words hit her like a blunt instrument. She froze. The great, expressive blue eyes suddenly went opaque. Then, quickly, she pulled down her cuff. "I don't know what you mean," she said, and she laughed; it was a tinny sound.

"The scars. On your wrist. What did you use—a *rasierklingen?*"

"A razor-blade? What are you talking about, Mr. Allison?" Erika's face was suddenly pale.

"You heard me." Allison suddenly seized her arm, pulled back her sleeve. The little white scars were dim, but perceptible. "There. And there."

She drew in a breath that made her breast rise. "I think my personal life is none of your affair."

"Then," Allison grated brutally, "neither is mine any of yours."

Erika stared at him.

Allison went on, bludgeoning her with questions. "What was it? An unhappy love affair? Did he throw you over or something? What gives you the right to pry into my life when you won't tell me about yours? How old are you anyway? Twenty-three, twenty-four, twenty-five? Why should you try at that age—?"

Erika jumped to her feet. "Shut up!" she hissed, pulling the ruffle even farther down her wrist.

Allison backed off, smiled sardonically. "Did you really intend to do it, or were you just playing? Trying to win sympathy? All right, Erika, you want all my secrets; suppose you tell me yours?"

The girl's face worked. "I said shut up," she whispered. "Shut your dirty mouth."

Allison's smile turned into a grin. "You know I killed a man; I know you tried to kill Erika Wolf. How would you like for me to broadcast that?" Then he suddenly broke off, went back to the whiskey bottle. "Think about it," he said in a flat voice. "We all have secrets it's vital for us to hide. I don't want mine published; you don't want yours published. Of course, I can't publish yours, I don't own any magazines. But I can hire people; I can turn your past inside out; you won't have any secrets left when I get through with you. And if there's anything there that will damage you, I can use it to hurt you until you'll wish you'd never heard my name—"

She pressed her wrists against her breasts. Her face was white as paper, her lips trembling. "You wouldn't—"

"The hell I wouldn't," Allison said brutally.

Then her eyes slid away from his, hopelessly, and he saw that he had won. "Well?" he said.

Erika's voice was dull. "I shall not write anything about you. If you will not . . . pry into my life, I shall not pry into yours."

Allison stared at her a moment longer. "That's a promise?"

She nodded. "A promise." Her right hand trembled as she picked up her glass. Not looking at him, she sat down again.

Allison felt relief, if not satisfaction. "All right," he said in a gentler voice. "With that understood . . . I suggest we sheathe our swords, then." He sat down on the bed, watching her as she drank. She clung to the glass as if it were a life preserver, drinking with long, deep swallows.

"You're a man without pity, aren't you?" she said at last.

"When I have to be."

She held out her glass. "Please. May I have another drink?"

Allison frowned. The whiskey had already got to her; he could see that. "Don't you want something to eat first?"

"I—I think not. I have no appetite. What has happened this afternoon—I told you, I have never seen anyone killed before. I am not very strong when it comes to things like that."

"Don't think I enjoy it, either," Allison said.

"But I should think you would be used to it. After Hungary. And then, especially, considering the things you sell. You sell things to kill people with."

Allison took her glass, made her another drink. He was aware that she followed his every motion, was looking at him differently now. Without any conceit, he realized that she was seeing him as more than just the subject of a story. He did not like that; she represented enough complications already. He had to get free of her somehow tonight before he crossed the bridge to see Marc. Then he looked down at the glass in his hand. With sudden resolution he added even more whiskey and gave it back to her.

He sat down on the bed again. She sipped the drink, made no comment on its strength. "Yes," he said. "I sell things to kill people with—if the people who buy them want to use them for that."

"And it doesn't hurt your conscience?"

"I told you, I am not going to be interviewed."

She shook her head. "You don't understand. I've promised there will be no story. But this is something ... for certain reasons, my own, this is something I am very interested in. How you feel about it, justify it."

"I don't justify it. But what I sell keeps wars from starting as often, maybe more so, that it starts them. If a country's armed, if it can defend itself, it's not so likely to become a victim."

"And you arm the weak against the strong?" Her voice was cynical.

"Not always. But it works out that way often enough. I depend on the major countries of the world for the weapons I sell—their surplus stock. To get that, I have to follow certain restrictions they lay down as to whom I can sell to. It's not usually that they let me sell to an outright aggressor."

"But sometimes—"

"Sometimes I have weapons that are under no restrictions. Then I sell them to whoever has the money to pay for them. What they do with them is no concern of mine—but first I make damned sure my skirts are clean with the big powers. In the long run, I probably arm fewer bandits than I do people who want to keep the bandits away."

"I see. Then, whatever one does, there is always a justification one can work out for it."

"I don't bother myself with justifications. In Hungary, during the revolution, they kept asking me, *When are the Americans coming? When will we get weapons?* The weapons never came. We fought tanks with sticks and rocks. The Russians crushed us. But maybe if there had been enough weapons, it would have been different."

She looked at him intently. "I think your experience in Hungary must have affected you very much."

"I told people a lot of things I thought were true. I helped incite them to rise against the Russians. When they did, what I told them turned out not to be true at all. Yes," he said, "I learned certain things from that. Now, that's all the talking about myself I'm going to do."

"Very well." Erika took a long drink, leaned back in the chair. She touched her hair, rumpling it a little instead of smoothing it. And suddenly, with that gesture, it was Allison's turn to feel something. All at once she came into focus for him as a woman, not an adversary. His eyes ran over the rumpled, silken, golden hair, the full breasts, the superb legs. She was a woman, all right, and one hell of a fine-looking one. But there was something about her not quite right, something discordant, jangling. Outwardly she was as sleek as a cat, sophisticated, self-confident. But those scarred wrists, the greedy way she drank, leaning on the whiskey, propping herself on it... Something was wrong with her inside, something drastic. She smoked one cigarette after another, and her hands still shook slightly. Something about her made him feel that she was on the brink of hysteria, holding herself back only by the power of will.

Instinctively, he warned himself against her. No normal man, sitting here across from her this way in the intimacy of such a room, could help feeling desire, and he felt it. But she was too complex, too complicated. And he had no room in his life for a complicated woman, or a neurotic one. There were too many available without complications.

She touched her hair again, rumpling it further. It was strange how that disruption of her sleek façade made her look childlike, curiously vulnerable. Abruptly, Allison got up, turned away from her, freshened his own drink. When he looked around, he caught her staring at him with a fixed and curiously intense gaze.

Her eyes shuttled away immediately. She drained her glass, then held it out again.

"You drink too much," Allison said.

She summoned a laugh. "Oh, yes. That's one of my bad habits. But it helps to make certain things bearable, you understand?"

"No, I don't." His eyes went to the scars again. "He must really have jilted you."

"What?" Then she followed his gaze. "Oh, yes, that. Yes, he jilted me, all right. He jilted me so badly that I no longer even know who or what I am. Except that I'm German, of course." Her voice was a little thick. "I have that much identity, anyhow."

Allison hesitated, hand on the Scotch bottle. Maybe he was wrong; maybe she would not attempt to follow him tonight. Yet it was a chance he could not take. He poured more Scotch, feeling like a hunter aiming at a sitting bird. "You're not quite making sense."

"Ah, but that's because you don't know my secret. If you knew my secret, you'd know I was making much sense. If you knew about these—" She touched her right wrist with the fingertips of her left hand. Then, seriously, intensely, she said, "I tell you, it was no play-acting, I was really trying. If the man I lived with at the time hadn't come home early, found me—"

"The man?"

"Yes." She laughed, a tinny sound. "My publisher. A much older man than you. I was his mistress. Of course, he was terrified. He thought it was because of him. That was when he made sure I got nothing but overseas assignments, with a very liberal expense account. As if "— she laughed again — "as if I would do such a thing over such a man as he . . ."

She sobered, looking down into the glass he handed her. "John. May I call you John?"

"Yes."

"Thank you. You see, John, I have been, as you Americans say, around. I am sorry, I see the disapproval in your eyes, but it is true. I drink too much and I— Perhaps am not wise about men. The kind of men who attract me." Suddenly she raised her head, looked directly at Allison. "But perhaps that's necessary," she said softly, "to find what I'm seeking."

"And what are you seeking?" He asked that automatically.

"I don't know," she said quietly. "Sometimes I feel that I am lost in a very dark, tangled forest. Maybe I am looking for someone to lead me out of it." Then her eyes dropped, and she laughed self-consciously. "Yes, I'm getting drunk."

"We'll go out and get something to eat."

"No. No, I don't want anything to eat. I am happy just as I am." She laughed with bitterness. "As happy as I ever get. Please don't make me go, yet. Please let me stay here a little longer." A kind of desperation had crept into her voice. "I don't like to be by myself when I feel like this."

Allison looked at her. Then he nodded. So it was going to be necessary . . . Otherwise, she'd be clinging to him all night. "Of course," he said. He got up and took her glass, went back to the bottle. The drink he made for her was merciless.

When he turned around, she was standing up. As she took the glass with her right hand, she put her left on his wrist. "I promise you," she said softly, "I shall be good company."

Her eyes met his, and there was no doubt about what she wanted. Her lips were slightly parted; he could smell the fragrance of her perfume, a light, clean smell. Quite instinctively, quite involuntarily, Allison bent his head and kissed her.

Her response was immediate, almost ferocious. Her mouth

ground against his, opening. He felt her breasts against his chest. Her free hand went to the nape of his neck; it caressed; its tips dug in. She moved her lower body against him hungrily.

Allison had been too busy for women for days. His own reaction startled him with its intensity. His caution, his carefulness, were all burnt out in its flare instantly. He put his arms around her, held her to him, and she moaned deep in her throat. His hand ran down her back, over the firm curve of her hip.

Then she pulled away, her breathing a rasp in the silence of the room. She set the glass aside, sloshing whiskey as she did so. "Wait," she said. "Wait." Her hand went to the blouse, fingers shaking. She unbuttoned it, threw it aside; her breasts were white, filling, overflowing the cups of her brassiere. She reached behind her, and then that was gone too; and she was naked to the waist. As if her hands could not move fast enough, she unzipped the skirt, pulled it over her head. In a moment more she stood there in superb nakedness. She came to Allison again, and this time, as he kissed her, he pulled her down onto the bed.

CHAPTER 3

DEL RIO, TEXAS, was not a large town; but this was Friday night, and there was a flow of traffic which gave the place a temporary air of feverish activity. Servicemen from the local Air Force installation, tourists, Mexicans returning home from jobs in town or shopping, and Texans who preferred to do their weekend carousing in the cheaper and less inhibited atmosphere of Del Rio's sister border town, Ciudad Acuña—all these were bound for the International Bridge on the outskirts. Allison, caught up in traffic, had no trouble finding his way.

His mind should have been ranging ahead to his meeting with General Marc, but he could not get it off the girl, Erika Wolf, who lay now in drunken sated sleep back in his motel room. This was far from being his first chance encounter with a woman looking for a quick bedpartner, nor of taking immediate advantage of such an encounter when the girl was attractive and interesting enough. That part of it neither puzzled nor concerned him. What did bother him was that this girl had struck some unexpected chord within him, and that, instead of walking away from the room coldly grateful that she had passed out and would not hamper his getting to Marc, he felt curiously guilty, as if he had somehow taken advantage of a child or a cripple.

That was ridiculous, of course. She was far from being a child, had been around, as she said, and in bed she had been experienced, adept, very, very good. But there had been a curious quality of desperation in her lovemaking and in the way

28

she clung to him afterward; as if, he could not help thinking, she were someone drowning and he the rescuer. "No," she had said when it was long over and he had thought her sound asleep and had tried to move. "No. Don't go away. Don't go away."

So he had lain with her for a long time, with her arms locked about him in that desperate fashion. Presently, sure she was asleep, he disengaged himself again. Even then, one arm came up, groped for him, missed, and fell back. Her breathing was regular, hoarse.

He stood there over her, looking down at the long, curved white flawlessness of her body. The arm that had reached for him was outflung, the ugly little scars unconcealed, almost blatant, on the wrist. They were, so far as he could see, her only blemish. Allison had rubbed his face thoughtfully, then unfolded the blanket at the foot of the bed and drawn it up over her. He turned away, oddly disturbed, and went to the shower.

When he was dressed, she had not even changed position. He wrote a note: *Back late tonight. Allison.* He put it on the bed table, weighted it with the Scotch bottle. Then he'd slipped out, making no sound as he closed the door.

Now, with deliberate effort, he put her out of his mind and turned his thoughts to Marc and Acanara.

Allison was by necessity thoroughly informed on the small wars, rebellions and separatist terror movements always seething with more or less intensity in one or another part of the world—in this case, West Africa, in what had formerly been one of the British Empire's showcase colonies.

Acanara was a big country, part jungle, part high plateau; agriculturally prosperous; rich with oilfields in its southern portion. When the British had pulled out, they had left behind an ample cadre of capable, well-trained administrators, and the country's first president, Randolph Shodombe, had been, from all Allison could gather, honest, efficient and forward-looking.

But Shodombe was dead now, executed by his former army

chief-of-staff, Victor Nadunda, in a bloody military takeover. And now the country was rent by civil war—tribal warfare, really—between the N'kula and the N'terua.

It had been Nadunda who had unleashed the ancient hatred of the N'kula for the other tribe. The N'kula of the north were Moslems; the N'terua of the south, Christians and pagans. Moreover, as Allison understood it, the N'terua were one of the most remarkable people on the entire continent—highly intelligent, energetic, acquisitive, with a tribal structure that was an ancient, efficient, naturally evolved democracy; and they had long been hated by the more numerous, but less dynamic N'kula. Nadunda, an N'kula himself, had set out to purge Shodombe's coalition government of N'terua, and the purge had turned into persecution, terror, massacre and religious warfare. N'terua had been slaughtered by the hundreds and, recoiling, had seceded from the country, setting up their own state of Southern Acanara. But Southern Acanara was unrecognized by any major country and had received no military aid from anyone, while Nadunda's government, promptly recognized by the British, the United States and most other large nations, had plenty of tanks, planes and guns. It was an unequal struggle and one that would have been long since over if it had not been for the military genius of General Marc.

He was a legend—enough of a legend so that even Allison had been drawn all this distance as much by curiosity as by any hope of profit. Nobody really knew anything about Marc except that he had suddenly sprung to leadership among the N'terua and, like a black Lee or Jackson, had out-generaled and outfought Nadunda at every turn. Some said he was a professional soldier of great experience; others that he was a tribesman of natural genius with hardly any experience at all; among the N'kula, Allison had heard, it was even rumored that he was a devil, an evil spirit. Whatever he was, he had held off the N'kula for a year, though by sheer force of numbers and superior equipment they had driven him ever farther back into the southern jungles. And now he waited for John Allison somewhere in the Mexican town of Ciudad Acuña across the Rio, undoubtedly in the hope that Allison would sell him the arms he needed to survive and could obtain nowhere else . . . Which, Allison thought, was something that remained to be seen.

The line of traffic swung right. Ahead, in the twilight, Allison saw the bridge.

With footways on either side, it spanned the wide, shallow, muddy river, connecting the United States and Mexico. It swarmed with traffic, vehicular and pedestrian; but Allison had no intention of taking his car across. He knew how much difficulty the slightest traffic accident could cause an American in Mexico and he was in no position to be involved in even a minor dispute with the law. So he parked on the side of the road near the bridge's approaches, thoroughly locked his car, paid his toll, and joined the throng along the walkway.

As he passed a toll booth and checkpoint guarded by brown-uniformed police, he was acutely aware of the Python in the shoulder-holster beneath his specially tailored sportcoat; but no one gave him a second glance as he entered the narrow main street of the town.

It was lined with souvenir stores, liquor stores, bars and restaurants. Show windows were jammed with goods ranging from junk to fine lace, leatherwork and magnificent bridles and saddles; free of tax, all brands of whiskey were displayed at a fraction of their cost on the American side; in the eating places, rows of lambs and kids, split and roasted whole, revolved on spits over glowing beds of charcoal. The street was jammed with American cars, its curb lined with ramshackle taxis, and in the midst of this, an occasional horse-drawn *carreta* clacked past. The evening air bore the spicy smells of cooking, woodsmoke and the raw kerosene odor of the untreated natural gas used for fuel here.

There was still some time remaining before he was to meet Marc. Allison rambled around the streets; entered a bar, drank a Carta Blanca, sipping the excellent beer slowly, while a jukebox lilted a Mexican love song and men in overalls and straw sombreros played cards in a corner. Then he looked at his watch; it was time to go.

At the curb the cab drivers sprang at him like wolves fighting for a single piece of meat. He said, "Boys' Town," and got in the first open vehicle.

By now it was quite dark. The old Packard, its upholstery tattered and the door on the driver's side wrapped shut with baling wire, coughed and wheezed as it took him through the labyrinths of the town. Meanwhile, Allison fished in his pocket, brought out an extra wallet, an empty one—the gunman's. He surreptitiously shoved it down behind the Packard's back seat: the last of the evidence, and surely never to be connected with the dead man fifty miles east in the chaparral ... Ahead, the dark streets exploded in a carnival of light, a rainbow of flashing neon. They left the pavement; the old car bounced over rutted dirt. The light engulfed them, and so did the thunderous, raucous whang of music pouring from a myriad of bars and dancehalls. The driver slowed. "*Señor,* this is Boys' Town. Where to?"

"Here," Allison said. "Here will do fine." He got out, paid, tipped generously.

As the cab growled away, he looked around with curiosity and wariness. Nothing spawned a redlight district like the presence of the military; and the American military, with more money to spend than any other, always spawned the biggest and gaudiest.

He was in the middle of a phantasmagoric scene. The neon flickered and blinked; added to its glare was the guttering light of torches used by pushcart vendors who had taken up stations, here and there at the curbs of the dirt streets. As far as Allison

could see, there was bar after bar, honky-tonk after honky-
tonk, and the whores were everywhere.

In solid ranks they lined the sidewalks, clustered in the door-
ways of saloons. As Allison began to walk, they called and
grabbed at him, shrieking obscene propositions, clutching at his
sleeve, his coat. "Hey, sweetie, I hot girl, you want—" Ranging
from almost-children to withered hags, they were like birds of
prey: the flickering light played over faces corpse-white with
powder, glinted from gold teeth in mouths painted gaudy red.
As he ran their gauntlet, Allison was confronted with body
after body, flaunted, thrust at him; their screeching and chattering mingled with the mind-breaking slam of music crashing
from every doorway with the deafening rhythm of a giant
heart. In such a place as this, it was always well to know the
layout in case you had to get out fast.

So he made a complete circuit of it, almost a dozen square
blocks crisscrossed by unpaved streets only lightly policed by
gun-hung officers in brown uniforms. Marc, he thought, had
chosen a fine place to meet—in this throng of carousing servicemen, tourists, sightseeing American girls, touts, pimps and
whores, two strangers could come together without notice.

Then it was time; he came back almost to where he started,
and he was at the Club Hollywood. It was an enormous building with a huge neon sign and a façade of plastic adorned with
glossy photographs of vacuous-eyed strippers, all alleged to be
direct from Mexico City. When he pushed through the swinging doors and entered, he was in a vast room, high-ceilinged,
loud with laughter, voices, music, foul with smoke.

Allison looked carefully around the room, then started for the
bar. Inevitably, a plump harpy confronted him, bosom welling
from a lowcut gown. "Hey, sweetie, you buy me drink?" Before
Allison knew what she was about, she reached up, seized his
head, and forced his face down between great piles of moist,
perfumed flesh.

Allison jerked free. "Get the hell out of my way."

"Shit on you, sweetie." She pouted, faded away. There were others, clustering, chattering, grabbing like monkeys as he made his way to the bar, hand protecting his wallet. Then, suddenly, their laughter ceased, their chattering died, they faded away. Allison turned to see why, and the girl was there.

Her hair was blue-black, long, her face unpainted, her skin pale, with an undertone of olive. She wore a tight white blouse, a black satin skirt, and she would have made heads turn anywhere in the world with that figure and her cameo-perfect features dominated by black, melancholy eyes. Unlike the others, she did not accost Allison, but only took a stool beside him at the bar, her movements graceful, almost regal. For an instant Allison found himself wondering if she actually worked here. But the bartender put tequila before her, and as she sprinkled salt on the back of her hand, she asked in heavily accented English, "You will pay for my drink?"

"Yes," Allison said and ordered a Carta Blanca for himself. There was a significance in the way she had come to him, and he had spotted no other possible contact . . .

She drank half the tequila. Then she said, "I think your name is John."

"Yes," he said. "Who're you?"

"My name is Maria. Would you like to go upstairs with me?"

"That depends."

She looked at her glass. "I am the most expensive girl here— the cost is eight dollars. Fortunately, I may pick and choose my customers." There was no touch of conceit in her cool, almost dead voice. "Some nights I do not work at all. Really, I do not feel like working tonight. But my room is a good place for people to talk."

"It depends on who the people are."

"People who have traveled a long way," she said.

"I think I would like to talk to them, then."

"Bueno." She finished her drink, got off the stool. Allison followed her across the crowded room to a door in the far corner. "You go first," he said and opened it for her. She moved ahead and he came after her, up a dimly lit stair, ready to do two things simultaneously if necessary—draw the Python and use her for a shield.

But nothing happened; and the narrow corridor into which they emerged was empty, save for a gray cat that ran past them, though from behind the closed doors in either wall came sounds of a brothel. The floor sagged and creaked under their weight as he followed her down the hall; the place was flimsy. She halted before the last door, knocked. "It's Maria," she said clearly. There was the click of a lock turning; the door opened. She entered, and with double wariness Allison followed her into the dimly lit room.

Then he halted as Maria stepped aside, closed the door behind him. The man who got up off the bed was not tall, but he was enormously wide in the shoulders, barrel-chested, long-armed. He wore a blue denim work shirt and blue jeans molded to thick, powerful thighs. In the light of the single bulb dangling from above, his face was as black and shiny as freshly melted tar. His voice, when he spoke, was deep, soft and thoroughly American. "Hello, John Allison," he said, coming forward and thrusting out a big hand. "It's been a damned long time."

CHAPTER 4

IT HAD INDEED been a long time, and so much had happened to Allison in the intervening years that he only stared blankly. Then his brain with computer swiftness darted back the requisite space of years, eliminated everything and everyone in between. He saw again that dark face beneath crash helmet and goggles, the thick torso in combat jacket protruding from the turret of a Sherman tank. "For God's sake," he said as he put out his own hand. "Gil Markham!"

The black man smiled, showing gold-crowned teeth. "I didn't really expect you to remember. Or did you know—"

"No," Allison said. "No, I didn't. But you— You're—"

Markham laughed softly. "Yeah," he said. "Yeah. I'm General Marc."

Then he released Allison's hand. "Quite a rise in rank, huh? From tech sergeant to general in twenty years?" He laughed again. Then he sobered and turned his head. "Roy," he said.

Allison whirled around, his hand instinctively going to the Python. "Easy," Markham said quickly, as the shadow detached itself from the murky corner of the room and moved forward into the light. "Easy. This is my bodyguard, Roy Hausa."

The man was tall, towering over Allison by three inches. Not more than twenty-five or six, he wore his hair bushed out in a frizzy, African coiffure, and his skin was dark brown, his features sharply chiseled, almost Egyptian. His eyes, looking down at Allison, were strangely lambent. His lips moved soundlessly

36

in a word that might or might not have been a greeting. If it were, there was no warmth in it; his whole bearing radiated hostility, and his right hand rested on the butt of a Colt .45 automatic thrust into the waistband of his jeans.

Marc's voice was harsh. "All right, Roy. Climb down off it. I've told you about Allison. We were in the same outfit in Europe. I was his platoon sergeant. He came in a green lieutenant and I helped make a tanker out of him. He's a good man."

"Yeah," Hausa said tonelessly. "Yeah, okay." He still did not put out a hand.

Marc sighed, seemingly a trifle embarrassed. After a second he said, "Roy's paid to be suspicious, Allison. You understand."

"I guess," Allison said. He looked around the room. One chair, a washstand, pitcher, basin, a cheap, iron-steaded bed. From the wall above it, next to a framed print of Jesus, a sepia rotogravure portrait of Humphrey Bogart clipped from a magazine looked down at the mattress.

Marc turned to Maria. "What about some *cerveza*, honey?" He gestured to a bucket at the foot of the bed; it held iced beer. Maria nodded, opened two, gave one to Markham, the other to Allison. Hausa did not drink, fading back into the corner, a shadowy presence.

"Royal entertainment, huh?" Marc looked appraisingly at Allison, then gestured to the chair. "Well. So you sell guns. Money in it?"

"Sometimes." Allison sat down.

"Yeah. I can look at you and tell." His eyes darted to the door. "You weren't followed, were you?"

"Yes," Allison said. "But I'm not any more."

Marc's eyes narrowed. "What do you mean?"

Allison looked significantly at Maria. Marc read the glance instantly. "Don't worry. She's all right. She knows my business. And when I leave, she's going back to Africa with me."

"Just the same—" Allison said.

Marc nodded. "Okay. Honey, you go downstairs, have a beer. Look out for yourself though, *sabe?*" His eyes softened oddly; he smiled. Obediently, smiling back faintly, she turned, let herself out. When the door had closed behind her, Marc waited a moment. "All right," he said, as her footsteps died down the hall, "what's the story?"

Allison hesitated, then told him tersely what had happened in the afternoon. When he finished, Marc drew in a long breath, let it out soberly. "Yeah," he said. "That was Rinaldi's doing, all right. Son of a bitch." His voice was grave. "So it's leaked. You hear that, Roy? It's leaked; we got to keep our eyes double-peeled. They know where we are; they'll try to sew us up from this end just like they tried to get Allison. Rinaldi don't leave anything to chance."

"Who's Rinaldi?" asked Allison.

"The brains behind Nadunda. I'll get to him in a minute." Then Marc's voice changed. He raised his beer. "Well, here's to old times, Lieutenant Allison, such as they were."

They drank. When Marc lowered his bottle, he went on. "Yeah, I'm General Marc. And I appreciate your coming all this way to meet me; I really do. I couldn't risk coming to see you. I'm not wanted in Mexico, but I'm still a deserter from the U. S. Army."

"You deserted?" Allison was surprised. Markham had been a career soldier.

"Uh-huh. Not long after you left the outfit." Marc's voice was matter of fact. "They brought in a new platoon leader, guy from Michigan. You wouldn't think a Yankee'd be a worse redneck than any Southerner, would you? But, God, he hated niggers. And when he found out I had a white girl friend, that really tore it. He laid on the old treatment, you know? And so I finally did what he wanted me to—I knocked the living hell outa him. Then I bugged out. I had to. They'd have thrown me in the stockade, kept working me over, piling charge on charge—it would have been years before I saw daylight again."

"I'm sorry," Allison said.

From the corner, Hausa made a sound in his throat.

Marc's lips compressed. "I might as well tell you about Roy too. He's wanted in Los Angeles. He was a very big man in the Black Power movement there until he killed a cop."

"A pig," Hausa said from the shadows.

"Whatever he was, Roy killed him. Took off for Mexico, Cuba, then came to Africa. I won't tell you his real last name; Hausa's like Jones in Acanara. No point in hiding it; Roy hates your guts. Not your fault, not his; matter of skin color."

"That's his problem." Allison took out a cigarette. "How'd you get to be General Marc?"

"Fighting," Marc said promptly. He sat on the bed, took a swig of beer. "In those days it was still possible to join the French Foreign Legion, no questions asked. But I deserted it too after they sent me to Algeria. Didn't like the tactics they used. So I went over to the other side."

He drank again. "Well, that's water over the dam. Katanga, Biafra . . . and now Southern Acanara. I always seem to be on the losing side." He laughed with a touch of bitterness. "You know what? There are times when I'd like a little less reputation and a little more winning."

Allison said nothing.

"But I'm always outgunned," Marc went on. "You know, Allison, I'm really a pretty good general. Maybe not as good as all those stories they tell about me, but pretty good. Men'll follow me and die for me, and if you know as much about generals as I think you do, you know that's pretty rare. But, goddammit, I never have the guns." He drained the bottle, set it down with a savage thump. "I never have the fucking guns."

"They cost money," Allison said.

"Yes, by God, don't they? Unless you're a *recognized* government or you go to the Russians." His face gleamed sweatily in the dim light as he looked at Allison. His brows were great ridges of bone, his nose broad and flat, his mouth wide, lips thick. The curly hair against his skull was thinning, tinged with gray. "You know the situation in Acanara?"

"Yes," Allison said.

"It could have been such a damned fine country. It was a damned fine country under Shodombe." There was pain in Marc's voice. "When I had to hightail it out of the Congo, I went there and all of a sudden a funny thing happened to me." He looked at Allison, then looked away. "I went down South, to Terua. That's a good country, down there in the south of Acanara. Maybe a little isolated, remote, but that's the way I like things, with the number of people who want my head. But the N'terua, their allied tribes—they're fine people. Anyhow"— he cut the air with an inarticulate gesture— "this funny thing happened. I began to feel at home."

He arose, began to pace. "Now, you got to understand, Allison, that I have never felt at home anywhere in this world since the day my mama bore me. That was in the worst slum you've ever seen, in Charlotte, North Carolina, nearly fifty years ago; alongside of it, the roughest part of Acuña still looks like where the aristocracy lives. Anyhow, when I was able to get up and walk, I went; and from that day to this, I've roamed the face of the earth and I never felt at home until I was in Southern Acanara, among the N'terua. They took me in, and then I knew I was where I belonged."

His face twisted. "But you ain't interested in all this crap. Anyhow, the point I'm trying to make is that Acanara had a lot going for it before Nadunda pulled his *coup*."

"There's always a coup," Allison said.

"There shouldn't have been, this time. Shodombe was a good president. Nadunda was his chief of staff. Then Rinaldi came."

"You mentioned him before."

"Yeah. He's stayed behind the scenes until lately. Just recently he came out into the open; not long ago Nadunda appointed him minister of defense."

"Rinaldi's not an African name."

"No, he's a white man, an Italian. Incidentally, he was a tank man too in North Africa during the Second War. Anyhow, he showed up in Acanara a couple of years ago, got buddy-buddy with Victor Nadunda. And he's the one talked Nadunda into turning on Shodombe like a treacherous dog, executing Shodombe, making himself supreme ruler. Then he and Nadunda turned the N'kula loose on the N'terua, declared open season on 'em—and, hell, we had no choice but to rebel!"

"Yes," Allison said. "Well, considering everything, you've done well since then."

"*Well?*" Marc almost spat the word. "If you call making bricks without straw *well,* maybe so. Sure, we're outfighting 'em. But they're outgunning us. The British hold those oil concessions in Southern Acanara, and they want to keep 'em, so they recognized Nadunda before Shodombe's corpse was even cold and started pouring in the weapons. While we— Well, we get nothing from nobody." He broke off, turned to look directly at Allison. "Now you know why I asked you to meet me here. We need guns."

For a moment the room was silent. Then Allison said, "All right. Tell me what you need and how much you've got to spend."

Marc drew in a deep breath.

"What we need," he said, "is everything. What we've got to spend is nothing."

Wearily, then, Allison arose and helped himself to another beer. Of course, he had known it was going to be this way. What he had not known was that General Marc would turn out to be Gil Markham. And he owed Gil Markham a great deal.

Markham had already been a combat-seasoned veteran of the Second War and of Korea, too, when Allison had taken over the armored cavalry platoon in Vienna, a raw youth directly out of Armored OCS. Had he chosen, he could have given Allison a rough time, in the way that seasoned enlisted men know; instead, he had played it straight, seeming to like Allison, had taught the green lieutenant more about handling both men and tanks than Allison learned from any other source, and that tactfully and respectfully. For the year they had served together, they had made a good team, and Allison had long since become aware how important that year had been in changing him from boy to man. In some measure, at least, he owed what he was today to Gil Markham, and, he thought a bit regretfully, it was too bad he was not going to be able to pay the man back.

"I'm sorry," he said as he opened the beer. "In that case you'll have to go to some government. Not the British or Washington, of course, but maybe France or—"

"Or Russia?" Marc said quietly.

"Not if you're smart." Allison said. "But that's your affair. I'm sorry, but I can't help you."

"Why not?" Marc's voice was still careful, controlled. "Listen, Allison, it's true we got no money now. But if we win this fight, we'll have oil. Lots of oil."

"I know," Allison said. "But the oil is exactly why you'll never win it." He turned to face Marc and took a swallow of beer.

"Listen," he went on, "it all goes back to the oil. Why do you think the British recognized Nadunda right away; why do you think they poured weapons in on him? Because they don't want to lose that oil, that's why. All right, if somebody comes in and helps *your* side, it's going to make the British very, very unhappy—right? It puts their oil in jeopardy. And if that somebody is me, they're going to raise hell to Washington about it. And if they raise hell with Washington, Washington's going to raise hell with me."

Marc's faced twisted. "I thought you were in business on your own, not some kind of damned captive—"

"I'm in business, all right. And I need merchandise to sell. And a lot of that merchandise comes from Defense Department surplus. On top of which, I have to have State Department export permits to ship it out of the country. If I make trouble for Washington, they make trouble for me. They can cut off my surplus, stop the permits—hell, for all practical purposes, put me out of business, and maybe give me income tax trouble on top of that, just to make sure I've learned my lesson." His eyes met Marc's. "The people in Washington don't like to be embarrassed. And I try to be damned careful not to embarrass them."

Again silence fell. Allison heard the rasp of Marc's breathing. Then Hausa said from the corner: "I told you, General." His voice was scathing. "I told you it was a waste of time to ask any damn chuck dude—"

"Be quiet," Marc said. He looked at Allison. "All right," he said. "I'm sorry I didn't handle it the way it's done in big international circles. I'm sorry I didn't invite you to my war ministry, serve you pheasant under glass, have a reception with white gloves . . . I'm sorry you had to come to a room in a whorehouse, drink cheap beer, listen to somebody beg . . ."

"General—" said Hausa fiercely.

"I said hush." Marc never took his eyes from Allison; and his voice gathered intensity. "But that's the way we operate. We operate on the cheap, close to the bone. Northern Acanara's got us outnumbered two to one, it's got planes, tanks, it can get more. All Southern Acanara's got is ten million people who decided not to let themselves and their wives and kids be slaughtered by a bunch of fanatics, and a willingness to trust a damfool named Marc and expect him to work a miracle every other day." He chopped the air with his hand. "Well, I'm outa miracles. All the same, Allison, there's something you got to understand. Despite the surroundings, despite the fact that you remember me as nothing but a nigger platoon sergeant in an army that wasn't crazy about niggers, I *am* General Marc. And I got to be General Marc by fighting most of my grown life, and I've learned my trade and earned my title the hard way.

When I tell you I'll do something, I mean I'll do it." He paused. "At the very least, I got to have tanks. When the British pulled out, they left Nadunda with forty-eight Centurions, 105 gun. I got to have tanks to fight him—M-60's, West German Leopards—or Russian T-54's if I can't get anything else. Now, if you can't get us anything else, I'm asking you to get us some tanks. And I promise you that if you do, as soon as we've beaten Nadunda, we'll pay a dollar and a half for every dollar those tanks cost. I'll make you that promise and I'll keep it!"

Allison shrugged. "You could make it two dollars, three, and it wouldn't change things." His voice was hard, final.

Marc stared at him. "That's gospel?"

"That's gospel."

Marc stood perfectly rigid for a moment. Then suddenly, furiously, he threw his beer bottle. It slammed against the wall, smashed into glittering shards. "Well, what the hell difference does it make anyhow? he roared. "All right, they'll use all their weapons to drive us back and pen us up like hogs and slaughter us! But what the hell goddam difference does it make?" His face worked. "They ain't nothing but niggers anyhow, not but ten million of 'em, runnin' around nearly naked all the time, talkin' funny, like in the Tarzan movies! They don't import no cars from General Motors, no steel from Bethlehem—they ain't no market! They ain't anything but men, women and children that Nadunda and Rinaldi are gonna kill, starved to death or slaughtered like sheep if I don't get some tanks from somewhere! But who gives a goddam, anyhow? Who gives a goddam for a bunch of black, naked niggers?"

He strode across the room, whirled to face Allison again. "Listen," he said, regaining partial control with visible effort. "I *got* to have tanks. The rainy season's coming on; when that hits, Nadunda's planes can't fly. I could go on the offense then, break out of the south, take M'nanda, the most important road junction in the country, and then I'd have a base to move against Ogoro, the capital. But this rainy season's my last

chance, and if I don't make it now, I'll never make it at all."
His eyes narrowed. "And if I don't make it, Allison, you know
what you'll see? You'll see genocide! I don't mean just a few
civilians killed, I mean a whole tribe, a whole race, wiped out,
like Hitler wiped out the Jews. And now you stand there and
tell me that you can't help me, that I got to let that happen."
He shook his head, spread his hands. "For God's sake, I don't
want to go to the Russians. They're like tapeworms, they eat
you alive from the inside out. I don't—" Then he broke off.

"I'm sorry," he said in a flat voice. "I reckon I had just
invested too much hope in you because I used to know you.
But we never were all that close anyhow, were we? I'm sorry,
Allison. Sorry I called you down on a wild goose chase, sorry I
came this far myself. I was a fool to think that maybe you,
anyhow—" He turned away.

Now Hausa came out of the corner, his hand on the butt of
the automatic. "All right, Whitey. You get the hell out, now. I
told the general— You better get the hell out before I—"

Allison's temper snapped. "Hausa, how would you like to eat
that goddamned gun?"

Marc whirled, was between them in a step. "Roy, dammit!
Take your hand off that pistol. This man could draw and kill
you before you ever got the sight loose from your belt." His
eyes blazed at Hausa. "Allison came a long way to see me and
hear my song and dance. He—" Then he broke off. Slowly, as
if very tired, he turned to face Allison. "All the same, maybe
he's right," he said wearily. "Maybe you better go."

"Maybe I had." Allison went to the door, turned the key in
the lock. Then he halted, with his hand on the knob. No, he
thought. No, you're deadbeat tired and you're not thinking
straight. Not even those, dammit. Crider would find out and it
would only make trouble. Besides, they're too old, too obsolete.
He'll laugh in your face and go to the Russians anyhow.

Nevertheless, Allison let go of the doorknob and turned
slowly. "Marc," he said.

Marc stood there, looking at him with narrowed eyes, great chest rising and falling. "What?" he growled.

Allison raised a hand and dropped it in a gesture that was almost helpless. "I've got twenty tanks you can have," he said.

For a moment Marc continued to look at Allison. Hausa started to speak, but Marc cut him off impatiently with a wave of his hand, "Twenty tanks?"

Allison nodded. "They're not much. M4-A3 Shermans with 76-millimeter rifles. No match for new Centurions with the 105's. I bought 'em six or eight months ago and haven't been able to unload them. But they're in good shape; they run."

Still Marc looked at him digesting this. "Twenty old Shermans. That all you got?"

"That's all."

Marc shook his head as if he did not comprehend, and there was suspicion on his face. "And how much you want for that kind of junk?"

"I don't want anything," Allison said. "I was going to give them to you."

Hausa cut in then with a single terse obscenity, and added, "What's the catch?"

"There isn't any catch." Allison carefully addressed only Marc. "I haven't been able to find a buyer for 'em and they'll have to be junked soon, so you might as well have them if you want them. It's not much against four dozen Centurions, but it's the best I can do."

"What is this?" said Marc slowly. "Huh? You think this will keep me from going to the Russians?"

Tiredly, Allison said, "I don't give a hoot in hell where you go," and he turned to the door again.

Suddenly Marc was there, back pressed against it, face close to Allison's. "Now, you wait a minute. You hold on. One minute, you say you can't sell me *any* tanks, then next you haul off and say you're givin' me twenty old Shermans. I don't under-

stand this, and you ain't leavin' here until I do. You just
told me that even if you had tanks, the government wouldn't let
you—"

"It won't," Allison said. "If it finds out, I'm in trouble. But
I'm just damned fool enough to stick my neck out for you that
far, no farther. I'd have to arrange with a dummy purchaser in
Mexico or South America that I could trust to tranship the
tanks in their name. It's complicated, but I could manage it.
Your port at Terua's still open; delivery would be by tramp
steamer and might take awhile. The tanks are complete and
operational—guns, radios, spare parts, a small inventory—
though you'll probably have to cannibalize eventually . . ."

"Yeah? But what about ammo?"

"That I've located, high-explosive and armor-piercing both,
back when I hoped to sell the damned things. It's well stored
but old as hell, and one round out of three will probably be a
dud. But it's already stockpiled out of the country, so I won't
need an export permit, and I've got first refusal of it . . ."

Now Marc stepped away from the door. He rubbed his chin
thoughtfully. "We might be able to scrape up money for that."

"I'll furnish it on the dollar-and-a-half for every dollar basis.
I'll pay the freight on the same terms. And you'll pay me in
hard currency—after you've won the war." Allison looked from
Marc to Hausa. "But if either of you lets the source of these
tanks leak out—"

"No, don't worry about that." Marc began to pace again.
"What kind of tracks they got?"

"Steel, twenty-four inch, self-cleaning."

"Then I'd have maximum flotation," Marc muttered. "With
the M-4 weighing thirty tons, those Centurions nearly fifty, that
would count for something in the rainy season. Anyhow, I'd
have something to try with. To *try*—"

Hausa stepped forward. His lip curled, showing very white
teeth. "Twenty tanks," he said. "Twenty old tanks against

forty-eight new ones with guns that can go right through those old Shermans' armor like a knife through butter. Big deal. Very big deal. General, we can do better with the Russians—"

"Maybe," Marc said. He rubbed his palms along his thighs as if they were sweating. "But it's mortgaging your goddam soul. And besides, they got to get there before the rainy season." He turned on Allison. "Could you get 'em there before the rainy season?"

"I'll do my best," Allison said. Now he felt a sinking sensation and realized that, subconsciously, he had not expected Marc to accept; that he had only wanted to make the gesture to salve his conscience.

But Marc was already coming forward. "All right. If you mean it, I'll take you up on it. Will you shake hands on it? Will you take my handshake? Then you can work out the documents to suit yourself."

Allison put out his hand slowly. "Of course," he said. Then his reluctance vanished. "What the hell," he said. "Nadunda tried to have me killed. I owe him one anyhow."

CHAPTER 5

THE AGREEMENT REACHED, a host of details remained. The girl, Maria, reappeared and Marc dispatched her to get some coffee. Allison did not miss the way the two of them looked at each other, and when she was gone, he turned questioning eyes on Marc. "You say she's going back to Africa with you?"

Marc nodded, his expression almost defiant. "That's right." Allison said nothing, but Marc read the doubt on his face anyway. "Okay," the general went on harshly. "So she's a whore. So what?"

"So nothing," Allison said. "It's your business."

"No," Marc said reluctantly. "No, I reckon it's your business too, now that she's seen you here with me." He looked a trifle embarrassed. "Anyhow, I've been here long enough to know her, now, really know her. You can sense who you can trust and who you can't, when you been around as long as me. She and I— Well, we make it together. Really make it. I can't explain to you how it is, but— Only, it's like I had been looking all over the world for a part of me that I had mislaid somewhere, and all at once I found it. You ever had anything like that happen to you?"

"No," said Allison.

"Me neither, until now. Anyhow, I'm buying her out. The people that run this racket didn't want to let her go, but they agreed when she threatened to kill herself if they didn't turn her loose—and they could see she meant it. And it's not Southern

49

Acanara's money, either," he said defensively. "I made some in Katanga. Mostly it's gone into this fight. But there's enough left to bail her out."

"I still think you're a fool," Hausa put in bluntly from the corner.

Marc showed no offense, as Allison turned to look at the big gunman in the corner. "What's wrong with him, anyhow?" he asked sharply.

"You'd have to grow up black to know," said Marc. But it's nothing personal against you or Maria, either. He just don't trust anybody with the wrong color skin."

"And you let him talk to you like that?"

Marc smiled. "He's earned the right. We've been through a lot together. He's not only my bodyguard, he's my adjutant and sometimes my chief of engineers. He pulled a hitch with the Engineers in Vietnam, and he's a damned genius. But it's not easy to be a black genius in the United States, John."

"You don't have to make any apologies to this mother for me," Hausa said.

"Don't worry," Allison said brusquely. "I don't give any more of a damn about you than you do about me." He turned back to Marc. "Let's get down to business."

Once they did, it went quickly. Maria returned with the coffee, and by the end of the second cup, Allison was scribbling furiously in a code of his own on a small pad from his pocket.

"So that's it," Marc said. "Where I'm going to operate, the rainy season really socks in about the first of October. Then Nadunda's planes can't fly. And I've got to have the tanks before then if I'm going to make my break-out. I need time to shake 'em down and train the crews."

"Where are you going to get crews?"

"Oh, I'll get crews. A lot of Africans have learned to handle tanks in the past ten years, and they'll come to me like iron filings to a magnet. They won't know Shermans, but give me two weeks and I'll teach 'em."

"All right," Allison said, rising stiffly. He looked at his watch; it was nearing two in the morning. "You keep your port open, and I'll have 'em there in time."

"Don't worry," Marc said. "We'll keep it open somehow." He put out his hand. "Allison, I thank you."

Allison shrugged. "Forget it. You know and I know, it's a drop in the bucket."

"Maybe so. But it's the first time anybody outside of Acanara has stuck out his neck for us. That's something I'm not likely to forget. And if you get your tail in a crack over it, you've got two arguments. The first is that these'll keep me from going to the Russians—for a while, anyhow. The second is that even if I don't win, these tanks will at least postpone a massacre like nothing Africa's ever seen before."

"Washington doesn't pay any attention to arguments," Allison said. "But I hope you win, Marc." He turned to Hausa. "I even wish you luck."

Hausa said nothing. But, as Allison went to the door again, he drew the Colt and stepped in front of him. "Wait a minute," he grunted then. He unlocked the door and, with the gun ready, peered cautiously up and down the corridor. Then, pulling back into the room, he said, "Clear."

"Good," said Marc. "All right, John. You go ahead. Go out the front, like anybody after a big night upstairs here. Roy and I are gonna leave by a back door. You don't want to be seen with us and we don't want to be seen with you. But . . . watch your back, for God's sake. Nadunda and Rinaldi are damned thorough people. Roy and I haven't had any trouble yet, but that doesn't mean there won't be any. And the last thing we need now is for something to happen to you."

"Before the tanks are shipped," Allison said wryly.

"That's right," Marc grinned. And he slapped Allison on the back. "Good luck and be careful."

John Allison did not have to simulate the fatigue of an all-night debauch as he went down the stairs and into the big room, which was still crowded. He felt as if he'd been on one, and his weariness was so obvious that even the whores left him alone as he threaded his way between the tables and past the little stage, where a dumpy stripper in G-string and tasseled bra capered awkwardly. It took a considerable effort of will to remain alert, but he was perfectly aware that Marc's warning was not to be taken lightly, and he forced himself to be vigilant as he went out onto the street.

Its bawdy nightlife was somewhat diminished, but the indefatigable whores were still on station, their powdered faces drawn and haggard, their mewing, obscene cries a little more urgent, desperate, as morning neared. Again, Allison stepped out into the street to avoid them and looked around for a cab. But apparently the beginning exodus from Boys' Town had them all in use; there was none in sight.

He cursed softly and, wearily, began to walk, remembering having seen another cab stand one street over. The Club Hollywood was on a corner where two streets came together to make a blunt point, so Allison passed its entrance again and went around to its other flank. Sure enough, fifty yards down the street, a driver stood beside an ancient Pontiac at the entrance to another big dancehall. Allison increased his pace, lest somebody else get the cab before he did.

It was on the opposite side of the street, and he swung over to the other sidewalk. There was only a scattering of prostitutes along here, and their only apparent prospects were a pair of young Negroes wearing Air Force caps and civilian clothes, engaged in conversation with a couple of them. They hardly gave Allison a glance as he stepped around them.

Then he reached the cab. The driver said eagerly, "Taxi, *Señor?*"

At that moment Allison realized what he had actually seen. "No," he said quickly, and went on walking, hardly breaking step.

He went another fifty feet, came to the entrance of a bar, in front of which three or four tired girls still kept lookout. This time, when they all reached for him at once, he let them draw him into their group. They swarmed around him eagerly, and he said, "Okay. Okay, in just a few minutes. I'm waiting for a friend."

"You buy me drink while you wait," one urged. He shook his head.

"No. I might miss him. I'll stand out here, watch for him." Almost absently he fended them off, yet glad of their presence as camouflage, as he looked back up the street, past the parked taxi, toward the Club Hollywood on the right, and saw the two young blacks still chatting with the girls on the left. Maybe he was crazy, Allison thought; maybe he was all wet, but— No. No, he had seen them, all right; it was just that they hadn't registered until he was well past; his brain was that tired. But they had been there, thrown into relief by the neon brightness of the Club Hollywood's big sign across the street—deep marks on the cheek of one of the young men that could only have been African tribal scars.

They were still talking with the girls, laughing, joking; there was nothing in their appearance—sport shirts, slacks, brown loafers—to set them off from any of the other black Air Force men who thronged Acuña. Except, Allison thought, those scars—and the wearing of the uniform caps with their civilian clothes—and perhaps it was only coincidence that they stood where they could watch both the front entrance of the Club Hollywood and the dark alley that ran behind it ... Nevertheless, Allison slid his hand under his coat and found the grip of the Python comforting.

He waited. The girls had temporarily lost interest in him. One of them turned and went back inside. The cab driver found another fare and pulled away. Then the two men Allison was watching entered a bar with the girls. Allison let out a gusty breath. He was just about to step out of the doorway in which he stood when there was movement in the blackness of the alley behind the Club Hollywood. Cautiously, Roy Hausa appeared, looking this way and that, one hand in his pocket. As he moved into the light, Marc followed him.

They paused for only a moment, surveyed the street. Then they turned their backs on Allison and began to walk, Marc in front, Hausa behind. They rounded a corner and were lost to sight.

Allison waited a moment more. He was about to walk out to the cab stand when the two men in Air Force caps came out of the bar. A girl clung to the arm of one of them, but he shook her off impatiently. Quickly, they began to walk in the direction Marc and Hausa had taken.

"Hey, sweetie!" One of the girls in the doorway grabbed at Allison as the pair disappeared around the corner. But Allison dodged her, was already trotting along the sidewalk. He reached the corner, halted, then turned it carefully.

Two blocks farther on, past the boundaries of Boys' Town, the wide dirt street was swallowed in darkness. There was no sign of Marc, of Hausa. But the young blacks in Air Force caps were striding purposefully down the center of the roadway, and as Allison watched they disappeared into the shadows.

Allison hurried after them, not quite running, along the sidewalk. He stopped before he reached the edge of the light, breathing hard. Ahead the street narrowed; there were rickety fences on either side, behind which sat wooden shanties. The sidewalk ended here; the darkness beyond was almost absolute. Allison held his breath; somewhere up ahead he could hear the sound of running footsteps.

Allison hesitated; then he drew the Python. With it held low, ready, he entered the darkness. He walked swiftly along one side of the street, every nerve taut. He could hear no footsteps now, but their sound could have been drowned in the rasp of his own breath through his nostrils, the drumming of his own heart. He thought of yelling at the top of his lungs, warning

Marc, Hausa, that they were being followed. But that would
make him a target too. Besides, nothing had happened yet;
maybe nothing was going to happen. He did not want to rouse
the neighborhood, be picked up by police . . .

He went a block, another one. The alleys that marked them
off were stygian; only here and there in this slum of ramshackle
hovels did any dim light burn. All four of the men ahead of
him seemed to have vanished from the earth. Allison slowed
down, more cautious now. No point in blundering about in this
darkness; one more block and he'd turn back . . .

He made it, reached the sidestreet, halted there, trying to
pierce its darkness. Nothing. He let out a long breath. Whatever
was going to happen now was beyond his control; he was
in too deeply already; he had to get out, back across the river.
He turned to go back in the direction from which he'd come;
in that instant there was a tick of sound behind him. Before he
could whirl, an arm had clamped around his throat with tremen-
dous force, shutting off his wind, nearly crushing his larynx;
a big hand gripped his wrist and squeezed brutally, so that he
dropped the Python to keep bones from being broken. Then he
was jerked off balance, pulled back into the alley.

He tried to fight; the grip that held him was unbreakable.
His air was shut off; lights danced crazily before his eyes, lights
that didn't exist. He clawed at flesh that was like rock, and a
voice hissed, spraying warm breath across his cheek: "Hurry
up, damn it! Use the knife!"

Another blackness, a great amorphous shape, confronted Allison; there was a tiny click: a switchblade snicking open. Desperately Allison forced his last remaining breath through his
throat, formed two tortured words. "Marc. No!"

There was a single frozen second. Then the man who held
him snapped, "Wait." The pressure on his throat eased. Allison
sucked in a sobbing breath. "Marc, let go. It's Allison!"

Immediately his throat and wrist were released. Allison
crumpled to his knees, sucking desperately for air, rubbing his

aching throat. For one instant a tiny penlight's beam played on his face. Marc cursed. "Hell. It is." He dropped to his knees beside Allison. "John. Goddam it, John, you all right? For Christ's sake, I didn't know it was you . . ."

Allison's head was clearing now. He kept rubbing his throat. "There were two men . . . black, scars on cheeks . . . Air Force hats. They followed you . . ."

"Yeah. Didn't they?" Roy Hausa whispered.

Allison's voice was all right now. "You saw them?"

Hausa chuckled; it was not a pleasant sound. "Yeah. We saw 'em. You think we were born yesterday? They ain't going to follow anybody any more, those mothers."

"Where are they?"

"Where you'd be if you hadn't managed to identify yourself," Marc said, and his voice was shaky. "About ten feet up this alley with their throats cut. It's just God's mercy you didn't get the same treatment. Listen, you all right? We gotta bug outa here."

"I'm all right," Allison said.

"Okay. Here's your gun. Go back the way you came. Nobody can tie you to this. Roy and I head the opposite direction to the place we're staying. Look—" He pressed the Python into Allison's hand. "This wasn't your fight. You shouldn't have come after them."

"I thought if they jumped you, I could take 'em from behind." Allison holstered the Python.

There was a pause. Marc whispered, "Thanks." Then he said, "But get out of here now. And for God's sake, be careful; don't let anything happen to you. I need those tanks. Get 'em to me before the rainy season and I'll burn Victor Nadunda a new one and settle all scores . . . Goodbye, Allison."

"Goodbye," Allison whispered. Then, almost as if they were wraiths, fog borne on the wind, Marc and Hausa were gone. Allison stood there only a moment longer, waiting for his legs to lose their shakiness. Then he hurried back up the dark street to the brightness that was Boys' Town, where, to his relief, he almost immediately found a cab.

Drunk with weariness, Allison crossed the bridge, reclaimed his car, and drove toward the motel. Where, he thought, another problem awaited him—one with which he would just as soon not have to cope tonight. Undoubtedly, Erika would have awakened by now and found him gone; just as certainly, she would have realized that his aim all along had been to work free of her for the evening, and that she had played right into his hands by getting drunk and leaping into bed with him. What he could not imagine was how she had reacted to that realization.

But he'd had enough challenges for the day. Whatever challenge she posed, he'd face tomorrow. When he reached the motel, he pulled into its drive, parked, and got out before he was aware that her car was not where it was supposed to be, alongside his own space. He cursed, a certain concern breaking through his fatigue. Damn it, if she'd waked up and figured out that he'd gone to Acuña, wandered down into that massive brothel alone and something had happened to her— His eyes searched the drive, scrutinizing every car. Hers was not among them.

Allison strode to the door of her room, knocked softly. "Erika? Erika!"

There was no answer. He knocked again, harder, called once more. Still only silence.

Thoughtfully Allison took out a cigarette, looked back toward the town. Maybe she had just awakened, had been hungry, had gone out seeking an all-night restaurant. If that was it, she wouldn't have much luck, was bound to be back soon. He puffed jerkily on the cigarette; the smoke burned a mouth already tender from too much of it. Then muttering another curse, he unlocked his own door, went in, and switched on the light.

The bed was empty and had been neatly made. The bottle of

Scotch sat on the table, further diminished by only a single drink. And then Allison saw that the note beneath it was not the one he had written.

He strode to the table, jerked the slip of paper from beneath the bottle. The words were in English, but the script was Germanic.

> Dear John Allison,
>
> I do not hold you responsible for the fact that, as usual, I made a great bloody fool of myself. And I am assigning myself my own punishment. I leave for San Antonio immediately, and you need have no fear that my magazines will ever carry a story about you written by me. Nor will any secret we share be brought to light. I shall advise my editors that I have failed miserably on this assignment. Since I do not think we will see each other again, I wish you the best of luck in everything. Yours.
>
> E

Allison sat down heavily on the bed and read the note a second time. He thought about the girl, undoubtedly still tired and shaken and hungover, driving alone through all that desolate country between here and San Antonio in the middle of the night; mingled with a disappointment he had not expected, there was a surprising amount of helpless anger and concern at her foolhardiness. There was guilt too; if anything happened to her, he would be in some measure responsible.

Then, ferociously, he crumpled the note into a ball and hurled it toward the trash basket. "God damn it," he said aloud, "I didn't tell her to follow me in the first place." Shaking with fatigue, he arose, stripped off his clothes, and went to the shower, where he sluiced off the unwholesome miasma of Boys' Town. Then he had an enormous drink of Scotch and went to bed. But even as he drifted off to sleep, he was acutely aware that the pillows still smelled of her perfume.

PART TWO: NOVEMBER

CHAPTER 1

SOMETIMES THE WINGS of the old DC-4 actually seemed to flap. Which, in this weather, John Allison thought, was probably an asset; now, if she only had webbed feet too . . . Peering out the window, he watched lashing rain dissolve in spray against the wing's leading edge as the airplane plowed doggedly through the downpour, unable to rise above the murk from which it sluiced. With appalling frequency, she seemed to hit an invisible wall and rebound; again she jumped and plummeted as if tossed in the hand of a playful god; but somehow she kept on going. Considering what lay below, she had to.

Looking down, Allison could catch only glimpses of that great tropical jungle through whorls and tatters of mist, but it was awesome. It slid away beneath with seeming endlessness, from this height looking rather like thick, curly wool. And it was dominated by a great river that coiled through the heart of it like an immense, coffee-colored snake: the Acanara, from which this country took its name.

Allison turned forward, took out cigarettes. Immediately the Englishman who'd sat down by him at Monrovia snapped a lighter into flame. Allison inhaled and nodded. "Thanks."

"Not at all." The man was young, with a rawboned outdoor look—a working, not sporting, one. Dennis somebody; he was an oil company engineer returning to Acanara from leave. "I say, I rather doubt we'll make Ogoro in all this soup. Ten to one he'll set her down at M'nanda."

John Allison frowned. "If that happens, how do we get to Ogoro?"

"Oh, in the military convoy, of course. There are two a day each way, a detail of armored cars escorting any civilian vehicles that have to make the trip. The natives ride the buses, but you don't want to do that; they're dreadful, always jammed, since they only travel when the escort does. You can either rent a car, or if your business is with the government, the garrison will fix you up with transportation. My advice, if you're a VIP, is to see Kopapo, the commandant at M'nanda. I'm sure he'll take care of you."

"Thanks," Allison said. "I'll do that." Then he braced himself as the aircraft banked sharply.

"You see?" Dennis crowed. "This turn means we're not going to Ogoro. It's M'nanda for us."

Allison did not answer. Furious at the prospect of wasting another day making his way overland two hundred miles from the interior to the coast he thought, *Damn Crider!*

And, staring out at the rain, his mind went back to the confrontation in the State Department four days ago.

It had been unscheduled, unexpected, the result of a sudden phone call from Larry Moore in Washington. "I'm sorry," Moore had said. "But he won't give me any hint of what it's about. All I know is that somebody's thrown an awful lot of stuff in his fan, and you'd better get down here quick and catch it before it hits him."

That was enough for Allison; he dropped everything; and on the following morning, facing Crider across the big walnut desk in the pleasant, spacious office on the fourth floor of the State Department, he saw immediately that, if anything, Moore had underestimated the intensity of Crider's anger.

Crider opened the conversation without preliminaries. "All right, Johnny. Let's get down to cases, shall we?" He was a small, dapper man with an oddly homely, rural face and a voice touched with New England twang.

"It's your move," Allison said. He did not betray anxiety, but it was there. Lloyd Crider was one of those invisible men who

kept the gears of international relations from ever quite jam-
ming, no matter which administration held power. His title was
meaningless, his name never made headlines. And his job was
to supervise the considerable clandestine traffic in arms in
which the State Department found it expedient to use private
contractors rather than dealing directly, and as a matter of
public record, with the countries involved.

It was Crider's frequent use of Allison Trading Company in
that traffic that had brought the firm to such prosperity so
quickly and had made John Allison a millionaire. More than
one government too unsavory to Congress and the voters to
warrant direct military aid had been shored up against collapse
or Communist takeover for State's own purposes in such secret
deals. Crider would see that the Defense Department made
weapons available to Allison as "surplus." Allison would buy
them at rock-bottom prices, resell them to the dubious countries in question for a handsome profit in State Department–guaranteed hard currencies. Outwardly the transaction
was private, free enterprise in action, and State's skirts were
clean; if there were any repercussions, Allison took the brunt of
them. The payoff was more than handsome, but the risks were
large. Although he and Crider had known each other for a long
time—it had been Crider who had recruited him for that ill-
fated mission in Hungary—if things went so sour that the public demanded the blood of a scapegoat, Allison knew who
would be the one thrown to the wolves.

And now, Allison could see, something had gone sour. What
it was he could not imagine, but it was something that had
flapped the normally unflappable man across the desk. Crider's
face was without expression, but his eyes were angry, and that,
in Crider, meant that he was furious. "It's your move," Allison
repeated, and began to light a cigarette.

"Very well," Crider said harshly. "I called you here to find
out why you sold arms to Southern Acanara!"

"What?" Allison blinked, his confusion genuine. He had

nearly forgotten his meeting with Marc; the twenty tanks had long since been landed at their destination. Then, because he had covered his tracks well and there was nothing Crider could pin him with legally, he decided, at least temporarily, to play a role of innocence to the hilt. He snapped his lighter into flame. "What do you mean?"

"Don't play games with me, John. You know damned well what I mean. Tanks. Last year you had Nichols at the Pentagon release twenty M-4 A3 Shermans to you for a song. Now they've showed up in the hands of the Southern Acanara rebels. And that's put us in a hell of a position."

Allison closed the lighter and blew smoke. "As a matter of fact, Lloyd, I sold those tanks to Xavier Steel and Foundry in Tampico, Mexico—I guess for junk. Anyhow, you issued valid export permits and Xavier had import permits . . ."

Crider's mouth twisted. "Knock it off, Johnny! CIA's already checked out the whole routing."

"And found nothing out of the way—right? I can't control what Xavier does with the merchandise it buys from me."

Crider's eyes shuttled away; and Allison knew he'd scored that point. Nevertheless, Crider's voice was still sharp. "It's not the first time you and Xavier have connived to pull a fast one on us—and I don't appreciate your being disingenuous about it. With this little trick you've opened a whole Pandora's box." His eyes came back to meet Allison's. "You've dragged us into another war we didn't want to be mixed up in. You've screwed up our relations with the British. And you may be responsible for setting off guerrilla warfare right here at home—in the streets of every major city in the United States!"

Slowly Allison came upright in the chair. "Lloyd," he said. "What in hell are you talking about?"

"I'll tell you what I'm talking about," Crider said. "And I'll take it point by point, so there won't be any misunderstanding on your part." He arose, came around front, sat on the corner of his desk where, despite the difference in their height, he could look down on Allison.

"First point," he said. "At least one of those tanks has been captured by the government of Acanara—and its serial number traced back to that lot you bought from Nichols. So don't try to claim they weren't your tanks."

"They were Xavier's."

Crider disregarded that. "Second point: As soon as the Acanaran government found out the rebels had American tanks, they went to the British government with a hell of a protest, and the British fired right back at us."

"Tell the British to go screw themselves."

"It doesn't work that way. It gave the government of Great Britain an excuse to lean on us."

"Lean on you?"

"Yes," Crider said. "They're finding out that Nadunda and his crowd are a pretty unsavory lot, and that it was a mistake to recognize them and give them aid. Still, they had to do it to save their oil concessions. But the whole thing is turning stomachs among their voters at home—it's been blown up in their press as their very own Vietnam. What they're looking for now is a way out—or, rather, a way to suck us in and get them off the hook. Make Nadunda's government *our* protegé. And you may just have given them the lever to do that with."

"For God's sake, Lloyd, you're not going to give Nadunda any military aid, are you?"

Slowly Crider nodded. "As things stand now, we are—to a limited extent. Nadunda's threatened to make a big stink in the U.N. about us arming his enemies. He's already badgered Norris Middleton, our ambassador to Acanara, until that old hack has made a recommendation that we give him aid. And, as I said, we've got the British pushing us. So—Yes, we're going to give Nadunda aid. Or, rather, you are."

"Me?" Suddenly Allison was angry. "Now, listen—"

"No," Crider snapped. "You listen. I'm not through yet."

"Go on," said Allison tensely.

"Nadunda claims that Marc's got at least a hundred tanks. You know and I know that's a lot of crap. Marc has twenty— or had, before he lost some. Still, there's no way we can disprove Nadunda's claim without a lot surfacing that we don't want to become public. He wants us to give him a hundred too . . ."

"You aren't going to do it?" Allison half rose from his chair.

"No. But we're going to give him exactly double the number Marc has and then tell him to go chase himself if he asks for more. We're going to give him forty M-60's—or, rather, you're going to sell them to him. As a matter of fact, they've already been loaded on a rush-rush basis and are on their way; I've got the documents here for you to sign."

"Lloyd," Allison said slowly, "do the people upstairs on the seventh floor know about this?"

"Of course they do. It's their decision."

"But do they know that they're sealing Marc's death warrant? Goddammit—" Allison's voice rose. "They're making the United States party to what's liable to be one of the biggest, worst massacres of civilians in the history of the world! If Marc's resistance collapses, if the N'kula can get at the N'terua with a free hand, no one to stop them—"

"We're very acutely aware of that," Crider said thinly. "But thanks to you, we've no choice now, except to hope that by this gift of tanks we'll be able to exercise some small amount of restraint on Nadunda when the time comes." He stared at Allison and his face was as deadly serious as Allison had ever seen it. "For your own sake, you'd better hope we're able to do that. If we can't, if the massacres do occur—and most particularly, if anything happens to Marc himself, if he's taken and executed, say, or even killed in combat—then I'm afraid it's the end of Allison Trading Company."

Now Allison did stand up. "Wait a minute," he said. He was

looking down at Crider. "Wait one damned minute. Let me get this straight. First, you're forcing me to sell Nadunda tanks to use against Marc. Then, if he beats Marc with them, I get the axe?"

Unemotionally Crider nodded. "If what we fear happens here at home." He turned, picked up a folder from his desk, opened it.

"This is a report from the FBI," he said. "A quite current, thorough and very dismaying report on a Black Power organization called simply Black Liberation. Have you heard of it?"

"I've heard of it," Allison said. "It started on the Coast, Los Angeles. An armed, underground black revolutionary movement. They even approached me for weapons. I turned them down, gave the FBI information on the request. It's probably in that report."

"So it is. But that doesn't help your situation any now. Listen, do you remember what happened after the assassination of Martin Luther King? The riots, the fighting—?"

"Yes."

"There was fear then, very genuine fear, of a full-scale black uprising. Fortunately it didn't occur. Do you know why?"

"No."

"Because the armed, organized black revolutionary groups in this country, the truly radical ones, the heavily armed ones, didn't identify with King." His eyes met those of Allison. "But they identify with Africa, Johnny. And they identify with General Marc. Now do you see?"

Allison drew in a deep breath. "I'm beginning to."

Crider arose, went to a window, pulled back the drapes, and looked out. "Black Liberation isn't the biggest militant Black Power group. But it's the wildest, roughest and most heavily armed. And it's allied with others like it, and with a lot of the New Left, as it's called. They're all interlocked, they're all waiting for an excuse to explode—and General Marc, since the death of Che Guevara, has become their idol. If he's brought down, and if the American government has contributed to bringing him down—" Crider turned. "Well, according to the FBI, that's what they're really waiting for, hoping for. That would pull the trigger."

Allison, considering this, found nothing to say.

"Now." Crider's voice had turned almost gentle. "Now, Johnny, do you fully understand the ramifications of the mess you've got us into? We've bent over backward to stay clear of the Acanaran war, knowing that if we helped Marc, we'd alienate the British; if we helped Nadunda, we might precipitate revolution here at home. We didn't want to make that choice— and now you've forced it on us. You've got us into this; it's up to you to get us out."

Allison sat down heavily. "All right," he said. "What do you want me to do?"

Crider also seated himself behind the desk. "The usual. Take legal possession of the tanks. Nadunda has certain convertible credits with which he can pay you. And—make yourself very, very visible."

"What do you mean, visible?"

"We don't want any doubt about this being a private transaction, one we have no hand in, can't control. So you're to fly personally to Acanara and deal with the government there. Nadunda will make sure the press knows why you're there; Middleton will make sure there's a leak; and we'll make sure that everyone understands that while we deplore what you're up to, you're a free agent and there's no way we can stop you. We're going to hang the whole thing around your neck. And there won't be any allowance for profit anywhere along the line. You're not going to make money out of putting us in a bind."

"I've got to amortize my overhead," Allison said automatically.

"You get nothing above the actual cost of the tanks and the freight except what you can legitimately negotiate out of Nadunda—and since Nadunda knows all about the deal, my guess is that will be zero. And if I were you, I wouldn't complain. You can consider yourself damned lucky that you're being given a chance to atone for your blunder. That way, if things blow up here at home and the people upstairs decide to hang you in public, maybe I'll be able to persuade them not to hang you so high."

Allison's lips thinned. "Thanks," he said.

"Anyhow," said Crider, "there you have it, with the gloves off. I've delivered my official spiel. But, Johnny—"

Allison looked at him. "Yes?"

"The tanks will satisfy the British. But it's this country I'm concerned about. A black revolution here can't succeed, of course. But a lot of innocent people will get killed before it's over, and the seeds of divisiveness and hatred it would sow would set race relations back another hundred years. If Marc goes, there'll be all that; there'll be hell to pay."

"He'll go," Allison said. "He can't help but go with all that's being thrown against him. This will just be the finishing touch."

"I know. Still ... This is unofficial, Johnny, and I'm not asking you to take any additional risk, put yourself in any more jeopardy than you're already in. But you and I have worked together for a long time, and ... damn it, I know how resourceful you can be when you want to. If there's any way, any way at all, while you're in Acanara that you can see to postpone Nadunda's victory over Marc ... Well, you'd be acting on your own, of course, but considering the situation you're in, it would be to your advantage. And— it might save a lot of lives in Los Angeles, Detroit or New York."

Allison stared at Crider. "Hell, Lloyd, you're asking me for a miracle. First, you want me to sell Nadunda forty tanks; then you want me to figure out some way to keep him from beating Marc with them. It's impossible."

Crider sighed. "Yes," he said after a moment, "I guess it is." He shoved another folder forward. "Well, anyhow, Johnny, if you'd like to examine these documents ..."

The airplane stopped again in mid-air, as if it had hit that invisible wall. Then it churned on, through rain so heavy that it seemed the craft was floating in it. Now, though, the plane was losing altitude.

Dennis nudged Allison out of his reverie. "There. What did I tell you? You can just see it —M'nanda."

Allison looked down. In the distance that immense jungle at last came to an end, dribbling out into a region checkerboarded with tiny farms, oil-palm, and cocoa plantations. Then the land rose steeply, leveled off into a high, flat, enormous bench; and in the center of that sprawled the city, a hub from which spokes of highways radiated to every point of the compass. It was the second largest city of the country, and probably the most strategic, and it was the one Marc had talked of taking, if he could use Allison's tanks to break out of the tight perimeter into which Nadunda's army had forced him.

So far, Allison knew, he had not been able to do that. And, of course, when the new M-60's which were still on the high seas were landed, finis would be written to whatever slim chance he might have had. Nadunda would have enough tanks then both to defend the principal cities and to mount a strong, final offensive in the field, encircling the rebels, squeezing them until there was nothing left. Rainy season or no, with the new tanks Nadunda would not need his planes—that is, if he understood armor well enough to move it through that great southern rainforest they had just flown over, and in which Marc and the rebels sheltered.

It would, though, take a master of armor to operate in such terrain. Laymen thought tanks could go anywhere, overcome any obstacle. Actually they were fairly delicate vehicles, with severe limitations unless well handled. "It must be rough to try to move heavy equipment off the road in this weather," Allison observed innocently to Dennis.

The oil man laughed. "Pretty rough for anything heavier

than a weasel. We've had some bog-downs you wouldn't believe. Once, while we all stood around helplessly, one of your
American D-8 Caterpillars just went straight down in quick-
sand. We retrieved it, of course, but it was like exhuming a
body. Actually, in the rainy season, we *never* take equipment
off the roads. If we have to penetrate the jungle, we build our
road as we go along. And even that's not very practical at this
time of the year."

"What about out here on this plain?"

"Oh, that's much better: a different type of soil entirely. But,
unfortunately, there's no oil there; it's all down south in the
jungle." He sighed. "I do wish this war would end. Right now,
we're just marking time until we can get back into our main
field."

"I don't imagine it'll last much longer. Marc's pretty hard-
pressed, isn't he?"

Dennis laughed, with a touch of bitterness. "That's what we
like to think, and it's what everybody keeps saying. And yet,
somehow, the government never seems quite able to administer
the *coup de grace*. One would think that with all their overwhelming superiority—" He lowered his voice. "Really, if you ask
me, it's the Eyetie's fault."

"The what?"

"The Eyetie. Rinaldi, the defense minister. He's Italian, you
know. And, well, frankly, when you come right down to it, the
Italian isn't very good at that sort of thing, is he? I mean, he's
just not naturally aggressive. At least that's what my father
always claimed, and he fought against them in North Africa;
he should know." He checked his seatbelt. "It's Rinaldi who
really runs the show, you know. Nadunda's just a figurehead."

"So I've heard," Allison said. "I've also heard that when the
government wins, there'll be one hell of a massacre of the
Southern tribes. What's your opinion?"

Dennis hesitated, looking uncomfortable. "Oh," he said finally, "I shouldn't care to speculate on that. After all, I'm not a prophet; I'm just an engineer." Then he was silent. Allison turned back to the window.

Now he had a good view of M'nanda. Its center was startlingly modern: wide boulevards, sleek, new high buildings, all steel, concrete, glass. Flung out from this were attractive sections of villas and bungalows, rainwet lawns gleaming green; the whole thing rimmed with a thick, dark rind of scabby dwellings in which corrugated iron seemed to play a major part: the native quarters and the slums. The single runway of the civilian airport was a white slash on the outskirts; a military airbase on the city's opposite side was neatly ranked with jets. Allison's eyes were, though, more for those all-important highways, like the main strands of a spiderweb, and for the fortifications that protected them.

They were not heavy; apparently M'nanda was considered secure. There were anti-aircraft emplacements, crosswebs of trenches two or three deep between the roads, probably some hidden bunkers and pillboxes. Allison noted, however, that the trenches were thinly manned, at least on this side of town. Then the wheels kicked down; they were past the fortifications and sloping in toward the civilian runway.

The terminal building had been a bedlam, swarming with competitors for seats on outgoing planes, and with the pitiable wrack of war: refugees. It was jammed with blacks; in every vacant space, families huddled around whatever pathetic possessions they had rescued from their homes. Children cried, laughed, shouted, ran loose; mothers suckled babies; men with lost, hopeless expressions shambled about aimlessly; the place smelled like a cattle pen, and the task force of soldiers, nuns and priests working frantically to alleviate the misery seemed not to have made a dent in it. Dennis halted, staring. "I say, this is something new. It wasn't like this when I went on leave. What do you suppose has happened?"

Allison felt a throb of excitement. "Looks like the fighting is getting close to home."

"It shouldn't be; Marc's supposed to be penned up tight below the Laramba—that's a tributary of the Acanara in the south. He can't have got forces through all that jungle in floodtime—can he? Well, we'll see. Come on, there should be a car waiting for me and I'll give you a lift to the barracks. Perhaps the driver will know."

However, the driver was black and his command of English left as much to be desired as Dennis' facility with the native dialect. Finally Dennis gave up. "I don't know. Something about Marc shooting up villages and missions. It doesn't seem to make much sense the way he tells it."

"No," Allison said carefully. "Not from what I've heard about Marc, it doesn't."

"Well, I'll find out at the office and the military will give you the gen at headquarters. Move on, please, driver."

The trip to the barracks took them through a nightmare slum, the worst Allison had seen; not even the *favelas* of Brazil could match it for sheer squalor and human degradation. Its core was a jumble of jerry-built shacks, tin-roofed, jammed along narrow streets and alleys really no more than garbage-strewn mires where dogs, pigs and naked children wallowed. Now, though, Dennis said, its population appeared to have doubled or tripled overnight, the incoming swarm sheltering under tatters of corrugated iron, in packing boxes, beneath improvised lean-tos of scrap lumber. Hunched there in idleness, the refugees watched the passing car with eyes glazed and incurious, apathetic with hunger and despair, and a stench penetrated the vehicle's closed windows that made Allison swallow hard. "Jesus," said Dennis. "I don't understand this. I don't understand this at all."

Then, after a buffer strip of sheet-iron warehouses and light industry, they reached the barracks, an old military complex that apparently had been recently expanded and modernized. Wending through it, crossing several different parades, they finally found the headquarters building proper, and there they said goodbye. Now, in the office of the commandant of the Military District of M'nanda, Allison sat across a desk from Major General Lewis Kopapo.

The general was small, compact, in his middle thirties, soft-spoken, courteous, a Sandhurst graduate. His immaculate khakis were void of ribbons and meaningless decorations; nevertheless, Allison did not think he was a man to be taken lightly.

"Yes, Mr. Allison." Kopapo's English was perfect. "As soon as your airplane changed course, we had a signal to expect you. I've reserved a suite for you at the Central Hotel, and I'd be delighted to have you dine with me tonight. Tomorrow we'll convoy you to Ogoro." He arose, taking down helmet liner and raincoat. "Now, if you'd like to go to your hotel . . ."

Allison stood up. "Thank you, General. And as for that dinner invitation—by all means."

"Very good." Kopapo smiled, and Allison found himself liking the man. They went out through a complex of offices, Kopapo giving orders that his car be brought up. By the time they reached the gallery of the headquarters building, fronting on a paved barracks square, it was there—a fairly new Mercedes. As they got in, Allison noted an infantry company at PT in the square; stripped to shorts, the black men were lean, muscular, tough-looking; they were well drilled, their movements brisk, precise. Their noncoms saluted sharply as the car pulled away. The rifle salutes of the military policemen were equally taut as the car passed through the gate in the massive wall around the military enclave; and Allison, impressed, decided that whatever the merits of the rest of the Acanaran army, Kopapo's command would be a tough adversary.

Now they entered a wide esplanade, where pink villas nestled behind high walls, tile roofs gleaming beneath tropical foliage. Military policemen stood on every corner; not, Allison imagined, as protection against Marc so much as protection against undesirables entering this genteel suburb. And that brought his thoughts back to the refugees clogging the airport and the slum. "General," he said, "how is the war going?"

"Oh, very well," Kopapo answered. "Very well indeed."

"Is Marc still choked up south of the Laramba?"

Kopapo hesitated. Then he said, "Not entirely."

"What do you mean?"

Kopapo bit his lip. Then he said, "I suppose we shall catch up with it eventually. But for the moment, we're concerned about a—what shall I call it?—terrorist detachment, guerrilla, that he's set loose in this area. Oh, it's not a new tactic, but it's a new one for him."

"What is it?"

"Terrorism," Kopapo answered. "I said, terrorist detachment, didn't I?" He gestured vaguely. "My military district, Mr. Allison, encompasses a huge area. I can't guard every village, every mission, every hamlet in it. And Marc's taking advantage of that fact. As of about ten days ago, he somehow infiltrated several tanks and a certain amount of infantry into my area, and he's been raiding quite without mercy. Taking a leaf from the Vietcong's book."

"How so?"

"Hitting undefended places and killing anything that moves, men, women, children . . . No regard for the rules of civilized warfare, just a determination to demoralize the countryside, undermine the prestige of our regime. He'll pick some village with no conceivable tactical or strategic value, appear out of nowhere with tanks, blast in and slaughter anything that moves. He's hit four hamlets and one mission so far—and, of course, thrown the whole countryside into panic." Kopapo's eyes were hard, his face bleak. "It's cold-blooded murder. And worse than murder. At Sinawa, the mission, and at two of the villages, there was torture in addition—atrocities." His voice rose angrily. "No other word for it, Mr. Allison—atrocities! All

to convince the people that we can no longer protect them—
and to send them swarming into M'nanda to clog up the works,
hamper us that much more."

Allison looked at Kopapo carefully; the man's anger was
real. Nevertheless, Allison could not keep incredulity out of his
voice. "*Marc* did this?"

"Yes. No doubt about it. The pattern's constant: five Shermans and a force of infantry. And savagery—typical N'terua
tribal brutality! I suppose it's desperation. He knows his end
isn't far, and this is a last vicious spasm. Well, he'll pay when
we get him; I promise you he'll pay!"

Allison was silent for a moment, grappling with this. Kopa-
po's sincerity, outrage, was undoubtedly genuine. And yet—
Marc? Mingled with disbelief, he felt sudden apprehension.
This was a new, an ominous complication. "How do they do it?
They don't come up through the jungle, across the rivers, every
time they make a raid?"

"No, of course not. The rivers are in flood; besides, we hold
every bridge, ford and ferry. They have a base somewhere here
north of the Acanara, in our territory—" Kopapo broke off.
"I'm afraid I can't tell you any more. Military security, you
know."

"Certainly," Allison said. He settled back thoughtfully. If
what Kopapo said were true, if Marc were using *his* tanks . . .
Disbelief and anger mingled within him.

Then they were in the central city of M'nanda. The rain had,
for the moment, stopped; people took advantage of the respite.
The sidewalks swarmed, every tram, bus and jitney was
crowded. Colorful caftan and fez, shorts and tattered under-
shirts, long, swathing dresses and miniskirts, breechclouts and
business suits—it was an exotic mélange. Allison was surprised
by the number of whites. But, unlike East Africa, Acanara had
made no attempt to force out those who had settled under
British rule, and Marc's terrorism would have sent them
flocking to refuge in the city.

As the car wound through the crowd, Kopapo's head
swiveled from side to side, and his hand was on the holstered
pistol at his belt. The guard in the front seat beside the driver
was equally alert. It would be simple for terrorists to conceal
themselves in such a throng, and Kopapo, of course, would be
a prime target for assassination.

Then the Mercedes halted before the hotel, a soaring structure of glass and concrete rising from a contrasting compost of
older wooden buildings. Its lobby repeated the chaos of the
airport on a loftier scale. Well-dressed Africans and whites alike
jammed around the desk, fighting for rooms. Allison caught
tatters of phrases amid the clamor: "Dammit, man, I'll pay
double, triple—" "But you don't understand, we've no place to
sleep—" Then, with the guard running interference, the crowd
parted. Allison felt curious, envious eyes upon him as Kopapo
spoke briskly to the clerk, was answered deferentially. The general scribbled on a card and a uniformed porter materialized to
take Allison's bag. Kopapo turned away from the desk and
smiled. "All in order, Mr. Allison. I've given quite specific instructions. If there's anything you need, you're to have it at
once." He thrust out his hand. "Now, I'm afraid I must get
back. Seven-thirty? I'll ring you up if there's any change."

"Fine. Thanks for everything." Kopapo left, with his guard.
Allison followed the porter through the throng. Somebody
caught his shoulder as they reached the elevator. "Look here,
old chap. Have you a room? I'll pay your cost and double it for
the use of half—"

"Sorry." The door of the crowded lift closed behind Allison,
and he was carried smoothly to the seventh floor, where he
emerged into a deeply carpeted corridor. The porter unlocked a
door not far down the hall, and Allison was ushered into the
living room of a suite furnished in luxurious, space-age,
modern. Then he frowned. On the coffee table a cigarette still
burned in an ashtray. He looked at the porter. "Is there somebody here?"

At that moment the bedroom door opened. The tall, cadaverously gaunt man who came through it had thinning hair, haunted, circled gray eyes, and wore the white tropical garb of a priest. At the sight of Allison, he halted. "Oh, I'm sorry," he said. "I was just checking to make sure we left nothing behind. But it's quite clear, and I shall leave you now."

Allison motioned to the porter to set down the bag, pressed a few Acanaran shillings into the man's hand and dismissed him. "Who're you?" he asked the priest.

"Father Terence O'Kerry, from the mission at Sinawa—or what's left of it."

"Sinawa." The name had stuck in Allison's mind. "Isn't that one of the places Marc raided?"

Father O'Kerry nodded. "Aye. We were driven in from there." He sighed. "Well, everything's in order here. Father Devlin has already gone; so have the Sisters. I was just checking to see we'd left nothing that would inconvenience you." He looked at Allison with curiosity. "You must indeed be a person of importance to rate a suite to yourself in these times. Are you an ambassador or—?"

Allison gestured impatiently. "Never mind what I am. I didn't mean to drive you out of here; the government made all the arrangements. I didn't even know the suite was occupied. Look, I don't need all this space. Let me phone—"

O'Kerry shook his head. "Thank you, but it's not necessary. We're through giving our official testimony and we'll be going back to the mission, now—at least, we men will. We can't subject the women to such risk again; they'll stay here and help with the refugees for the time being." He took a step toward the door. "I'll leave you now—"

"Wait!" Allison said sharply.

"Eh?" O'Kerry halted.

"I'd like to ask a favor," Allison said. "I'd like to know what happened at Sinawa. If you've got just a moment . . ."

"I'm sorry. We're not allowed to talk to newsmen. Not until

after the investigation. Then the government will issue its own
press release." Again O'Kerry let out that unutterably weary
sigh. "Nor do I care to talk about it. As it is, I'll see it over and
over again in my dreams for the rest of my life."

"I'm not a newsman," Allison said. "I'm a businessman, and
it's important to me to have some information—"

For a moment O'Kerry was silent, his slate-colored eyes ranging over Allison. Then he said, "Aye. I know now who you
are. The American weapons salesman." As Allison reacted, he
laughed shortly. "Oh, don't look so startled. There are no secrets
in Acanara. You're here to sell Nadunda some tanks, aren't
you? It's been made quite thoroughly public, and what other
big-wig would rate a suite in times like these?" His voice was
harsh. "You'll pardon if I stare. I've always wondered what a
man like you would look like. It's very odd; you look like other
men."

"Thanks," said Allison dryly. He opened his suitcase. "I'm
going to have a drink. Would you join me?"

O'Kerry stood hesitantly; but Allison did not miss the glitter
that came into his eyes. Presently the man nodded. "Aye," he
said. "Father Devlin does not approve; but it is a surcease I
need badly at the moment." His eyes followed the bottle of
Scotch. "But since you're an American, you'll need ice. That
will be difficult."

"Never mind the ice." Allison found two glasses in the bath.
The priest watched intently as he poured the drinks and, with
no preliminaries, took a long swallow as soon as Allison handed
him the glass. Then he let out a long, shuddering breath and
dropped onto the sofa, almost a collapse. "Ah, what a blessing . . ." His voice faltered, that of a man suddenly released
from unbearable strain.

"Now," said Allison softly. "Can you tell me about it?"

The priest stared wordlessly at his glass. The rain had begun
again, drumming at the window. At last, O'Kerry said, having
drunk once more, "Aye. I think I can talk about it now.

"Sinawa," he went on, "is one of the oldest missions in the country. A school, a hospital, a church . . . for nearly sixty years now, members of our order have ministered to the tribes around it, particularly the N'terua."

"It was in N'terua country?"

"Yes. A hundred kilometers southeast of here; that was primarily N'terua country until the secession; then the government pushed the N'terua south. For a long time, then, the area was a combat zone, and we treated casualties on both sides, N'kula and N'terua alike. We tried to be impartial—"

"What do you mean, *tried?*"

"Well, after all, man, we *are* missionaries. The N'terua are Christians, the N'kula Moslems. Still, in need and suffering we did not differentiate. But—" He broke off.

"But you sympathized with the rebels," Allison said.

"I made no such statement," the priest answered crisply. He drank again. "Still, the N'terua were our charges, had been for years . . . Anyhow," he went on, "Marc was driven south. The N'kula came in, took over the N'terua lands with the government's blessing once the area was secure. For a time the countryside was almost peaceful. Then"—his mouth twisted—"not many days ago, Marc began his raids." He set down his glass.

Allison poured more Scotch and waited.

"They came with startling suddenness. Places so small, so remote, so inconsequential as to have no military value—and thus no defense. And what happened in them—" He broke off, looked at Allison. "Do you know anything of the Mau Mau in Kenya years ago? Or of the atrocities committed in the Congo by the Simba guerrillas?"

"I know about them," Allison said.

"The same sort of wanton brutality . . . Not warfare: sadism. And at first, when the news trickled in, we refused to believe it. Perhaps other guerrillas, some splinter groups, bandit gangs— but not Marc, not the Army of Southern Acanara—" Then he took a long, almost spastic gulp of whiskey and shuddered.

"We were fools. And because we were, dozens are dead now who might be alive ..." His hand trembled as he held out his glass. "Dozens."

"How did it happen?"

"Like a sudden thunderstorm on a summer afternoon. One moment all was peaceful; the next—" O'Kerry seemed to be staring into the distance, as if he were seeing it all again. "Only four days ago. It was raining terribly hard. The tanks came out of nowhere ..."

"Tanks?" Allison said, feeling an odd chill.

"Aye. Five of them, with men riding all over them ... The old-style tanks of the American Army in the Hitler War ..."

"Shermans?"

"Yes, so I was told. They blew down the wall around the mission compound with their guns, surged in ... we were all caught cold, by surprise. The men jumped off the tanks, already firing their guns, shooting at anyone they saw—women, children, it made no difference. Officers urged them on—"

"Wait," Allison said. Then he asked, "Were they N'terua?"

"Aye." O'Kerry nodded with bitter certainty. "They were N'terua. Soldiers, uniformed soldiers, wearing Southern Acanara insignia, and no doubt about their tribe. No doubt about anything—the tanks, their old weapons, their identity. It was like the strike of a thunderbolt, but there was time to see, to verify ... no time, though, for anyone to escape—except five Sisters whom Father Devlin managed to hide in a cellar. But the others—" He broke off.

Allison waited.

With effort, O'Kerry pulled himself together. "I'll not go into detail. I can't bear to. Everyone in the compound was rounded up. And then, the women—the soldiers took the women." His voice rose. "Raped them. Over and over again. In every conceivable, hideous, perverted fashion ... There in the center of the compound ... They ..." He broke off. "And then when they were through, they killed them. Not mercifully ... Not—"

He stopped, set down his glass, almost knocked it over. "Meanwhile," he said in a different tone, a dead, cold one, "a detail went through the hospital. It slaughtered every patient there. There were ... many children. Even babies ... And then the men ... They were killed too in cold blood—tortured, executed ... Two of them were ... were bound together, gasoline poured over them, a match thrown ... The soldiers laughed..." He looked at Allison with dazed eyes. "You see, they were N'kula, those two..." He broke off. "I don't want to talk about it any more. Not even drunk."

"No," Allison said. "No, don't. Except— How did you escape?"

"Myself, Father Devlin, Father Kelly? We didn't. We were spared."

Allison stared at him.

"The N'terua colonel in charge spared us. Oh, we were beaten, humiliated, but allowed to live. We, he said, were to spread the word. To let everyone know that no matter what the government claimed, it could not protect the countryside. To let everyone know, great or small, that there was no safety from General Marc, no hiding place anywhere ... That was how he put it. That all must cooperate with Marc or die— We three were given back our lives; as quickly as they came, the soldiers mounted their tanks again, roared off, after sending rounds from their tank cannons into our buildings, destroying them... We waited until we were sure they were gone..." His voice broke again. "They were dead, all dead but us and the five Sisters hidden in the cellar. There was nothing we could do for any of them, nothing..." He picked up his glass, drained it, slammed it down hard, got to his feet, swaying a little. "Please don't tell anybody about this conversation, please. Thank you for the whiskey. Now I must go. We have got to return to Sinawa, begin our work all over again ..."

CHAPTER 2

THE TELEPHONE did not ring; it buzzed.

Allison came up groggily, looking at his watch as he did so; it was past six. A second or two to remember where he was, and then he picked up the phone. "John Allison here."

"Mr. Allison? Lewis Kopapo. I'm afraid I won't see you for dinner tonight after all. I've just had a report that Marc's hit another town, some distance south. I'm going over immediately to take personal command."

Allison was immediately awake. "Like the others—the tanks, the Shermans?"

"Yes. Five tanks, according to first reports. In and out, a lightning raid. It was just a crossroads hamlet in the back country, of no importance. The casualties, from first report, are heavy." His voice changed. "Here's good news for you, though. You'll have a more entertaining dinner companion than myself. When I phoned General Rinaldi to advise him you were safely in, he was delighted; and he's already left Ogoro in special convoy and will easily be here in time to dine with you. He's very eager to meet you."

"All right," Allison said. "I'll be here. Good luck down the line, General."

"Thank you, Mr. Allison." And Kopapo rang off.

Allison took two aspirin and dressed.

Wanting coffee, he went down to the lobby. It was still crowded, its chaos unabated. Probably the crowds would be worse tomorrow, after this new incident. The whites would be

83

especially nervous, haunted by memories of Mau Mau atrocities in Kenya, Simba massacres in the Congo . . .

He found the restaurant packed and dozens waiting, and, indeed, most of them were white. Giving up at once, he turned back toward the elevator, having to edge through a throng growing more desperate as evening came and many of them were still without places to sleep. He had not made much progress when he became aware of a sudden change of tone in the clamor and gabble of the crowd. Then, moving from the door backward, silence spread, like oil on water. The press of people rippled in a sort of wave as those closest to the lobby front drew back. Magically, a lane cleared from the front door to the elevator, and Allison, on the very edge of it, saw then that it was not magic at all, but a wedge of splendid-looking black soldiers with machine pistols. "Back, please, back!" They spoke in English and in some native dialect. "Make way. Please make way there." The crowd became so compacted that Allison had no place to go. Then he saw the big white man coming behind the soldiers: a giant in immaculate khakis, his shirt front decked with ribbons. Beneath curly, steel-gray hair, his forehead was high, his face bronzed, his nose a great blade; his eyes were dark, commanding, yet not without good humor, and the teeth between which were clenched a slender black cigar were very white, in a wide, mobile mouth. The man radiated masculinity and authority; and Allison made no further move to draw back—this could only be his host for dinner: Rinaldi.

The Italian laughed, waved, as somebody called to him from the crowd. Then he spoke to the woman on his arm, whose face was blocked from Allison's view by the man's great chest, his huge, sloping shoulder. A guard shoved at Allison. "Make way, please. Make way."

Allison tried to, planning to let the man pass him by, then go to his own room to await word from him. But suddenly Rinaldi halted, frowning. He spoke to the woman again, then said something to the guard. The man looked frightened, moved back.

Rinaldi's eyes met Allison's directly. Again that smile; it lit his face almost irresistibly. He took the cigar from his mouth with his left hand and strode forward. Allison had a momentary sense of being dwarfed as Rinaldi, who must have stood six feet four, towered over him. Then Rinaldi put out his right hand. "Mr. John Allison, is it not? I am General Alessandro Rinaldi."

"How do you do, General?" He frowned. "How did you pick me out of the crowd?"

"Second sight," Rinaldi said and chuckled, a deep, virile sound. "Welcome to Acanara, Mr. Allison." Then he released Allison's hand. "Actually, the young lady with me pointed you out to me. I believe you have met before."

Only then did Allison's eyes go to the girl, who stood there in the middle of the corridor the soldiers had created. She wore a short dress of silver brocade on white, cut low at the bosom; her pale blonde hair was short now, and it emphasized the bone structure of her face, giving it an almost Slavic cast. As Rinaldi turned and Allison automatically stepped forward, her blue eyes, heavily made up, met his and then moved away. But now he understood. "I believe you know Miss Erika Wolf," said Rinaldi.

As Allison came up to her, Erika slowly, almost reluctantly, put out her hand. "Hello, John."

"Erika," Allison said. "It's good to see you again. What are you doing here?"

She hesitated. Then said, "I am reporting the war for my magazines." She withdrew her hand, stepped back, and slid it through Rinaldi's arm. It was a smooth, possessive gesture. "How have you been?"

"All right. You?"

Still her eyes did not meet his. "Well, thank you," she said almost tonelessly. Her fingers played back and forth restlessly over Rinaldi's thick forearm, and Allison sensed that, far from being glad to see him, she was intensely uncomfortable. He looked from her to Rinaldi; they made a handsome pair, though the Italian was easily twice her age.

There was a second or two of strained silence. Allison was aware that Rinaldi's eyes, keen, penetrating, were shuttling from him to Erika appraisingly. Then Rinaldi said in a jovial voice, "Well, shall we go up? We'll dine in my suite, Mr. Allison, if you have no objection."

"Certainly," Allison said. He fell in on the other side of Rinaldi.

As they walked toward the lift, Rinaldi said, "I trust you've been well treated? If you've any complaints, please let me know."

"No complaints. Except that I feel guilty about taking up so much space when it's at a premium."

Again Rinaldi gave that deep chuckle. "Never feel guilty about anything in Acanara, Mr. Allison. Here, everyone gets what he deserves. If you had not been of value to us, we'd have made no effort to accommodate you. We're awfully practical about such things."

"All right," Allison said as they got into the lift, "I'll remember that."

Rinaldi chuckled again. "Yes, do," he said.

Guards surrounded them; the lift door closed; they began to rise. Now Allison could get a good look at Erika. It had been what—five months? If anything, she was lovelier than before. Instinctively his eyes went to her wrists; standing rigidly beside Rinaldi, she became aware of his gaze. Almost defiantly she moved her arms; now Allison could see the insides of her wrists and there were no scars there; he guessed they were concealed with heavy makeup.

Rinaldi missed that byplay. "I'm sorry you were inconvenienced by the weather. Unfortunately we have not yet installed radar control for civilian aircraft. Still, it'll give you an opportunity to see something of the countryside tomorrow."

"Surely," Allison said. "I'm in no hurry."

"Oh?" Erika's brows arched. "I thought you were always on the go."

"I stay where I am as long as my business warrants it," Allison said. "What about you? How long have you been in Acanara?"

"Almost exactly one month."

Rinaldi put his hand on her back. He smiled down at her. "Erika's one of our favorite correspondents—one of the few who writes of the situation as it actually is. Normally I'm not very fond of the press, but in her case I make an exception." His voice was soft, and her cheeks flushed slightly. In that instant Allison realized that the relationship between them was no casual one. It was strange; that realization unsettled him. Thirty days, he thought. She works fast . . . But, of course, it was no business of his.

Then the lift stopped, sighed open. The corridor into which they emerged was swarming with guards who snapped to attention as Rinaldi led the way, pausing before a door bearing the engraved bronze designation *Presidential Suite*. A lieutenant opened it, bowing slightly.

It was big, yielding nothing in luxury to the better hotels of Europe. In the sitting room a waiter stood in attendance over chilled champagne and hors d'ouevres. A squad of men in uniforms which were not those of the army emerged from another room; Allison guessed they were local police. Their captain saluted. "All is in order, sir. We made a thorough search."

"Thank you. Dismissed. You, too, there." Rinaldi indicated the waiter. "We prefer to be alone until I order dinner served." They went out and, noticing Allison's eyes following the police, Rinaldi said, "There have been three attempts on my life in the past sixty days. And the rebels can be damnably clever sometimes. One must never take anything for granted."

Allison thought back to the man with the shotgun. "No," he said.

Rinaldi strode to the champagne, opened a bottle with a twist of thick, strong wrists. He smiled at Allison and Erika. "I know something of the circumstances of how you and Erika became acquainted, Mr. Allison. I understand that you're occasionally the object of such attempts yourself—as a man in your business, must, I suppose, inevitably be."

"Yes," Allison said. "Inevitably."

"I've long wanted to meet you—for several reasons. Her account of how you dealt with the assassin gave me another. It displayed qualities I admire in a man—quick-wittedness, decisiveness, and accuracy with a weapon under combat conditions. Did you ever learn who hired the assassin, Mr. Allison?"

"No," Allison said.

Rinaldi poured champagne. "My dear." He gave Erika a glass, passed one to Allison, poured another for himself. As he did, he said, "I don't imagine there was anything personal in it. Not like the attempts on me. Marc, for instance, has great personal hatred for me. But I should think that, in your case, the gunman was hired by someone who felt no personal animosity toward you, but found it necessary that you be prevented from consummating one or another of your deals."

Allison nodded gravely. "That was very probably the case."

Rinaldi picked up his glass; his eyes met Allison's. "For all you know, the same person who once tried to have you killed might someday become a customer of yours, with every incentive to keep you alive. I wonder— When that happens, Mr. Allison, are you inclined to bear a grudge?"

Allison looked back at Rinaldi. "In my business, General, there are no friends and no enemies—only customers."

Rinaldi laughed. "Well said!" He raised his glass. "Now—to a long and pleasant stay in Acanara!"

Dinner was broiled sand-grouse, baked carp, roast beef and a

wide variety of side dishes, including yams and cassava, staples
of the Acanaran diet, prepared in the native way. It was deli-
cious, and by the time the cheese and fruit were served, Allison
and Rinaldi were, at the Italian's insistence, on a first-name
basis.

As Rinaldi ate and drank, he grew more voluble. His range
of knowledge was wide, his wit sharp, his grasp of his profes-
sion sound. It was almost impossible not to respond to such a
personality; and Allison's caution grew. Men who wielded so
much power had no need to be charming; when they were, he
had learned, it was usually for an end they could achieve in no
other way. Allison was thoroughly aware that he was being
courted; and he was pretty sure he knew why.

Meanwhile, Rinaldi talked about himself without any apparent reserve. His mother had been Florentine, his father a
titled Roman who had been an early backer of Mussolini. He
himself, he said, was apolitical, as befitted a man who had been
a professional soldier nearly all his life. He had begun his career
as a lieutenant in the Littorio armored division in North Africa
in the Second World War. Remembering that, he lost some of
his ebullience, his bronzed face clouded. "It was not," he said,
"an auspicious beginning. Our surrender in North Africa put a
blot on the escutcheon of the Italian fighting man that we shall
be a long time in erasing. I know that my own subsequent
career has suffered from it." His mouth twisted. "Since then,
the Italian soldier has been a joke."

"Not necessarily," Allison said.

"Oh, you need not be diplomatic with me. Nobody's more
acutely aware of it than I am. And yet, it was not our fault—
not the fault of the common soldier, the junior officer. It was,
as always, the generals." For a moment Allison thought Rinaldi
would pound the table with his fist. "The old, tired, incompe-
tent generals into whose brains not a new thought had filtered
since Caporetto! It was a failure of leadership, John, not any
lack of will to fight in the ranks! It was—a shameful betrayal!"

"I don't know," Allison said. "I wasn't there."

"But you do know, must know, that an army's effectiveness is only as good as its leadership!" Then he regained his self-control; the bitterness left his face; he smiled a bit ruefully. "And now I am a general myself. Well, I hope that what I learned then I shall never forget. I may be accused of many things but, I assure you, lack of aggressiveness shall never be one of them!"

Relaxing, he poured more champagne all around. "Well, another advantage; in the British POW camp I acquired a certain polish insofar as my rather shaky English was concerned. That's stood me in good stead. Be thankful for small blessings, I always say. Anyhow, after the war, I was able to work with the British army in Italy for a time; then I went back to the Middle East. Ah, there's a place where there's always something doing for a fighting man. And will be, I warrant you, for a long time to come!"

Allison nodded. "How'd you wind up in Acanara?"

"Quite by chance. One wants a change occasionally, you know, and I was offered the management of an import-export agency here by a friend. I really intended to retire from the military, make my way as a businessman. But the past, it seems, never dies. I inevitably became friends with Victor Nadunda, who at that time was Shodombe's chief of staff. And when it became evident that it would be necessary to depose Shodombe, it was to me he turned for advice—"

"And you advised him to go ahead?"

"Of course!" Rinaldi was emphatic. "John, you've no idea what a bloody mess things were here under Shodombe. The N'terua were being given free rein in the government and it was only a question of time before they took it over completely themselves. Then it would have been a minority government, with the N'kula, who after all are the majority, completely out and powerless. Something had to be done, order had to be brought out of chaos, or the state wouldn't have survived. So I suggested to Nadunda that he not only go ahead, but move quickly and decisively, and he did. The loose democracy the British left behind simply had too many shortcomings; the only solution was to overthrow it and set up a corporate state."

Allison paused with his glass half-lifted. "Corporate state? Isn't that the euphemism Mussolini used for Fascism?"

Rinaldi shrugged. "Whatever it's called, it's the mustering of state and private enterprise in concert under a strong leader to solve the problems of a backward, stagnant society." He looked at Allison. "You're a man of the world, you know that despite what your country says, there simply are some countries not suited to the kind of government the United States and Great Britain are so damned determined to impose on the world. This is one of them. Maybe what we do have here is Fascism, but whatever it is, it works. And I have no hesitation at all in saying I'm proud to have been one of its chief architects!" He relaxed, laughed. "If the thought of Fascism offends you, let's just say that the government of Acanara aims for maximum efficiency and is staunchly anti-Communist."

Allison shrugged. "It's none of my business how you run this place."

"Oh, but it is," Rinaldi said quickly. "It is indeed."

"Why?"

"Because," said Rinaldi, "I want everyone who comes here to go away with a good report. Especially one like you—who obviously has certain connections in high places in your own country."

"I'm afraid you overestimate me," Allison said carefully.

"Ah, but do I? I think your mission here, your very presence, confirms my estimate. Forty tanks, John—the very first aid I've received from the United States since the war began. That's a milestone. A fine beginning."

"And an ending too, I'm afraid," Allison said.

Rinaldi looked at him. "Oh, I hope not," he said. "We badly need more arms."

"You'd have a hard time explaining that to the State Department. You've got Marc outnumbered in men, tanks, airplanes, everything. This was a special circumstance. I'm afraid they wouldn't understand why you'd require anything more."

Rinaldi smiled. "Ah, but a clever man like you could explain to them why. Especially if a profit were involved in it." The smile vanished. "You know of Marc's new tactic—these terroristic raids of his on undefended villages?"

Allison nodded.

"Then neither you nor your government should doubt that I still need arms—far more than forty tanks. Like Vietnam—there your side has overwhelming superiority in men and materiel, and still it's not enough. That's because guerrillas aren't limited by considerations of decency, humanity. Like Marc, like the Vietcong, they don't hesitate to slaughter the innocent if it furthers their cause. And we have to guarantee the safety of the countryside without knowing where they'll strike next. To do that, we've got to double, triple our weapons base. Theoretically there's no limit to the arms one needs in such a situation—and your own joint chiefs would be the first to agree with me."

"Yes," Allison said, "but—" Then there was a knock at the door.

Rinaldi frowned. "Excuse me." He went to answer; Allison got a glimpse of an officer standing there. Then Rinaldi went out into the corridor and closed the door behind him.

Allison looked at Erika. They'd had no chance to talk; Rinaldi had conducted a monologue. But he had not been able to keep his eyes off her; he had almost forgotten how superlatively beautiful she was. He felt a quick thrust of envy of Rinaldi, almost jealousy. But, he told himself, of course that was only a primitive reaction; when you had made love to a woman, some part of you always begrudged her another lover. Still, he was surprised at the effect her presence had on him. To offset it, he made his voice very cool, almost ironic. "Well, I see you're having less trouble with your assignment here than you did in Texas."

Quite poised, she nodded. "Yes. Sandro's a wonderful man. Utterly fascinating."

"Good," Allison said. "I'm glad you've found somebody to lead you out of the dark forest."

"What?" She frowned, then remembered. "Please, let's not even discuss that awful afternoon."

Allison smiled. "Totally awful?"

Her cheeks turned pink. She half-smiled, then sobered. "I made a fool of myself, an absolute, bloody fool. I talked a lot of gibberish, I'm sure. And when I awakened, I knew what an idiot I'd been and I couldn't bear to stay there one minute longer." She hesitated. "I'm surprised you even remembered it. I . . . hardly thought you would."

"I remember it clearly," Allison said. "When I came back to the motel and found you gone, I was . . . disappointed. I was worried about you too. Driving to San Antone in the middle of the night, alone. That was a *fool* thing to do."

"I'm at least quite competent at driving, thank you. Besides, I should think you would have been relieved if something had happened to me. Anyway," she said, "that's all past, just an incident."

"What about Sandro. Is he just an incident too?"

She raised her head, looked at him directly. "No!" she said. "For the first time, I've found someone who— Never mind. I think, however, you'll see that I'm a changed person now. I was a child in Texas; now I am a woman."

Allison looked at her steadily, appraisingly. Indeed, in a way she was right; she *had* changed. There was something of a new confidence in her bearing; and the glow of a woman in love was unmistakable; he had not missed the way she seemed actually to shine with it in Rinaldi's presence. All the same, he thought, she might not have changed as much as she imagined; there were the same nervous gestures, that same affecting vulnerability, that intangible quality that challenged a man's ability to protect her, look after her. All right; she was Rinaldi's woman, and he was not in the market for a woman of his own. Yet, he could not quite put out of his mind the feeling that there was unfinished business between himself and Erika Wolf.

Then Rinaldi returned. "Sorry." His voice was wrathful. "That was a report from General Kopapo. You knew there'd been another raid?"

"Yes."

"He's at the scene, directing the search—with not much success. I'm afraid I'll have to go take personal command myself. I've ordered up a helicopter at the barracks. Maybe you'd like to come along, John? See at first hand Marc's way of making war."

Allison pushed back his chair. "I think that would be a good idea."

"Excellent." Rinaldi turned to Erika. "And you too, darling. Run and change."

Allison stared at him. "Do you think she ought to—?"

"Of course. She's a reporter, isn't she?"

"Yes, sure, but—" Allison turned to Erika. "This will be pretty rough, I expect. Not exactly the sort of thing a woman ought to see."

"Nonsense," Rinaldi said promptly. "It's an exclusive story for her. Besides, I refuse to have my evening totally ruined by Marc. Now, *carissima,* go change. Hurry."

Erika hesitated, then stood up. "Yes, of course," she said. "Just give me a minute." Then she went into the other room.

Rinaldi poured himself another glass of champagne, his eyes lingering on the door she closed behind her. "A remarkable girl, John. Did you and she know each other well?"

"No," Allison said. "She hounded me for a story and I wouldn't give it to her. That's all."

Rinaldi laughed, a deep, rich sound. "I'm afraid your resistance is higher than mine. The first time we met, she complete-

ly enchanted me. The longer I know her, the more enchanted
I become."

"You need the publicity, I don't."

Rinaldi looked at him and laughed again. "Yes," he said.
"You're right. But there's more to it, I assure you; much, much
more. She's a person of great potential, John, but much of it's
unrealized. I find that one of the most fascinating things in life
is to help such a person explore herself, become aware of her
own powers. When I met Erika, she was like a child. Now she
is rapidly becoming a woman. All she needed was a strong
hand ..." He drank. "By the way, do you have bush clothes
with you?"

"No," said Allison.

"Very well; we'll have you outfitted quickly at the barracks."
Rinaldi lit a cigar. His voice roughened. "Those poor people.
God damn Marc!"

CHAPTER 3

ERIKA WAS VOMITING.

Allison, listening to the agonized sounds of retching coming from the darkness behind a hut, did not much blame her. Hardened as he was, his own stomach was queasy as he surveyed the shambles that had once been a native village.

Now, pounded by torrential rain, lit by the floodlights of military vehicles, the place was at once a slaughterhouse and bedlam. Mingled with the roar of engines was the shrill keening of grief-stricken women, the wailing of children, an occasional scream of agony from one of the few huts left standing in which medics worked furiously over wounded. And over it all roared the voice of Rinaldi, everywhere at once, barking orders.

And it was my tanks, Allison thought savagely, *my* tanks that did this! He turned again to the lieutenant who had been assigned to him as interpreter. "What did you say the name of this place was?"

"Nepwa."

Nepwa, Allison thought. It was not a name he would forget.

The helicopter had set them down here fifteen minutes ago—not long after midnight. By then, the worst had been cleared up—but it was still bad enough. And so goddamned senseless! he thought. This miserable little cluster of wattle huts and board shacks, isolated in the back country, had neither strategic nor tactical value. What had happened here was not warfare; it was an exercise in sheer bestiality.

Allison looked down at the row of corpses at his feet. They

were covered with tarpaulins now, but they had not been until Rinaldi had given the order, and it was the sight of them that had caused Erika to gasp, then disappear behind the hut. The bullet-stitched bodies of men and women had been bad enough; what was left of the two children who had been crushed beneath tank treads had shaken even Rinaldi, sent him raging off into the darkness like a madman, bellowing orders furiously.

Now Allison turned away from the bodies. The sounds Erika was making ended in a kind of rattling gasp. He slogged through the mud, rounded the hut to find her leaning against the wall, face upturned to the pouring rain. "Are you all right?" he asked.

"*Gott,*" she whispered. "*Gott im Himmel...*" Her eyes closed, she shook her head, dabbed at her mouth with a sodden handkerchief.

Allison took her arm. "Erika! I asked if you're all right?"

"John," she managed. "Oh, God, John." She fell against him, buried her face against his streaming poncho. Instinctively Allison held her. "Okay," he said inanely. "Okay, okay." He patted her back as if she were a child.

Presently she drew in a long breath and straightened up. Her face beneath the helmet liner she wore was a white blotch in the darkness. "I— Thank you, I'm all right now." She was still breathing hard. "But—"

"I know. It's pretty bad."

"Bad? It's terrible, horrible! That humans could do this to one another..." She shook her head. "Whoever they are, Sandro has got to catch them. He can't let this happen again..."

"No," Allison said. "It shouldn't." He took her arm. "I think you'd better go back to the helicopter or wait in a vehicle." He led her back into the shrapnel-churned center of the village, where the corpses lay.

Erika leaned weakly against Allison as he led her to the helicopter. Aided by the pilot, she climbed aboard. "Thank you," she managed to whisper.

"You shouldn't have come," Allison said.

"No, it's that I should be stronger. I should learn to bear such sights."

"Don't be a fool," Allison said, turned away, and slogged back to the village.

Africans, he'd heard, bore pain more stoically than whites; but there was nothing stoic about the screaming coming from the hospital hut. He strode past rapidly, to where Rinaldi and Kopapo conferred, raingear shining in a spotlight's glare.

Rinaldi turned to him as he came up. "Well, you've seen it now, eh? The use to which Marc puts his American tanks?"

"I've seen it," said Allison.

"Five Centurions are on the way from M'nanda to follow him. They should come up soon."

"For God's sake," Allison snapped. "Why so long?"

Rinaldi's mouth thinned. "Our armor is limited. And we must keep M'nanda covered. The tanks could not be dispatched until replacements for them could come into the city." He flung out an arm. "This is a vast country, John Allison. Four dozen tanks aren't much with which to protect it. But it'll be a different story when the M-60's come."

Allison nodded. "Well, your detail shouldn't have any trouble tracking them, anyhow. In this mud five Shermans leave a hell of a trail. Not even this rain can wash it out entirely. You ought to be able to run them down to their base."

"We hope so," Kopapo said. "We intend to try." His face was weary, his eyes, in the yellow light, bloodshot.

"You'll not *try*," Rinaldi said with an edge to his voice. "You'll *do* it. This time there will be no excuses."

Kopapo looked at him. "Then you authorize me to keep the five tanks assigned to the trail until they catch up?" Allison sensed tension between them. "With the head start they have, it may take some time."

"I authorize you to keep them assigned to this mission until further notice," Rinaldi said. "That's all I can tell you."

"Very good," Kopapo said tiredly. "Thank you, sir. Now, if you will excuse me—" He turned away.

Rinaldi stood there for a moment, watching him slog into the darkness. Then he let out a long breath. "I suppose I was too hard with him. All the same—" He cursed. "Damn it, it's difficult to know what to do. If we put five Centurions on the trail tomorrow morning, we may need them somewhere else tomorrow night. That's what's happened to us in the past, one of the reasons we've never caught up with these raiders nor found their base. We can only afford to follow them for so long . . . And they always have such a damned head start before we get the word and can move armor in."

"Helicopter reconnaisance," Allison said.

"We've tried it; not profitable. Our copters are as limited as our armor—and damned vulnerable to anti-aircraft fire. We sent one out after the Sinawa raid and apparently the raiders brought it down. We can't risk any more that way. Damn it, John, while this is going on, you know, we've still got a war to the south. We can't respond so heavily to a diversion like this that we leave ourselves open for an offensive." He flung away the cigar he'd had clenched between his teeth. "We're in exactly the same position as you were in Vietnam before your massive escalation. We've got *apparent* superiority—but not real superiority."

"I see." Allison's voice was toneless. He was too new to the ground, the situation here to make any judgments. Too stunned right now he supposed, by the carnage his own tanks had wrought, too full of resentment at Marc for committing the very crimes with them that he'd sworn to use them to prevent.

CHAPTER 4

THE NEXT MORNING they went from M'nanda to Ogoro by helicopter. Below them the high plateau fell away to thick jungle, cut by the gleaming asphalt band of an excellent highway. Only once did Allison see traffic—a long string of military vehicles and civilian conveyances, the latter mostly crowded buses. Headed and rear-guarded by armored cars, this was the morning convoy between the two cities.

Ogoro was on the coast, with a big port full of ships. Allison's trained eye did not miss the heavy fortifications that encircled it. Its defenses were stronger than those around M'nanda, though it was in a far more secure position. Nadunda, he thought—and perhaps Rinaldi too—was looking after Number One.

There was little conversation, even in the car that took them from the heliport in the barracks to the center of the city. All three were pinched with weariness, groggy from lack of sleep, and Rinaldi was preoccupied with a massive file of official business. Erika leaned against him as if she drew strength from the physical contact. Allison, remembering her disjointed conversation in the motel room at Del Rio, thought that whatever she had been seeking, she had found at last. That was good, he told himself. She was one of those women who needed a man to stabilize her. Her very fatigue seemed to emphasize a curious quality of inner fragility, of vulnerability, which cried out for a strong protector. It was something to which Allison could not help feeling his own response; and apparently it had captivated Rinaldi too. Even as he riffled through his files, he kept an arm about her.

Then they pulled up before a soaring structure of glass and steel: the Ogoro-Hilton; and Rinaldi withdrew it. "Well, John, here's your hotel. I've reserved one of the best suites for you. I hope you'll be comfortable and get some rest. I'll have a car put at your disposal. I wish you could meet President Nadunda immediately, but I'm afraid it's not possible until ten tomorrow. Meanwhile, I hope you won't feel neglected. I'd like to entertain you, but these—" He indicated the files and sighed. "You know how it is."

"Sure," Allison said. "Don't worry about it. I've got a full day, anyhow. I need to check in at the embassy, and also send some cables to my offices. I'll be fine."

"Very good. Then I'll see you in the morning." Rinaldi got out of the car, and Erika and Allison followed him. He took Erika's hand, kissed her briefly on the lips. "My dear, you get some rest. You have a taxing day ahead of you tomorrow too, you know."

"Yes, Sandro." Then she said, "Sandro."

He looked at her. "Ah?"

"You need rest too."

Rinaldi laughed. "After we've won the war, I'll rest. When there's no more General Marc, I'll retire and we'll spend the rest of our lives swinging in a hammock. But for now—" He kissed her again, shook hands with Allison, and got back in the car.

As a porter took their bags, Allison asked, "You stay here too?"

Erika was watching the car pull away. "What? Oh, yes, I have a room here."

"Fine. Then you'll have lunch with me?"

She shook her head. "I'm sorry. I'm really not hungry. I'm just ... absolutely exhausted. What I need is a nap."

"Okay," Allison said. "Then let me buy you a drink. It'll help you sleep."

She hesitated, then nodded. "Yes. Perhaps you're right. I keep seeing what I saw last night over and over again. Maybe a drink is what I need."

Allison sent their bags up and led her to the bar, almost empty just now. They took a table in a corner. "You're an old hand here. What would you recommend?"

"I think a Martini," Erika said dully. "The Acanaran gin is very good."

Allison ordered. There was an awkward silence then, which he masked by lighting a cigarette. Finally he said, "Thanks for not doing the story on me."

"Did I have any other choice?" Her voice was wry. Instinctively she pulled down the cuffs of her blouse. Then she shrugged. "It worked out well. If I had not failed there, I would not have been reassigned here."

"It's hardly the place I expected to find you. I thought violence wasn't your cup of tea. After last night, I'm still pretty sure it isn't."

"Originally I only came for a quick interview with Sandro. But after we had met, he persuaded me to stay and my office agreed. As for last night— Well, I suppose I shall eventually become accustomed to such things."

"Knowing you, I doubt it," Allison said. "I don't think Sandro should have taken you along."

She looked at him strangely. "Knowing me? I think there are a great many things you don't know about me, John Allison."

"Things that Sandro knows?"

"Yes, as a matter of fact, he does. He knows, too, what is best for me in a way that you do not, that you could never understand. At least he has not used me the way you used me in Del Rio."

"I used *you*?"

"Of course you did. You evidently had some business that

night, you didn't want me tagging along. So you got me drunk, deliberately got me drunk, made love to me, I am sure, in quite cold blood, and was relieved when I ... passed out. It was what you were aiming for all along, wasn't it? Just to get rid of me?"

After a moment, Allison nodded. "Yes. I guess it was."

"Then you should be content. You got everything you wanted. I made a fool of myself and you helped me. At least Sandro has not tried to make a fool of me. He helps me to grow, to strengthen myself. And at a time when I no longer thought there was such a thing as a future, he gave me one. For that, I shall be eternally grateful to him."

Her voice was full of emotion. Allison was silent for a moment. Then he said, "All right. I'm glad you found what you wanted."

"Not only what I wanted," she said. "But what I *needed*." Then she finished her drink, arose. "Thank you for the Martini. Now, I must absolutely have some sleep." Then she relaxed for an instant, her face softened, the resentment left her voice. She put a hand on Allison's. "And thank you for being concerned about me. It helps too. Perhaps I was not as great a fool as I thought." Then she went out.

Allison watched her go, puzzled at himself. She was right; he *was* concerned about her. And that was foolish. Another complication—and if there were one place he needed no more complications, it was Acanara.

He was about to sit down again when he heard a sound from across the room—a laugh, soft, feminine, sardonic. He turned.

The woman sat at the bar, the only other occupant of the room. Perhaps she was thirty; she could have been a little younger, a bit older. Her hair was mahogany-colored; she wore it piled high. The mocking eyes fastened on Allison were green; they matched the simple, yet very chic dress she wore. She just missed being a beauty, but she made up for that by good bone-structure and, Allison noticed, excellent legs.

She smiled at him. "Come here," she said. He realized then that she was more than a little drunk. He hesitated.

"Oh, come on. I won't bite you." She laughed again. "Not immediately."

"All right," Allison said, and he walked over to where she sat at the counter.

Her next words were like a slap in the face. "Who's the poor little bitch you were sitting with?"

"What?"

The woman laughed, gestured toward the door. "Her. The one with the long legs and the round little fanny. The next victim."

Allison said quietly, "Whose next victim?"

"Whose do you think? She's Sandro's new little thing, isn't she? What's her name? I've seen her around, but I don't know her name." She shook her head gravely now. "Little bitch. Poor little bitch."

"Why do you say that?"

She raised her head. "Because I *know* ... I've been the same course ... My name's Emily Ford. No, that's wrong, Ford married name, mustn't use that now. I'm Emily Whittington. Who're you?"

"John Allison."

"Umm." She pursed her lips. "Don't know it." Her eyes ran up and down him. "But you could do it, couldn't you? Give Sandro a run for his money with her."

"I don't have any intention of giving Sandro a run for his money."

"Oh, but you should, really. If you care anything at all about the girl. I don't know what you're like—John Allison, didn't you say?—but you're bound to be better for her than him." Then she broke off. "Never mind, I talk too damned much. Three Scotches before lunch. Always makes me twitter like a parrot. Have you got a cigarette?"

He lit one for her. She blew a plume of smoke and laughed

again. "Wondering, aren't you? Who's the crazy woman in the bar?" Her mouth thinned. "Well, I'm not really crazy. I was for a while, but not any more."

Allison said, "Whatever you're driving at, is there a point to it?"

"Oh, indeed there is." Then she was serious, even sober. "And I will make it by telling you a little story."

"Go ahead."

"Yes. Well. Once upon a time, there was a family. Like all families, there were a man and a woman—and a child, a son, only two years old, the very image of his father. It was a happy family, understand? Everybody in it loved each other very much. And the family came out to Acanara so the husband, who was an engineer, could work in the oil fields, making a great deal more than he could at home; and his wife had a lovely life of it, with a nice house and servants, and plenty of spare time on her hands, leisure, and all . . ." She pushed her glass with a fingernail. "Went merry as a marriage bell," she finished savagely. "Now, do you begin to understand?"

Before he could answer, she went on, her voice flat, abrasive. "Until the wife met Sandro Rinaldi. And became his mistress. And went quite mad and gave her husband no alternative but to divorce her and even"—her voice thickened "—insisted that he take custody of their son. So that everything they had was shattered, all for the love of Sandro, Sandro the Great. Sandro, before whom she wallowed and fawned like a spaniel only wanting to be touched, patted. Like," she ripped out the words, "a damned fool spaniel bitch." She raised her head and looked at Allison with eyes that were agonized now. "And do you know what I got for it? I got exactly what I deserved—a good swift kick in the teeth. Exactly what *she'll* get when he's had enough of playing his games with her and decides he wants someone new! So if you care anything about her, you'll go ahead and take her away from him before he has a chance to destroy her."

"I see," Allison murmured.

"No. No, you don't see at all." Her voice was fierce now. "Because you don't know what Rinaldi can do to a woman. You don't know what a damned clever sadist he is—how he can probe and probe for all the nerves, all the raw spots, and when he finds one that can make you scream, how he keeps hitting it over and over again. He finds where you're vulnerable, and he goes after it and after it and after it until there's nothing left of you, until he's made either a lunatic or a brainwashed zombie out of you—and then, when he's satisfied that he's done the maximum amount of damage, he lets you go, he turns loose—and starts casting about for a new victim." She slid down off the stool. "Excuse me," she said. "I'm sorry if I've bored you. I think I had better go have something to eat now, or I may behave in even more unpardonable fashion. Give the poor girl my sympathy, will you? Oh, and if you tell her about my outburst, tell her one thing more, will you? The fact of the matter is, I hate her. I hate her because I am so damned envious of her and jealous of her that it makes me want to kill her with my bare hands. That's the way Rinaldi can make you feel. Goodbye, Mr. Allison—for now, anyway." And, head up, she marched, a little unsteadily, out of the room.

Allison watched her go. Of course, she was drunk; she was jealous—the classic case of the discarded mistress. Still— He sat down on a stool, ordered another drink he did not really want. *He finds where you're vulnerable and he goes after it . . .* Suddenly he saw again the scars on the insides of Erika's wrists. Well, she was vulnerable, all right . . .

He took a sip of the drink, then shoved it aside disgustedly. But it was none of his damned business. She was of age and what she did with Rinaldi was her own affair. He had plenty on his own mind besides that. He got up and went from the bar to the dining room. The woman was seated in one corner. He took a table as far from her as possible, but every time he looked up, her eyes were on him. When he finished his meal and left, she was still sitting there.

The American Embassy was some distance from the hotel, an old stuccoed building on one side of a small, grassy square. Apparently Norris Middleton was well briefed on Allison and his mission, for as soon as Allison's name was sent in, an assistant led Allison up a great mahogany stair to Middleton's office on the second floor. The big double doors parted; Allison was ushered into the carpeted room, where an elderly man with thinning white hair and a reddish face that seemed to indicate a lifetime of heavy drinking arose to greet him from behind the desk beneath the Seal of the United States. "Mr. Allison . . ."

But Allison had stopped short, just inside the office. It was not Middleton he stared at, but the man in the chair beside Middleton's desk. "Cal! What are you doing here?"

Calvin Buckley stood up. "Hello, Johnny." He was a short, thick man in his late forties, his rumpled suit, as usual, dusted with cigarette and cigar ashes. His fingernails were bitten short, none too clean. Allison felt a mixture of pleasure at seeing Buckley again and a stab of apprehension.

"I came in on the next plane after yours," Buckley said. "Only mine managed to make it straight to Ogoro. What with the new developments in this situation, Crider thought he ought to have a representative on the ground."

"Yes," Middleton added, sounding none too happy about it. "Mr. Buckley just got here. We were talking about the ramifications of our involvement. Sit down, Mr. Allison."

Allison took a chair. "All right, Cal, what's the poop from Crider?"

"Right at the moment, he's climbing the walls. What's with Marc, has he gone crazy or something? You know about these raids of his—now they've hit the papers back home. And those damned M-60's haven't been landed yet, and already Nadunda's putting on the pressure for more help."

"Which I've recommended be given to him," Middleton said. When he talked, he exhaled a bourbon breath that Allison caught all the way across the desk. "These atrocities have got to be stopped. Nadunda needs more tanks, more helicopters, to stop them. You're aware of the latest one, last night, at . . . at . . ."

"Nepwa," Allison said. "Yes, I was there. Rinaldi took me, and we inspected it together."

"As bad as claimed?" Buckley asked. He and Allison had known each other for a long time; Buckley had been a member of Crider's team back in the days of the Hungarian disaster. Now Buckley was Crider's right arm in the field, ranging everywhere as trouble-shooter, problem-solver and, Allison thought, hatchet-man.

"Plenty bad." Allison gave them a terse description of what he had seen at Nepwa. Before he was through, Middleton broke in. "Exactly!" he exclaimed. "The very pattern to a tee!" He slapped the desk. "I said all along that this whole rebel movement was Communist inspired; this proves it! The same tactics exactly as the Huks in the Philippines—I was there right after the war, saw it—the same as the Vietcong! The whole thing, right out of all the handbooks by Mao and that North Vietnamese and Guevara!" He pointed a trembling finger at Buckley; his face was very red.

"That's why I cabled that recommendation. Allison's here now, and he could make the arrangements with President Nadunda and General Rinaldi. If we're going to fight Communism, this is a good place to do it, here in Africa, where we've got a strong government to carry the burden while we supply aid! Here in Acanara is where we can prove there's no future for Communism anywhere in Africa!"

Allison looked from Middleton to Buckley, whose face was carefully expressionless. "Wait a minute," he said. "I think I came in late or something. You *cabled* a recommendation, Mr. Middleton? For more weapons for Nadunda in addition to those tanks?"

"I did! And in the strongest terms!" Middleton sat back in his chair. "This farce with Marc has gone on long enough. Now's the time to put an end to it!"

Buckley nodded. "That's why I'm here, John. Fact-finding mission. Investigate the situation."

"Listen," Allison said. "Nadunda's getting forty tanks. Crider said that was the absolute limit."

"That was before Marc started these raids of his. Ambassador Middleton seems to think it's changed the picture. Maybe reconsideration's required. Anyhow, I'm here to gather as much information as I can."

"Well, you have my recommendations!" Middleton snapped. "Let's help Nadunda all we can!"

"I'm sure the Secretary wants to do all possible within feasible limits," Buckley said with a touch of weariness. Ponderously, he arose. "Well, I have to be going. John, I've got a car outside. Can I give you a lift?" Allison did not miss the faint motion of Buckley's head, almost a command.

"Why not? Ambassador Middleton—" They shook hands, Buckley hurrying Allison along.

When they had dismissed Allison's car and were in the embassy vehicle, Buckley said, "Jeezus!" He took out a handkerchief and mopped his face. "Old Blood-and-Guts back there hasn't had a new thought since the Spanish-American War. He'd love to see us sucked into a brand new Vietnam right here in Acanara. Well, Johnny, how've you been?"

"Lousy," Allison said.

"Well, it may get lousier before it gets better. These raids of Marc's open up a whole new bucket of snakes, and you're right in the middle of it."

Allison turned on him. "What the hell do you mean?"

"I mean that now there's a possibility that we *will* give Nadunda more aid. Since these raids started, he's asked for helicopters to help put an end to them. Actually, what he's looking for is an open-end commitment." Buckley took out a cigar. "After the helicopters, it'll be more tanks, maybe some rifles—"

Allison's flare of anger was immediate. "Well, you're not going to give them to him, are you?"

"I'm not going to give anybody anything. But, yes; there's a chance—" His voice was serious. "Look, when the word of these raids came in, so did Middleton's recommendation and an urgent request from Nadunda and Rinaldi—not to mention a quick shove from the British. Atrocities; they've got to be stopped. The result—for the first time the National Security Council discussed Acanara; that's as high as it's ever been bucked before. Rinaldi is playing both ends against the middle; we understand that he's inviting the Russians to contribute too. And they just might do it. Oh, they know he's a Fascist, they hate his guts. But it would give them a toe-hold in this part of Africa that they haven't got—the same way they got one in the Middle East with arms to Nasser and the Arabs. We may have to give Nadunda what he wants to stave 'em off." He blew a plume of smoke. "The CIA seems to think it's a good idea too."

"The CIA—" Allison said bitterly. Then he snapped, "Look, Cal, do you know about that FBI report—?"

"Black Liberation? I know about it."

"Well, goddammit, can't you see what you're doing? You give more weapons to Rinaldi, he'll smash Marc like a bug! And the minute Marc goes down, all hell breaks loose at home—"

"And you're hanged in public, so to speak, as the guilty party, the one who caused the whole thing." Buckley nodded. "I'm perfectly aware of the ramifications of it all, Johnny. It's rough on you. But, after all, Marc's violating the rules of civilized warfare. He's committing genocide on a small scale, himself—and it's *your* tanks he's doing it with." Buckley shook his head. "You're screwed either way, Johnny. You take the rap for Marc's atrocities. And you take the rap for whatever the black militants do at home if we help Rinaldi wipe out Marc. Frankly, I don't see any way out for you—unless you know how to work a miracle. Like, for instance, having Marc *win* this war—and win it in a hurry."

"Don't be an idiot," Allison rasped.

Buckley laughed without mirth. "I was only dreaming. I was just dreaming how nice and uncomplicated that would be, how it would get everybody off the hook. After all, the M-60's are still at sea. They could still be diverted; we wouldn't even have to land 'em. Then we wouldn't be involved at all, except for your Shermans. And the black militants at home wouldn't have an excuse to raise hell."

Then his voice was serious. "But unless you can pass a miracle on that order, Johnny, I'm afraid that no matter which way the cat jumps, you're cooked. We wind up with another Vietnam or Middle East here, you'll be the scapegoat for that too."

Allison was silent for a moment. "There's got to be some out," he said at last, although he knew very well there was none.

Buckley shrugged. "I don't know. Maybe there's a reason why we shouldn't give Nadunda anything else. Maybe somewhere there's something that would get you off the hook. If you find it, for God's sake, let me know. After all, you'll be dealing with Rinaldi and Nadunda. If they spill anything that might change the picture . . . Or what about this German broad of Rinaldi's? You always were a good man with the ladies."

"Erika Wolf? You know about her?"

"Yeah, we've got dossiers on everybody. She's a little bit nuts. Cut her wrists once. Suicidal, definitely suicidal. Unstable, slept around a lot . . ." Suddenly he looked at Allison shrewdly. "Anything there?"

"I don't know. Maybe you'd better tell me what's in her file." Allison's voice was careful, thoughtful.

"All right, if it'll help you. Of course, it's mostly hearsay. The bulk of it came from her publisher, who was also the man she was shacked up with when she cut her wrists." He blew smoke. "Guilt," he said. "I guess that's it. And I suppose it really isn't her fault. It's hard to be a German of any age, I guess, without being caught up in it. If you're old, you lived through it; if you're young, your parents did and you've got to look at them with a fishy eye ... All those millions of people executed in cold blood— It must be hell to be a member of a race that did that and have to, somehow, come to terms with it. Like having insanity in your family and wondering if it's hereditary ..."

"All right," Allison said. "Try some facts."

"Yes. Well, in the matter of Erika Wolf. Parents were Berliners; Friedrich Wolf, the father, owned a small metal-working plant in the outskirts of the city. Before the Russians came, he saw the handwriting on the wall and fled south to the American zone. In Munich, he was de-Nazified and hired as an adviser on light industry to the American government. Cleared of all pro-Nazi activity."

"Check," Allison said. "Go on."

"After that, under American sponsorship, he opened a hardware factory in Bavaria. It was a success; he died in comfortable circumstances. Those are the facts, as they exist on the record; the rest is pillow talk, picked up by the publisher. You see how important pillow talk is?"

"Damn it—"

Buckley held up a hand. "Gerhardt Felsenreich, the publisher, hired Erika and subsequently fell in love with her, installed her as his mistress. He was a man who looked very much like Rinaldi, older, big, handsome. Or like you, Johnny. Anyhow, she attached herself to him. Then he came home one day to find her in the bathroom, on the verge of bleeding to death." He crushed out the cigar; it filled the car with a vile smell. "She had just found out about her father."

"What about him?"

"Well, he'd fooled them all. The Occupation Authorities, his family, everybody. He was a Nazi, all right, a hell-roaring Nazi, but when the bombs blew the records to pieces in Berlin, he was smart enough to see which side his bread was buttered on. He immediately became a great humanitarian, you understand?

A confirmed hater of Hitler. And that was how his daughter grew up thinking of him . . . Then he had a heart attack."

"Go on," said Allison.

"He was disabled; he had to stay home; and he knew the next one would carry him off. For the first time he and Erika became really close. Up until then she'd been priding herself that she was in the clear, you know what I mean? All around her, her friends were trying to come to terms with those years; but she didn't have to come to terms with anything. She was that rare bird in Germany, somebody guiltless. Until the old man decided he had to make confession. Unburden himself. And did it on her. Told her everything. Including what he made in his Berlin factory."

Allison stared at him. "Which was—?"

"Gas piping," Buckley said.

The car wound on through traffic in downtown Ogoro.

"Gas piping," Buckley repeated tonelessly, "for such places as Auschwitz, Buchenwald . . . you get the picture. Not only made it, but was *proud* of having made it. He told her about it, the dying old man who had to unload on somebody. He told her, not only told but boasted, bragged." Buckley took out another cigar. "That," he said, biting off its end, "was the day she came home and tried to cut her wrists."

"Christ," Allison said.

"It was a hell of a shock to her," Buckley said. "According to Felsenreich, she's been a little bit off her rocker ever since. She had grown up, gone through life, guilt-free. Then this old man who was her father spewed out all his venom on her. And all at once . . . I guess I'm reading between the lines. They don't tell you that much in the cables. But, hell, I've got daughters myself. This thing in the Bible. You wouldn't understand it, John. But, *the sins of the fathers* . . . They pass down; they really do."

Allison nodded absently, thinking of Erika and understanding now. Understanding why she had hesitated to have him investigate her past, beginning to have some insight as to why she clung to Rinaldi. It was strange, he thought, how sick he felt.

"Anyhow," said Buckley, "that's her story. If it helps you understand what makes her tick."

"Maybe," Allison said, "it tells me more about what makes her tick than you can guess."

"Good!" said Buckley. "Then, if there's some way you can use her—"

Allison drew in a long breath. "Listen," he said. "I'll use anybody I can to get my company out of this."

"I thought you'd feel that way," Buckley said. Then he was deadly serious. "Johnny, there's more hanging on this than your goddam company. We were involved in the Congo too; but we got out lucky there, just by the skin of our teeth. We weren't that lucky in Vietnam. We still don't know whether we're going to be lucky or unlucky in the Middle East. But it's the same damn pattern building up here—chaos. Then the Russians fishing in troubled waters. Then our moving in . . . This is the way disasters start. We can't afford another disaster."

"Neither can I," Allison said grimly.

"Then you'd better not waste any time looking for your miracle. *Our* miracle. I'll be at the embassy; you can report to me there. And—Johnny."

"Yes," said Allison.

"Whatever you go, whatever you do, keep an eye over your shoulder. There are a lot of things in Rinaldi's dossier too."

"Yeah," Allison said. "I met one of them once." They were at the hotel now. He got out. "So long, Cal."

"So long, Johnny. Stay in touch." Then Buckley drove away.

Allison entered the hotel. At the desk the clerk stopped him. "A message for you, sir." He handed Allison an envelope.

It was smudged, grimy, as if it had traveled a long way—and yet it bore no stamp. Allison felt a sense of foreboding even as he opened it.

The words, written in a bold hand, leaped up at him.

> Now I know the price of tanks. Thirty pieces of silver.
> I could and should have your throat cut while you sleep.
> But the twenty Shermans will save it for you if you get
> out of Acanara right away. Advice—don't ever let your-
> self fall into my hands alive. We are savages, remember?
> And savages know how to make people hurt for a long
> time before they die.
>
> Markham

CHAPTER 5

A T ABOUT half-past six, the rain stopped.

The cessation of its constant drum made Allison look up from the table at which he'd been decoding cables from his offices, encoding answers and instructions. He rubbed his tired eyes, and as he arose and stretched, Acanara came crowding in on him again.

He picked up the note from Marc, which lay on the bed, read it again. Marc thought Allison had betrayed him, had given him the tanks only to make it easy to sell new M-60's to Rinaldi. Allison's lip curled; he threw the note aside. There was nothing in it about what Marc had used the Shermans for; he, Allison, was the one betrayed.

He began to pace the room, trying to analyze the situation coolly. At first he had found it nearly impossible to believe that Marc actually was responsible for Sinawa, Nepwa, all those other horrors. Yet it had been Shermans, all right; the priest had attested to that, and so had the tank tracks in the mud at Nepwa, which Allison had seen with his own eyes. And those tanks, the priest had said, were manned by N'terua.

So he had to accept that, hard as it was to believe. He had to accept the fact that Marc had reached the point where he would do anything to survive. And that he had made a mistake in giving Marc the tanks, that he'd misjudged Marc badly. He should never have yielded to impulse—after all, what did he really know of Gil Markham? Decades had passed since he and Marc had soldiered in the same platoon; and in those years

116

each of them had become someone else. He was not the same John Allison he'd been; there was no reason to have taken for granted that General Marc, after years of bloody, losing combat, was the same Sergeant Markham.

All right, he had been wrong; and being wrong was likely to destroy him. Now he had to do something right for a change and do it in a hurry. And yet, what could he do? There was nothing—except grope blindly, hope that luck, fate, something, would yield him some miraculous way of getting out from under. And to begin with, he had to find out everything he could of what was really going on in Acanara.

But he would have to do it without arousing Rinaldi's suspicions or enmity. There were talks ahead with Rinaldi, Nadunda. Some unexpected confidence, some slip of the tongue, might yield a scrap of information, give him a handle he could grip, a lever he could move, to take the pressure off Allison Trading.

He would not see them until tomorrow. He could not wait that long.

The bar was crowded at this time of day, most of its patrons black. Allison ran his eyes over their faces, wondering which one, if any, was Marc's man; that Marc had assigned someone to watch him was almost certain. Then he tensed as he caught sight of a signaling hand—and relaxed as he recognized the green dress its owner wore. Emily Whittington sat at a table in the corner.

Allison went over to her. "It *was* me you were waving at?"

She smiled. "As a matter of fact, it was." He had expected her to be under the weather; but she seemed perfectly sober and apparently was nursing the drink before her. She'd evidently taken herself in hand; her hair was sleekly done, her makeup fresh, and she looked younger than she had at noon. Allison sat down, not missing the way the dress hugged small but definite breasts.

"Actually," she went on, "I've been sitting here for a half hour, quite shamelessly watching for you. First of all, I'd like to apologize for being so ... well, crass ... at lunch. I'm not good at drinking on an empty stomach."

"Forget it." Allison signaled the waiter. "As a matter of fact, I found a lot of what you said very interesting."

She looked troubled. "I probably said a good deal too much."

"Don't worry. If you did, none of it will get repeated anywhere."

Emily looked at him closely; then relief touched her face. "No, I shouldn't think it would. Incidentally, I know who you are, now. I thought people like you always operated under a cloak of secrecy, but it's all over town about you."

The waiter brought Allison's drink. "Big Brother has spread the word."

"Yes. Well, I won't inquire further into what you do. Guns, weapons, that sort of thing—I'm thoroughly tired of all that. I heard quite enough about it from Sandro during our ... relationship."

Allison looked at her thoughtfully for a moment. "All right. Then, shall we talk about dinner? Here? Or do you know of a better place?"

For an instant her gaze flickered away, then returned with a certain boldness that Allison found exciting. "It will be pretty crowded here. But we could go to my house. I haven't made dinner for a man in a long time—but once I was a pretty famous cook."

"Your house? You're not at the hotel?"

"No, I have a place of my own. Even a job. Won't, though, if I take many more afternoons off as I did today." She sipped from her glass. "My ex-husband still sends me some money; he doesn't have to, really; he just does it. Even after the bad time I gave him. And I'm secretary to the managing director of a cocoa-shipping firm. All that enables me to keep the place Rob-

ert and I leased when we came." She toyed with her drink.
"It's really far too large for me now. I suppose I ought to go
back to England, anyhow. But"— she laughed a little brassily—
"women are such damned fools, you know. And hope springs
eternal in their breasts. Maybe when your blonde friend's term
is up—and I can assure you, it won't last much longer—well,
then, if Sandro should come looking for me again, I'd want to
be here, where he could find me." She drank, long and deep.
"You see what a hopeless idiot I am?"

Allison found nothing to say.

"I'm sorry. I didn't mean to bore you; as you must have
noticed this afternoon, I'm only too happy to discuss my most
intimate personal affairs with strangers. Please, may I have another drink? Only one more, I promise you—and then we'll go
to my place."

They took her car, a somewhat battered Renault. She drove
it with dash and verve through crowded streets, and before long
they were in a pleasant suburb of small houses, each with its
own walled garden. "This is the oil company's quarter," she
told Allison as they turned in the drive. "Robert used his influence with them so they let me stay on the term of the lease. But
I'm afraid I'm not very popular with the neighbors. It's a
crowd the gay divorcée doesn't fit into very well. Gay divorcée," she repeated sardonically. "Yes, I'm very gay." Then she
said, "Damn it, what I am is lonely. I'm lonely as hell. That's
really why I waited for you down in the bar."

"I'm glad you did," Allison said. "I had a long night ahead
of me."

"All my nights are long. That's one of the reasons I always
seem to drink a little too much."

The house was pleasant. There was even a piano, with two
pictures on it, one of a handsome, weather-beaten man holding
a baby; the other of Sandro Rinaldi in full uniform. There were
a lot of books, records and magazines about. Emily led Allison
into the kitchen. She indicated a cabinet. "Will you do the

honors while I put dinner in? It won't be long; I'd rather hoped things would turn out this way and I did some marketing, found a very nice hen. Anyhow, there's almost anything you might want to drink there. I wouldn't mind a Scotch and water myself."

Allison made the drinks while she donned an apron and went to work. When he handed Emily hers, she turned to take it, and as she did, her eyes met his and she tilted her face upward. Allison bent his head and kissed her and she responded greedily, straining against him, the hunger of her body obvious and unashamed. When it was over, she stepped back, breathing hard, breasts rising and falling. Then she laughed, a little shakily. "One more like that and we'll *never* eat. Hello, John Allison."

He touched her chin with his finger, liking her very much now and looking forward to the evening. "Hello, Emily."

Abruptly she turned away, back to the food. "Shall you be in Acanara long?"

"I hope not."

"Oh, that's too bad. Still, I don't blame you. It's a terrible place, isn't it? This dreadful war. One feels so sorry for the poor N'terua—or at least used to, before they began to do such awful things with their tanks. I don't see why Sandro lets them continue."

"Maybe he can't stop them."

"I don't know. He used to boast that he could crush Marc anytime he chose to. But maybe things have changed since we last ... were together. Anyhow, one never knows what Sandro's up to. After all, Machiavelli was an Italian too, wasn't he?" Then she shook her head. "You must be tired of hearing me talk about him."

"No. I have dealings with him. The more I learn about him, the better."

Emily turned. "Is that why you came home with me? In hope that I would tell you a lot of things you wanted to know about Sandro Rinaldi?"

Allison smiled, came to her, put his arm about her and kissed her again. She shuddered pleasurably, holding floury hands out and away from him. When he released her, he said, "That's why I came home with you."

"Much better, then." Emily's voice was a whisper. "That's why I brought you home. Do you know what? For the first time, I'm beginning not to envy that little German girl at all." Then she turned away briskly, as if it took will power. "I almost hope, for her sake, that he lets her down easily." She poured wine over the hen, slid it into the oven. "He won't, though. That would take all the fun out of it for him." She washed her hands. "If she's got dreams of being the power behind the power behind the throne of Nadunda's West African empire, she'd best forget them."

Allison did not flicker a muscle, but merely rolled his glass between his hands. "Nadunda's West African empire?"

"Oh, yes. He and Sandro are given to very grandiose dreams. All these little states that have just won their independence and are dirt poor and badly mismanaged ... If only it weren't for this war, Sandro says, it would be so easy to unite them into one big confederation with Nadunda at their head. Really, he says, it's the only way this part of Africa will ever thrive, and perhaps he's right. But, of course, this war has spoiled that dream for him—at least for a while."

"Yes," Allison said carefully. "At least for a while." He drank. "If he can't unite Acanara, how does he think he can unite this part of Africa? Countries that have just got their freedom wouldn't be anxious to give it up."

"Oh, he seems quite sure it could be done. The carrot and the stick, he says." Then Emily turned toward him, drying her hands. She unfastened the apron, threw it aside. *"Voilà!"* Her green eyes sparkled. "Exit the cook, enter the party girl! Maybe you're not tired of hearing about Sandro Rinaldi, but I'm tired of talking about him." She picked up her drink and tossed it off. Her eyes met Allison's. "It will be an hour before the hen's ready. And I want to be kissed again."

Allison came toward her. "Why not?"

She caught his hand, held him away. "No," she said, and her voice dropped to a whisper. "Not here. In the bedroom." Then she dodged away from him. "Just make us two fresh drinks and give me only a minute."

"Yes," Allison said. Her lips brushed his cheek as she went by. He took the two glasses and refilled them. Nadunda's West African empire, he was thinking. The carrot and the stick . . .

Then, from somewhere beyond the hall, Emily's voice called softly, "John?"

Allison picked up the two glasses. Almost with a click, he shut off all thought of Rinaldi. He went into the hall.

"In here, John," she called.

He found the bedroom, its door half open, entered it. One lamp burned beside the bed. Emily Whittington lay on the bed, a corner of the coverlet thrown across her loins. Otherwise, she was naked, her flesh white in the lamplight. Her eyes did not meet Allison's. "Bring me my drink," she whispered.

"Yes," Allison said, and he went to her.

CHAPTER 6

VICTOR NADUNDA, president of the so-called Republic of Acanara, was a short, brisk man in his late thirties who had already developed a pot belly, which he desperately and unsuccessfully sought to suck in when he stood up. He wore military uniform, and his shirt front was frosted heavily with self-awarded ribbons and decorations. His handshake was limp and damp; and it did not take many minutes for Allison to see that his attitude of briskness and decisiveness was pure sham.

Their interview was brief. "Defense Minister Rinaldi is, of course, empowered to handle all matters concerning armaments, subject to review only by myself. I'm sure you and he will have no trouble in reaching appropriate agreements. Meanwhile, Mr. Allison, all Acanara is yours for the duration of your visit."

"Thank you, Mr. President," said Allison, trying to look grateful. Then, surrounded by the omnipresent bodyguard, he and Rinaldi went to Rinaldi's office in the Presidential Palace.

It was large, but not lavishly appointed, furnished indeed with a martial severity. Once they were in it, Rinaldi motioned Allison to a chair and sat down behind a desk on which papers were neatly and methodically arranged. He leaned back and lit a cigar. "Well, John, I trust you got a good night's rest."

"A fine one, thanks." Allison was refreshed and the world looked much better to him, despite the incessant rain. The evening with Emily had been a pleasant interlude, one he'd badly needed.

"I'm sorry I couldn't entertain you last night. You know what a devil of a day I had yesterday. Then there was a call from Kopapo—"

Allison sat up straight. "Did he have any luck?"

"No. To be frank, Kopapo's aggressiveness leaves something to be desired. But in this case, the Shermans had too much of a head start. To top it all off, a couple of the pursuing Centurions got themselves bogged and had to be retrieved. It was pretty much of a botch all around. Anyhow, we couldn't keep those tanks out of position, just roaming around the back country, for too long. I understand the new tanks are due in a few days, and as soon as we can get them unloaded and shaken down, we'll mount a sweep that'll make short work of those damned Shermans. Meanwhile, we'll just have to hold our breath. Now, shall we get down to business?"

"A good idea," Allison said.

Rinaldi opened a file. "This is rather a tight price, isn't it? Doesn't leave you a shilling of profit, if my guess is right."

"Your guess is absolutely right."

"It's not fair, really. Of course, my hands are tied—on this shipment." He looked at Allison. "But maybe we could make it up on future shipments."

"I'm not sure there'll be any future shipments," Allison said carefully.

"Somehow," Rinaldi said, "I think there will be—if we all pull together."

"We—" Allison said.

"Yes. You. Ambassador Middleton. And I. If we all exert maximum influence with the State Department's Mr. Buckley with whom you and the ambassador talked yesterday—"

"Oh," said Allison. "So you know Buckley's here."

"And why." Rinaldi grinned. "John, nobody comes in or goes out of Acanara without my knowing who, when and why. Now, look. I don't expect your country to *give* us weapons outright, supply us with direct military aid. But there's no rea-

son at all why there can't be more deals like this one ... if
Ambassador Middleton's recommendations are listened to ...
and yours."

"I doubt that mine would be listened to."

"Oh, I think they would. I understand you and Mr. Buckley
are old friends. I get the feeling that your word might carry a
great deal of weight with him. Especially since you'd be willing
to handle future shipments at cost, as you did this one."

Allison snorted. "Why should I handle future shipments at
cost?"

"Insofar as your government would be concerned, you'd be
doing that. In actuality, you'd make a handsome profit. It
would work like this: You make a strong recommendation to
Buckley that we get more arms. You offer to handle them on
almost no margin at all. Your government sells them to you,
makes certain funds available to us to pay you for them, and
we do. Then, out of our own resources, we make direct to you
an additional payment of fifteen per cent in hard currencies.
Thus, we get modern arms, they cost us only fifteen per cent of
their real value, and you make a handsome profit. And, of
course, there would be a consideration for Mr. Buckley too,
arranged by you and paid by us, simply for accepting your and
Middleton's recommendations and adding his own."

Allison nodded, unable to help feeling admiration for Rinaldi. He'd not missed a trick in turning Marc's acquisition of
tanks, Marc's brutal new offensive, to his own advantage. "I
don't know about Buckley," he said. "That might be tricky."

Rinaldi visibly relaxed. "Salaries in the State Department
aren't very high, are they?"

"Not as such things go in America. Buckley makes about
eighteen thousand, I'd say. In Washington, that's not
much."

"He has wife and children?"

"Two daughters and a son."

Rinaldi's smile was confident. "Then I should think an additional three per cent on the total volume, deposited to his credit in a Swiss bank, would be most attractive."

"It might be."

"Then, most discreetly, you could approach him."

"Perhaps." Allison's eyes met Rinaldi's. "But you realize, the final decision rests with high-echelon people in Washington. And they're afraid you'll use these weapons to massacre the N'terua. Somehow, you'd have to convince them you wouldn't."

Rinaldi chuckled. "I'm far ahead of you on that, John. Are you free this afternoon?"

"Yes."

Rinaldi scribbled something on a sheet of paper, handed it to Allison. "Here is your pass to the main barracks. If you will have your driver bring you there at three, I believe you'll see something interesting." His face was sober now. "This afternoon I shall superintend the execution of four soldiers of our own army for atrocities against N'terua civilians."

Allison stared at him. "*What?*"

"These men, two of them officers, have been tried and convicted of violating the rules of civilized warfare. Rape, murder, looting—they're guilty of all three. I intend to demonstrate to the world at large that we'll tolerate no such atrocities, especially against noncombatants. I want our own troops impressed with that too. I think the affair will prove quite conclusively our live-and-let-live policy toward civilians. I'm tired of all this talk about genocide, and I intend to put an end to it. You come, see with your own eyes, tell your friends in Washington about it first-hand." Then Rinaldi added casually, "If you don't mind, please give Erika a lift, will you?"

Allison sat bolt upright. "*Erika?*"

"Certainly. She's a correspondent, and all members of the press in Ogoro have been invited to attend."

"Good God!" Allison snapped. "Didn't you see her at Nepwa? Things like that tear her all to pieces!"

Rinaldi's face was suddenly expressionless. "I'm aware of that, John. It's something she must learn to overcome. After all, she came here to report a war. One can't do that without becoming accustomed to violence."

Allison shook his head angrily. "But she doesn't need her nose rubbed in it!"

Frowning, Rinaldi took a cigar from a humidor. "You are concerned for her, eh? Well, of course your concern is appreciated. But I flatter myself that I know Erika better than you and that I know what is best for her. This is a violent world and Acanara a violent country. And if Erika intends to survive in either, she must accustom herself to violence. I've told her that it's my wish she attend, and she's agreed. That, I believe, ends the matter." He picked up a file folder. "Now. Shall we get down to business?"

Carefully suppressing the strange rage that smoldered in him, Allison nodded. "All right," he said. "Let's do that."

"Three per cent," Buckley said, almost dreamily. He drummed his stubby fingers on the table. "Three per cent of . . . how much? Millions. A fortune. A goddam fortune."

"Yes," Allison said.

"More money than I'll see in the next ten years. And me with a daughter just entering college." He laughed, a short, nervous sound. "Do you know what? I'd be a fool not to take it."

Allison said nothing.

"Goddammit," Buckley said, "it goes on all around me. I see it every day—congressmen, senators, the people on the regulatory commissions, in the Pentagon—damn it, they get theirs, you can bet on that! Why not me? Suppose we gave him five million dollars' worth of arms—just a drop in the bucket. But that would be a neat three-quarters of a million for you and a hundred and fifty thousand in a Swiss bank for me. Wouldn't that be something, Johnny? Just to walk in and tell my wife,

'Honey, pack up. We're going on vacation. We've got a hundred and fifty thou in a Swiss bank!' "

Then he sat up briskly. "Hell, she wouldn't let me keep it anyhow! No more than we'd let you keep any under-the-table profit from Rinaldi!"

"I don't want it," Allison said. "All I want is to get clear of this mess. But I couldn't turn him down flat."

"No. String along. Play for information."

"I've got some," Allison said. "I met a woman last night who used to be Rinaldi's mistress." He told Buckley about Emily Whittington.

"West African empire," Buckley said, when Allison was through. "Now that is something new. Unfortunately it's not the sort of thing I can put into my report."

"Why not?" Allison leaned forward. "Look, Cal—"

"For the same reason," Buckley said shortly, "that I can't use his bribery offer until he makes it to me personally; and he's too damned smart to do that. It comes from you, unsupported, and it's to your advantage for us not to give any more weapons to Acanara. Hearsay, unsupported. Now, if you had evidence—"

"Evidence? Emily Whittington will tell you—"

"No. Facts. Proof. Not the hearsay testimony of a woman Rinaldi dumped, who's got a score to settle with him." He nodded. "Look, John. I see your angle. What you're driving at is—"

"I'm saying that Rinaldi imagines himself as a goddam man of destiny, an Il Duce, junior grade. He wants to put together an empire of his own here in West Africa, and he needs guns to do it. That's why he's been carrying Marc along instead of putting an end to this war. That's why he's made no real effort to find those Shermans Marc's using in his terror raids. The longer the war goes on, the more chance he's got to sucker weapons out of somebody and stockpile 'em. Then, when he thinks he's got enough, he'll step on Marc like an ant and use those arms to hit his neighbors with."

Buckley nodded. "If it's true, it's damned convenient for you. If we had proof, there'd be no question of giving him any more weapons. Neither would the British—probably even the Russians would recoil. But—*proof*, Johnny!"

He straightened up. Allison did not miss the excitement kindling in his eyes. "All the same, you may be on the right track. I'll do some checking myself and you— When are you seeing the Whittington woman again?"

"Tonight. She's to meet me in the hotel bar at six."

"Good. Dig into the matter deeper with her. She's got a grudge against Rinaldi; maybe she knows more than she's told you. Maybe she even knows how to get some proof." Now the excitement had crept into his voice. "Johnny, maybe you *are* on the track of the answer. If we could get proof that Rinaldi really had plans like this . . . We could divert those tanks, we could get out of this mess completely! Listen, you keep playing along with him. You can tell him I was receptive to his offer. See if you can get him to spill a little more. Don't cross him, sucker him along."

"I'll do what I can," Allison said.

"You'd damned well better," said Buckley.

Erika was waiting in the lobby when he entered it. She got up off the sofa, trim and incredibly lovely in a fresh white dress; Allison was surprised at the way the sight of her stirred something within him. Then he cautioned himself. She was to be used; that was all. He must remember that. She was Rinaldi's woman, and he had to use her.

"I thought perhaps . . . would you like it if we had lunch together?" she said.

"Why not? Right now?"

"Yes, if you wish."

"Sure." He checked hat and coat and they went into the dining room. When they had been seated at a table in the corner, Allison ordered Martinis. Erika arched her brows. "A little early?"

"Not with what we've got ahead of us this afternoon."

She looked at him. "Oh. You mean the executions."

"Yes. Sandro asked me to bring you with me. That is, if you want to go."

Her eyes dropped away from his. After a moment she said, "Yes. Of course I must go. It's my job."

"Is it really?" Allison said caustically. "Or is it because Sandro insists?"

Erika frowned. "I don't understand what you mean."

Allison hesitated. No, it was wrong to try to talk her out of it. That was crossing Rinaldi, would only anger him. But then he saw how her hand trembled as she picked up the drink the waiter had brought. Sudden anger surged in him. *He finds where you're vulnerable* . . . still, he was cautious. "Have you ever seen anyone executed by a firing squad?"

"No."

"Well, if you liked Nepwa, you'll *love* the executions. Look, Erika—" His voice was suddenly earnest. "You don't really have to go. You're not on a daily deadline. You can pick up all the information you need from the other reporters. Hell, I'll go and give you a first-hand account, if you like. But seeing four men shot in cold blood— that's not for you."

She frowned as she looked at him. "John. Johnny. Why do you insist on being so concerned about me?"

"Because—" He groped for words. Then he said, "Because I know more about you than you think I do. I know about your father. I know why you cut your wrists. And I know that you're walking a psychological tightrope and it's not going to take much to push you off."

She stared at him. "You know about my father?" The horror in her voice startled him; so did the utter paleness of her face.

Then her tone was one of cold fury. "Damn you. You promised not to snoop—"

"I didn't. Someone else told me."

"Not Sandro," she whispered.

"No. But he knows, eh? You've told him?"

Suddenly she was defiant. "Of course I've told him. I've told him everything."

"Oh," Allison said. "So that's why he knows all the right buttons to push."

Erika's eyes were enormous. "And what do you mean by that?"

"Nothing," Allison said, retreating quickly. "Nothing at all. Forget it. You and Sandro are none of my business."

Erika shook her head violently; the motion made a golden blur of her pale hair. "I think perhaps we are," she said in a taut voice. "Since you seem so concerned for my welfare."

Allison said nothing.

"Listen," she went on fiercely. "The whole world fell out from under me when my father... When he told me. Until then I thought I knew who I was. And then I found out that I ... that I was something else entirely, and so was the one man I really loved   You don't *know* really what he told me or how he told it to me. It was unbearable! And... and the most terrible part about it was that, even after he told me, I still loved him." Her eyes glittered. "*I still loved him!* Do you know what that means?"

Before he could answer, she continued low-voiced. "It meant that I was like him, that his insanity was my insanity. Because I could *forgive* him for what he'd done! And that— When I realized that—" Now her voice was a whisper. "That was when I no longer wanted to live. That was when I went to Gerhardt's apartment and cut my wrists!"

Still Allison was silent, her intensity quenching speech. Then, quite surprisingly, she drank again and went on almost conversationally, almost archly. "I didn't succeed. It wasn't my fault.

But now I'm glad I didn't. Thanks to Sandro. Who else do you think has given me the will to live? My God, the men I went with, the men I slept with, trying to find one who could make some sense out of it all. You—do you know that day in Del Rio, I thought I had finally found someone. When we were talking there, I began to think, *Here at last, if I could only—* but I spoiled it all, of course. I got drunk, let you use me . . . And then I woke up feeling filthy, knowing what contempt you must have for me. And that was when I left . . . But that was a blessing in disguise; otherwise I would never have met Sandro."

Allison said, "I see. He's given you whatever it was you were looking for, eh? The answers?"

"Yes. First, he's taught me not to be *ashamed* of what my father did. That it was war, and in war people do what is necessary and have no choice. My father told me that too, but I did not believe him. Sandro has explained in a way that I can understand—"

"The end justifies the means," Allison said softly.

"You said the same thing. You do what is necessary to stay alive and in business. Everybody does it; it is not such a great thing. You Americans talk about German guilt. But Hiroshima, Dresden, Nagasaki—" She broke off. "I am not equipped to argue great moral issues. You must discuss it with Sandro sometime. For myself, it all boils down to the fact that he condemns neither me nor my father. And that he's teaching me to bear the things I have to live with—"

"How? With Nepwa? With the executions?"

"Yes. In a way. I was too soft. I needed to be harder, as my father was hard, as Sandro is hard." She drained her glass. "As you are, for that matter."

Allison said, "I don't expect you to believe this, but sometimes being hard costs more than you can afford."

Erika said quietly, "I think I shall take that risk. It is better than being soft and hurt by everything. And I think I have it within me to be hard. After all, I am my father's daughter."

"You think you are," Allison said. "Has it ever occurred to you that if you aren't, you're in trouble?" Then he said, "All right. We'll go to the executions together then. Do you want another drink?"

She stood up. "No. I'm afraid not. Please excuse me. This conversation has left me quite without appetite. I think I'll go to my room and rest. Please call me when you are ready to leave."

Before Allison could speak, she was gone. He cursed softly, then ordered another drink.

The car was there promptly at three. Allison, feeling curiously empty, drained, rang Erika and met her in the lobby. In the back seat, she sat well away from him in utter silence. Allison gave her no reason to break it.

The rain was falling hard from a sky that was one vast, gray smudge. The vehicle wound through town for fifteen uncomfortable minutes. Then it slowed as a high, thick wall loomed ahead of them, its massive gates swung open; a line of cars halted at a checkpoint. For the first time Allison spoke. "It's not too late yet. We can still turn around. But once we're inside the barracks, we won't be able to get out until it's over."

"I have no intention of turning around," said Erika thinly.

Allison shrugged. "Suit yourself."

They passed through the gate. The driver followed the other vehicles from parade to parade, and then, finally, they were in a huge, remote inner court. Here, troops were massed in the rain; on one side of the square, what looked like a covered reviewing stand had been hastily erected, raw new lumber glistening. A small group of officers in helmets and ponchos, several black civilians in hats and raincoats, and a group of newspaper correspondents had already mounted it. An MP opened the door of the car and Erika buttoned her trenchcoat and got out. Allison followed her. As the car drove away, he saw that, in the center of the court, paving stones had been removed and four thick posts, each six feet tall, had been sunk into the ground in a single rank at precise intervals. As they mounted the stand, he felt a chill that had nothing to do with the rain.

The officers and civilians had formed a kind of receiving line up there, and Sandro Rinaldi was in its forefront, just behind Victor Nadunda. As he took Erika's hand, he looked into her eyes. "Thank you for coming," he said simply. Then, unabashedly, he patted her. "It will not be too bad," he added.

"No," she said. Then she moved away, joining the ranks of correspondents. Allison took station with them, but well away from Erika.

The civilians were the minister of information and his assistants. They both looked uneasy, Allison thought, in contrast to Nadunda's lack of expression and Rinaldi's smiling self-assurance. There was a small murmur of conversation from the crowd; the soldiers in the ranks stood silently at parade rest. Then the murmuring died. A squad of an even dozen soldiers, under arms, marched with precision through a gateway and ranked themselves on the parade below, their 7.62 light automatic rifles slung muzzle-downward.

The minister of information cleared his throat, the sound very loud in the hush. He put on a pair of glasses and an assistant handed him a closely typed sheet of paper. "Gentlemen," he said. "Gentlemen, if I may have your attention . . ."

All eyes were on him. "Copies of the following press release will be distributed among you later. So will official photographs, on a pool basis; there will please be no private photography. Meanwhile, please allow me to read this. I am afraid it will have to speak for itself; there will be no questions later, and charges, specifications and court-martial proceedings remain classified." He coughed and began to read.

"Datelined this date, Ogoro, Acanara: In response to accusations made against its troops of irregular conduct and criminal acts against the civilian population in territories captured from the rebels, Victor Nadunda, President of Acanara, recently issued a secret order providing for the trial of any soldiers so accused and their execution if found guilty.

"A complete investigation having been made of all charges to date, four Acanaran soldiers with varying degrees of command responsibility have been tried on such charges and found guilty. Second Lieutenants Nkawe Okujukwe, and John Mebebwe, and Sergeants Tehno Kimbawe and Nio Mushatatwe were, therefore, executed by military firing squad today in accordance with the sentence of the court.

"The four were found guilty of the murder of noncombatants; the two sergeants were also convicted on charges of looting. It is hoped that by this stringent action, the Government's determination to observe the rules of civilized warfare toward the civilian populace of the other side will be made evident.

"The Government of Acanara continues to maintain the strictest standards of discipline among its troops, and the punishment of any future transgressors will be equally severe, regardless of rank."

He took off his glasses. "Thank you," he said. "General Rinaldi?"

Rinaldi stepped forward, handsome face grave. "Thank you, Dr. Imbaba. Gentlemen, it is a distasteful event we have asked you to witness today. No army likes to execute its own men—especially on such charges. Modern warfare is, by its very nature, often inhumane. However, these four have gone beyond the stringent limits our troops are required to observe, and they must suffer for it, not only as punishment to themselves, but as an example to their comrades. Now, gentlemen, if you will excuse me, I shall take personal command of the firing squad." He turned, and Allison was suddenly acutely conscious of the Browning 9-mm. automatic on Rinaldi's hip.

Allison moved over to Erika. "Listen," he said. "Last chance. If you want to go, I'll take you." He was surprised at the edge of anger in his voice.

"Leave me alone," she whispered. She did not look at him. Her face was very pale. Her eyes followed the massive man in the olive drab poncho as he went lithely down the steps.

Then a gasp went up from the crowd; there was even a sort of rush of breath from all those ranked soldiers. Through the same archway that had emitted the firing squad came the prisoners. There was no drumroll, no Rogue's March, no ceremony at all. Four black men, their hands cuffed behind their backs, were forced, poncho-less, into the rain; and it could be seen that one had already wet his pants, but the stain of urine was quickly lost as his clothes were totally drenched by the downpour. He stumbled and had to be half-dragged by the three guards hustling him along, but the rest of the group marched smartly and proudly, giving their escorts no reason to touch them.

Then each was taken to a post. Rinaldi barked a few orders. Their handcuffs were unlocked, their arms wrapped around the posts behind them, and the cuffs fastened again. The coward among them sagged to his knees, arms slipping down the post, and his whining, like that of a child in nightmare, could be heard all the way up on the stand, above the drum of rain. The other three turned their heads and looked at him with contempt.

Allison glanced at Erika. She was looking down at her feet. He saw her lips move, read their whisper: *"Ach, Gott . . ."* In a step, he was beside her. "All right," he said harshly. "Don't cop out. Look. Watch it all. It's good for you, remember?"

She shot him a glance that was half furious, half miserable. Then, in defiance, she drew herself up and her eyes fastened themselves on the scene below.

The official photographers were in place now, snapping picture after picture. Rinaldi barked another order. Now the soldiers of the firing squad separated, grouping three to a victim. They unslung their rifles. As they did so, two sergeants went to the men chained to their posts and offered them blindfolds. One of the upright, steadier trio nodded in acceptance and his eyes were bound; so were those of the whimpering man on his knees. The other two looked sullenly full into the eyes of their executioners. It was, Allison thought mordantly, of course too wet for such amenities as last cigarettes.

The sergeants stepped clear. The correspondents crowded up to the rail of the stand, bearing Allison and Erika with them. Rain poured from the edge of Rinaldi's helmet as he moved to one side, surveying prisoners, executioners and photographers, making sure that all was ready.

Beside Allison, Erika drew in a rasping breath. Her hand was at her throat, fingers moving nervously as if searching for beads. But she kept her eyes riveted on the men at the stakes.

Then Rinaldi's hand came up; his voice rang out. "Ready!" The rifles were raised, aligned. "Aim!" The man on his knees was looking ahead now, as if he could see through the blindfold into those three rifle muzzles trained on him; then he turned his head upward, lips moving as if praying, and the rain fell full into his face. He began to make a high, awful sound like a wounded dog. Rinaldi's voice bellowed solidly, clearly, the final, fatal command; at that moment Allison had an impression he would never forget of staring white eyes in contorted black faces. Abruptly the parade crackled with rifle fire. The man on his knees jerked; his head had got in line and a bullet ripped off the top of his skull; viscous gray matter flew, spilled onto the wet paving stones. Red spread at the same instant across his shirt and one thigh; no blanks were being used here. He slumped forward limply against the cuffs that anchored him. Two of the other three, their dark wet shirts suddenly scarlet, slid down their poles in ridiculous, clownlike fashion, legs sprawling ludicrously, heads flopping. The remaining man also sat down hard, bleeding copiously; but he was not dead; his head swiveled furiously and bulging eyes stared at the firing squad, at Rinaldi, at the spectators on the stand. He opened his mouth as if to yell, and bright blood poured from it. Then his heels began to drum on the paving stones; he sat there, bleeding through his mouth and the holes in his chest, jerking and kicking. *"Coup de grace,"* somebody near Allison said in a voice full of horror. "Jesus, man, hurry up; can't you see the poor bastard's suffering?"

Allison looked at Erika. Her eyes were wide, her face like marble; she had not averted her gaze from anything.

Rinaldi leisurely drew his pistol, strode over to the man whose heels were kicking. He put the pistol to the back of the man's head. Even in the heavy sound of the rain, the single shot seemed unbearably loud. The man instantly went limp. Then Rinaldi walked to each of the other men, although they were already corpses and one of them had no real head left, and administered a final bullet. A mixture of blood and water washed pinkly over the paving stones and around his boots. He stepped aside delicately, holstering his pistol, his face impassive.

A single great sigh went, in unison, out of the crowd. Victor Nadunda spoke for the first time in the silence that followed. "Thus the Government of Acanara deals with those who commit atrocities. Gentlemen, this has been trying for all of us. For those of you who would like a cocktail, a bar awaits—"

"Yeah," a man's voice said shakily. "God yes, let's have a drink." He led the exodus, which almost became a stampede. But Erika hung back. She was staring down at Rinaldi, out there on the parade. He looked up at her, his face unreadable. Then he came over to the foot of the steps leading up to the stand and waited.

Presently there was way open for them, and Allison gave Erika a push. "Come on," he said, and they went down the steps, she moving obediently ahead of him.

When they reached the pavement, Rinaldi blocked them, took Erika's hand. "There," he said. "Was it so very dreadful?"

"It was—" Erika's voice choked. She shook her head mutely, swallowed hard. Then, as Rinaldi smiled at her, Allison saw color come back into her face. "No," she said at last, breathily. "No, it wasn't so dreadful."

"Justice never really is," said Rinaldi. "Is it, John?"

"It all depends on what you mean by justice," Allison said.

"As I told you, in Acanara everyone gets what he deserves. That is our rule." Rinaldi stared at him, eyes curiously hard. Then he took Erika's arm and she leaned against him. "You did well," he said softly. "You did beautifully. I am very proud of you. Would you like a drink now?"

"Yes," she whispered. "Yes, I'd like a drink."

"So would I. Believe me, I'm not made of steel, either. Still, one does what must be done. One's duty overrides all else. John, you'll join us?"

"No," said Allison. "No, thank you. If I can have a car, I'll be going."

Rinaldi nodded. "Perhaps just as well. Your car will be here at once. I'll take Erika back to the hotel myself." He snapped an order to an officer standing nearby. "Good afternoon, John." Then he and Erika passed through a door, leaving Allison standing alone in the rain, watching as the bodies were unshackled from the posts and carried away on stretchers. By the time they were gone, the rain had washed the paving of the parade ground clean.

CHAPTER 7

SITTING IN THE hotel bar, waiting for Emily Whittington, Allison fought back the temptation to get drunk. Either that or violent action; he needed something to relieve the anger and frustration boiling in him.

Though Emily was late, it was not she whom he thought about. Erika Wolf was in his mind and would not get out of it. So were those four soldiers executed in the rain. Her pale face, enormous eyes, the man with his head blown off, Rinaldi pulling her against him—these images were all jumbled in his brain. Games! he thought savagely. Games! And the goddam little fool hasn't got sense enough to see—!

He drank his Martini. Emily was a grown woman, she had gone into her affair with Rinaldi with her eyes wide open. Whatever she got, she had, in a sense, deserved. But Erika— Hell, Allison thought, she was like a child or like something wounded; she was helpless, such an easy victim . . . Allison swore and ordered another drink, the rage he felt against Sandro Rinaldi ballooning in him.

He had dealt with unsavory people in his time; had dealt with them and remained detached. Like a whore, he thought bitterly, he could usually stomach almost any type if there were money in it. But even whores had to draw the line somewhere, and Rinaldi, he was beginning to think, was where he drew it.

Allison could almost forgive him for trying to have him killed back in Texas. That was, in the murky game they both played, a legitimate move, for Allison almost a normal occupational

140

hazard. But he could not forgive what Rinaldi had done to his company, enmeshing Allison Trading in whatever web he spun here, jeopardizing its existence. The company was all Allison had to show for his life; it was the only thing in the world he loved.

But least of all, Allison thought now, could he forgive Rinaldi for what he was doing to Erika.

It was all clear, The aging Don Juan, like a carnivore uncertain of its own powers, selecting as prey only the weak, the helpless and the wounded. And bolstering his own faltering ego with his perverse games, proving to himself his power over others by destroying them. He had thoroughly botched Emily's life, and she had been a far stronger woman than Erika Wolf. But at least Emily had survived physically. When Erika's turn came— Allison thought again of those scars. *Goddammit!* he snarled inwardly.

Feeling the drinks, he turned on the barstool and surveyed the room. He hated this place. He hated Rinaldi, he hated Nadunda, he hated Marc, he hated the rain. His eyes swept over the faces of the other patrons. Which ones, he wondered, were the spooks? Which were Marc's spooks, which were Rinaldi's? The place was bound to be swarming with them. He was under no illusion; both sides were watching him.

He turned back to his drink, glancing at his watch. Where was Emily? He was anxious to get out of here. At the thought of her, he calmed a little. She had given him the only pleasure he'd had in this lousy country. Last night, she had been ferocious at first; then slowly, as some of the fire was quenched, had turned tender, almost gentle, until at last she had been content simply to lie against him as if that, too, were exquisite pleasure. But what he wanted now was more of the ferocity; he needed it as an outlet for his own emotions. If she would only come on. He watched the door impatiently. Then he straightened up.

It was not Emily who entered but Calvin Buckley.

Buckley had not even checked his raincoat. He stood there in the doorway, dripping, eyes sweeping the room. Then he saw Allison. Their gazes met. Buckley turned and went away.

Allison got down off the stool, went to the door. There was no sign of Buckley in the lobby. Allison got his hat and coat from the check room and went out onto the street. It was raining hard. Buckley, in the back seat of the embassy car, signaled to him and Allison got in. The car pulled away from the curb.

"What's up, Cal?" Allison's stomach was taut.

"You were waiting for Emily Whittington?"

"Yes. I told you—"

"You can stop waiting," Buckley said. "She isn't coming. Ever."

Allison stared at him, feeling a curious chill. "What do you mean?"

Buckley drew in a long, weary breath. "It's not in the papers yet; will be tomorrow morning, I guess. I got it from the British Embassy. I know some of the people there, thought I'd drop by to check on the Whittington woman, make sure she's what she claimed to be. When I got there, they were all in a flap. She's dead, John."

Allison was silent for a moment. "The poor little bitch," he said when he finally spoke and then was startled at his own choice of words. His big hands clenched on his thighs. "How, Cal?"

"Hard. Damned hard. She worked for an export firm—"

"I know."

"Office was down at the harbor. She went out for lunch, didn't come back. This afternoon, the police found her in an alley between two warehouses. Badly beaten, raped, her throat cut."

"Christ," Allison said. He thought of Emily against him last night. He remembered kissing her briefly as she had let him out at the hotel this morning. The kiss of death, he thought. "Rinaldi," he said, but oddly, now, he felt no more rage. He was only very cold inside.

"No. According to the police, some wandering waterfront bum. Of course it was Rinaldi," Buckley said heavily. "She knew something he didn't want her telling you. He couldn't do anything about last night, but he could make sure she wouldn't have another opportunity to talk."

Allison leaned back against the seat. "All right," he said. "That ought to be the proof you were looking for."

Buckley said, "It will help, but we need more. Look. The German girl."

"Yes," Allison said. "The German girl." He sat up, his voice suddenly thick with anger. "You want her throat cut too, eh? You want her stretched out, gang-banged, behind some warehouse?"

"And what about Allison Trading Company?" Buckley said. "Where do you want that?" Then, as if he were very weary, he said quietly, "You decide, John."

Allison said thinly, "I'll do that, Cal." Then he got out of the car.

At the hotel, he returned to the bar. He felt empty, burnt out inside. The choice was forming now, shaping up in his mind. Everybody used somebody else. Crider used Allison Trading Company. Allison used Emily. Rinaldi used Erika. A daisy-chain of whores, he thought bitterly.

Well, he thought, as he had another drink, he was tired of it. He was tired of being used and he was tired of using people. He was finished with it. The hell with Acanara. The hell with Rinaldi. The hell with everybody except Erika. He had already used her once; he would not use her again.

He finished his drink and went to the elevator. He did not go to his own room, but to the floor above, on which Erika was quartered. He found her room and knocked on the door. He knew now what he was going to do; he knew exactly.

She let him in. She was wearing another silver dress; one that revealed a great deal of her breasts; very short, it also emphasized her legs. At the sight of him, she frowned. "Johnny—"

He shoved his way on into the room. "I'm not going to give you a lecture," he said. "But I have something to tell you. Are you alone?"

"Yes." As he sat down in a chair, she looked at him with eyes that were, perhaps, a little frightened. "What do you want?"

"To tell you to leave Sandro," he said.

She blinked. "I don't understand." Her voice was crisp, inimical.

"You will," he said. And then, very carefully, he told her everything. She stared at him as he spoke. When he was through, he stood up. "I'm leaving Acanara tomorrow, and I don't give a damn what the repercussions are. I'll worry about the repercussions later. Meanwhile, I'll tell you this. Rinaldi is playing games with you. That's why he took you to Nepwa. That's why he made you attend those executions. He's a warped, perverted son of a bitch, and he only wants to see how much you'll take before you crack." His voice was harsh, bitter. "He killed Emily Whittington, Erika. He'll kill you too, one way or the other, before he's through with you. Leave him."

"John," she said. He could tell from her voice that he had failed. She believed nothing he had told her. But then, she was a woman in love. "John, you must be drunk."

"No, I'm not," he said fiercely. "Goddammit, Erika, I was never more sober in my life. You didn't like it when I used you! Why let Sandro—"

"Stop it, John," she said. "I won't listen to this any more. I won't listen to you talk about Sandro that way. I don't know why you should—" Then she tensed. There was the sound of a key in the lock. Her face went pale. "That's Sandro now," she whispered. "Don't . . . don't mention any of this."

Allison said coldly, "All right. You know the score. From now on, you're on your own."

"I—" Erika put one hand to her breast. Then she turned. The door opened and Rinaldi came in.

He stopped there; his eyes shuttled from one of them to the other. Then, to Allison's surprise, he smiled. "Well, it's good you're both together. I rang your room, John, and you weren't there. We've had too much grimness today. And you haven't seen anything of the nightlife of Ogoro. I was going to suggest that the three of us make the rounds." His eyes met Allison's. "Unless you have someone else you're meeting tonight."

"No," Allison said. "No, I'm not meeting anyone else."

"Splendid!" Rinaldi clapped his hands together. "Then we'll take you on a tour! We'll really show you the town; shall we, Erika?"

She looked from Allison to Rinaldi. Then she went to Rinaldi and put her arm through his. Allison, standing tensely, saw how she rubbed her breasts against him. "Why not, Sandro?" she said.

"Well, Johnny?" Rinaldi's eyes fastened on Allison again, almost challengingly.

Allison looked back at him, then looked at Erika clinging to his arm. A strange weariness, a sort of despair filled him.

"Yes," he said. "That sounds like real fun, Sandro."

"Good!" Rinaldi said. "Then, shall we be on our way?"

"Africa!" Rinaldi said. He was expansive now, the first time Allison was sure liquor had got to him a little. It took a lot for that massive frame, but he'd ingested a lot in their circuit of Ogoro after dark. "The continent where something is always eating something else! By God, it's a marvelous place!"

"Any place is marvelous if you're the eater and not the eaten," Erika said thickly. She was far drunker than he, and clinging to him almost desperately.

Rinaldi slapped the table. "Didn't I tell you she was a re-markable girl? A Valkyrie, really, a literal Valkyrie! That's the German philosophy in a nutshell! They know things in their bones that we Italians must learn the hard way. But some of us learn them very well, nevertheless! Julius Caesar, Octavian, Garibaldi, Mussolini—"

"And Sandro Rinaldi," Allison said quietly, not feeling all the whiskey he had drunk.

"And Sandro Rinaldi! But why not? I'm starting late, but Africa's a good place to start! Alexander, Napoleon, Caesar, Anthony, Pompey, Scipio— even Il Duce. They all came here sooner or later. It's where you *have* to start. Believe me, John—" Then the sound of drums drowned his voice.

The nightclub was thoroughly modern, dim, with a look of expensiveness; except for the excellent service, this could have been New York. There was a sprinkling of blacks, but most of its customers were European. The drums were startlingly loud and primitive in such a setting. Allison turned.

Two great, muscular black men, clad only in loin cloths, sat at either end of the tiny stage. Then a girl, large-breasted, as naked as the drummers, came on, in the yellow spotlight, ebony skin shining. The drums were louder; she began to dance, a slow, mind-demolishing dance of utter eroticism in exact ca-dence to their blood-stirring beat. The beads that draped her otherwise naked loins gleamed and clicked as her hips began to rotate; her breasts joggled, damp with sweat. As the drums increased their tempo, so did her hips, her buttocks, her breasts, until at last, as they rose to crescendo, she was in a dazed, sprawled, erotic fervor on the stage, thrusting with her loins, and these naked as the beads spilled away. Allison's eyes went to Rinaldi; the man was watching intently, his own forehead shining with perspiration; he had his arm around Erika and was, unashamedly, squeezing her breast with relentless force. It had to hurt, those big fingers digging in far beyond the limits of a caress, with a mindless sadism of their own; yet, Erika only

put her hand over Rinaldi's and stroked it, her own eyes fixed
on the stage. Suddenly absolutely sober, Allison looked away.

Then they were back at the hotel, the three of them in Erika's room, with Rinaldi pouring champagne. He had been
drinking steadily, yet he was in full command of his faculties,
though still on a high horse. He handed out glasses all around.
Allison, watching him closely, did not miss the appraising
glance Rinaldi gave Erika as he handed her one.

She was pale, swaying, on the verge, Allison thought, of
being sick. She had eaten nothing, drunk an astonishing
amount. Her smile was ghastly, her hand unsteady as she raised
the glass to her lips.

"Wait!" Rinaldi said. "Wait, a toast." He raised his own
glass, bowing to Erika. "To the *Tedeschi!* The tough little
Tedeschi! By God, John, she was magnificent this afternoon,
wasn't she? Truly magnificent!"

"Yes," Allison said and sipped from the glass.

"She didn't even flinch when the top of that bastard's head
went off. Did you notice that? I thought surely she'd quail
when the brains spilled—" He put a hand under her chin,
tipped up her face until he was looking in her eyes. "But it
didn't touch you, did it? Do you know, I've seen even hardened
men get sick at executions. Especially when they get messy like
that one this afternoon. I hate to botch a killing. You know,
though, he didn't feel anything. Not like the one who kicked
and bled so much. Really, he was surprising how he bled. Like
in *Macbeth*. *'Who would have thought the old man had so much
blood in him!'* But, Erika—"

Her lips moved soundlessly, her face was paler. "Sandro,"
she said. "Please."

"Oh, I was so proud of you," he said. "It's the German in
you, of course. Germans don't mind blood, do they, John?
Blood and Iron, that's their motto! Actually, John, you know
Germans like the sight of blood—"

"For God's sake, Rinaldi!" Allison snapped. Erika was looking at the Italian like a bird at a snake. Her face was dead white, her throat working convulsively.

"They like blood," Rinaldi went on remorselessly. "Lots of it. Don't they—"

"Sandro!" She managed the one half-gagged word. Then she turned suddenly, hurried to the bath. From within it came the sounds of the girl being violently sick. Instinctively Allison stepped forward, but Rinaldi blocked his way. "Poor dear," he said smoothly. "She drank too much. She really should have eaten something." Then all at once he was quite, absolutely, sober. "Tell me, John. Mr. Buckley at the embassy. Have you talked to him?"

Allison stood there carefully, surprised at the almost indifferent tone of his own voice. "Yes. I felt him out in a roundabout way. He's going to be receptive."

"Excellent." Rinaldi drank. "I may chance talking to him personally as soon as you're sure he'll be with us. I think soon you and he will both have some very significant ammunition to use on your government, something very persuasive . . ." He broke off as Erika reappeared, face dead white.

She leaned against the doorjamb unsteadily. "Sandro," she managed, "please don't talk about . . . the executions any more."

Rinaldi looked at her. Then he shrugged as if it were a matter of indifference. "Of course not, my dear, if it bothers you. Though I'm a little surprised . . ." Gently, he took her arm, sat her down in a chair. "Now, rest a bit. I think you have drunk a little too much."

"So have I," Allison heard himself say. He looked from Erika to Rinaldi. "I'm pretty tired. I think if you'll excuse me."

"Well, if you must," Rinaldi said. "Then good night, John. Tomorrow, perhaps, you can further explore our mutual interests with your friend."

"Yes," Allison said. "I'll do that. Good night, Erika."

She hardly raised her head. She was, Allison saw, trembling

as if she had a chill. "Good night," she said dully as he went out.

In his own room, Allison donned pajamas, went to bed. Outside the rain drummed steadily. His mouth was sour and burnt from smoking. His head hurt. He thought of Emily. If her ex-husband did not, he would pay for her funeral; she deserved that much of him, at least. He thought of Rinaldi and felt the hot bile of hatred rise in his throat. That scene in Erika's room had been inexcusable; pure, unmitigated sadism. Now Rinaldi, aroused by all the killing, would be making love to her... Allison's stomach roiled at the thought.

But he had to stop thinking. He had to shut off his mind, had to sleep. He closed his eyes, tried to make himself think of nothing, absolutely nothing. Presently it worked. He slept.

As he sometimes did, then, he dreamed of Hungary. He saw Budapest laid out below him in autumn sunlight, as it looked from the Citadel, the great fortress above the Danube. He saw the multiple bridges spanning the river, the islands, the yellow houses of Pest spread out on the flatlands, the rolling hills of Buda... Then there were the executions, nightmares, nightmares he had lived through, the executions of the Secret Police, in the public squares, by the rebels. He had been a member of one firing squad himself, he had— In his sleep he cried out.

Then he came awake. He was bathed in sweat, his mouth was dry; he shook. He sat up, looking at his watch: nearly three. Suddenly he realized it had not been the dream that had awakened him. Instinctively his hand shot beneath the pillow, came out holding the Python. Then again there was the knock at the door.

Instantly alert, Allison jumped out of bed. Soundlessly, as the knock came again, soft, secretive, but urgent, he padded to the door. And also instinctively, he did not stand in front of the door but beside it, behind the protection of the wall, as he rasped, "Who's there?"

"John, please." It was a husky whisper. "It's Erika. Let me in!"

Allison hesitated. "You alone?"

"Yes. John, for God's sake—"

He unlatched the door, turned the knob, swung it wide, gun up. She was there in a frothy negligee, face sallow in the corridor light. And she was indeed alone. He stepped back. "All right," he said. "Come in."

She entered. He closed and locked the door behind her. "What's the matter?" he heard himself ask savagely. "One man not enough for you?"

"John, don't—" Her voice sounded exhausted. He turned on the light, looked at her. She was shaking. There were blue bruises on her throat, on the vee of skin revealed by the deep slash of the nightdress—the signs of savage lovemaking. He lowered the gun. "Okay, what is it?"

"I've got to talk to you, John. To somebody. I've—" She swayed; he caught her, took her to the sofa, sat her down. Her hair was touseled, she rubbed her eyes.

"Okay," he said. "Talk."

"Those men he killed today— it was terrible."

"I warned you it would be."

"I know. It's not that. That was bad enough. But the rest. What he told me after you left . . ."

Allison suppressed a growing excitement. His voice was calm, soothing. "All right," he said almost casually. "What did he tell you?"

He saw her swallow hard; she shook her head. "We made love," she said. Then she shivered. *"Christus!* I feel as if snails had walked on me everywhere he touched me."

Allison's calm vanished. He dropped to his knees before her. "Erika, goddammit, what are you trying to tell me?"

"The four men. The ones who were executed. They . . . they had had their tongues cut out."

Allison stared at her. "What?"

"They weren't government soldiers! They were Marc's! He had their tongues cut out so they couldn't yell anything before they were executed." Erika rubbed her bare, bruised arms violently, as if something slimy had indeed walked there "He was ... full of champagne and so proud of himself for having played such a trick. After all, there was no way any of us, the correspondents, could have known he wasn't really executing his own men. It was such a great joke! They were part of the crews of the tanks he captured . . ."

Allison sprang to his feet. "Tanks? What tanks?"

"I don't know. That's all he said. But, John, oh, God, John, after he left, I lay there . . . He had hurt me and I couldn't sleep. And I lay there and I kept seeing him shooting those men again, it just happened over and over again, like somebody running the same piece of film— And he wanted me to laugh too, laugh with him. About their tongues— About the joke. And I couldn't do it. I couldn't. And then I knew it was true. Everything you said." She put her hands over her face. "I've tried. I love him so, and I've tried and tried to be exactly what he wants me to be. But I can't. And I don't know what to do, Johnny. I'll go crazy if I try any more. What shall I do?"

Allison was hardly listening. Now he had begun to pace. "Tanks!" he said. "I knew he had *one*. But—" Then it had all clicked into place. Suddenly he turned, went to the phone. "All right," he said. "I know what I need to know. Don't worry. We'll get you away from here. We'll get you away from Sandro. I'll call the embassy and—" He picked the instrument out of its cradle.

At that moment there was a click from the corridor door. Allison, phone in hand, turned quickly, just in time to see it swing open. Then, behind two soldiers with automatic rifles trained point-blank at Allison, Rinaldi was there.

CHAPTER 8

"Master key," Rinaldi said, tossing it in the air, then dropping it into his shirt pocket. "Stand away from the telephone, John." Carefully, not blocking the line of fire of his riflemen, he came on into the room.

Slowly Allison lowered the receiver. The Python lay beside the phone, but there was no hope of using it now. Then Rinaldi scooped it up, looked at it briefly, nodded, and pointed it at Allison. "Both of you," he said, gesturing with the gun. "Over there."

Allison moved to stand beside Erika. Rinaldi stared at her with eyes like ice crystals. "My dear, my dear," he said. "How could I have so misjudged you."

"Sandro——" she said in a choked voice.

"No, be quiet." His voice was knife-edged. His uniform was rumpled, but there was no sign of the night's drinking on his face or in his manner. "You hardly waited until I was out of the hotel, did you? If I had not left my wallet in your room, returned for it— And you were gone. So I asked myself, where else could you be at this time of night; and there was one answer, only one." Suddenly his big hand flashed out, slapped her hard. "You bitch! Don't you know this room is monitored? I heard it all! Blathering my secrets like a schoolgirl! I thought . . . Well, I trusted you; the first woman I ever trusted. After today I was sure . . . But I was wrong."

He turned to Allison. "And you. I thought you were a businessman. So long as you get your money, what concern of yours is it what I do? But, no. At the first scrap of information, you think only of your embassy." His voice was vibrant with anger. "A spy. Nothing but a spy."

Allison said nothing. Rinaldi took another key from his pocket, handed it to one of the soldiers. "Go to her room. Get her clothes and bring them here. And you, John—get dressed. You're going to M'nanda, both of you."

Allison looked at him. "M'nanda?"

Rinaldi nodded. "Before you leave, you'll write a note—which I shall dictate—to your Mr. Buckley, and so inform him. It will account for your absence and Erika's."

"And what happens to us at M'nanda?"

Rinaldi laughed shortly. "What do you think? That's where the two of you die. I heard it all from the room next door. You know about the tanks. Do you think I can let you live with that knowledge?"

"I know about them," Allison said, "but I don't know how you got them."

"Oh, that was simple. Marc made a mistake—he entrusted a task force to the command of a mercenary. And mercenaries, John, sell out to the highest bidder. This one had not been paid by the rebels for a long time, so it did not cost me much. He simply bogged down the tanks and deserted them. There was no difficulty in retrieving all five of them intact. And believe me, they've been worth the investment."

"Yes," Allison said thinly. "I imagine they have. So you raided Sinawa, Nepwa, those other places, with them . . ."

"Indeed. Now, get on your clothes." He wagged the gun. "Watch her," he said to the other guard and followed Allison into the bedroom of the suite.

In there, he sat almost relaxed and casual in a chair while Allison began to dress. "I value your judgment, John. You know my plans. Tell me, do you think they will work?"

"No," Allison said. "Not if you kill Erika and me. Do you think Buckley or Middleton will let you get away with that?"

"Ah, but *I'm* not going to kill you," Rinaldi said, smiling. "Marc will."

Allison froze, his fingers on the buttons of his shirt.

"Ah, yes," Rinaldi said. "At M'nanda. You see, at dawn, day after tomorrow, Marc commits his greatest crime. I'm afraid you and Erika shall be among the victims. Do you remember Stanleyville, John, in the Congo?"

Allison felt cold. "I remember."

"As in M'nanda, the whites from the countryside had taken refuge there. Then the guerrillas took the place and slaughtered them without mercy and in the most horrible fashion. After that, a great stream of aid poured in to the Congolese government. Well, what happens once can happen twice. My earlier raids served their purpose; they terrorized the countryside, sent the whites flocking to M'nanda to refuge. And there they huddle now—like sheep waiting for the wolves to come."

Allison drew in a long breath. Then he shook his head. "No. You can't get away with that. Stanleyville was isolated, cut off. M'nanda's a major city, under government control. You've got forces concentrated there. You'd only make yourself look stupid, inefficient, if you supposedly allowed Marc to strike like that."

"Correction," Rinaldi said easily. "I'd make Kopapo look stupid, inefficient."

"He's not in on this?"

Rinaldi shook his head. "No, John, he's not. Let me outline the entire plan. You see, I have no one else of sufficient sophistication with whom to discuss it. But you— Even the expression on your face tells me a great deal. And I'm sure you will be quick to point out any flaws in order to dissuade me." He smiled. "*You* have the brains to pick them out immediately; and you don't know how I've yearned to go over all this with a man of your caliber."

He leaned forward. "Kopapo has already been ordered to move against Marc in one great general offensive, a sweep far to the west and then across the river crossings we hold and down into Marc's territory. And he is to take everything he has with him, especially his armor. When he's well away, we strike—shoot through the screen that's left, slash into the city itself, round up the whites, and— Well, when we get through, Marc's name will be a symbol for frightfulness all over the civilized world. What a stink there will be! Killing blacks is one thing; but no Western country will remain indifferent to the slaughter of whites. Under the pressure of public opinion, they'll vie with each other to give us aid . . ."

"They'll vie with each other in blaming you for leaving the city defenseless."

"Ah, but Kopapo shall bear the blame for that! Oh, he protested strongly at leaving the city uncovered, but I insisted, and he obeyed orders, relying on me to protect it from the east. But I've worked things so there will be no written record of my orders—and after the raid, General Kopapo shall be court-martialed in secrecy for dereliction of duty in leaving M'nanda defenseless and will be promptly shot. Thus—our scapegoat." He stood up, still smiling. "And it will work, won't it? I can tell by the expression of dismay on your face that it will work. Five Shermans—they *have* to be Marc's; no one knows we have them. A terrible killing, in the most primitive, uncivilized, African tribal way—and, unfortunately, you and Erika among the victims. And I think then no one will quibble at giving us the help we say we need. Now, you must write a note to be mailed to Mr. Buckley. In it you shall say that Erika insisted on going to M'nanda and you have accompanied her. I daresay he'll get the implication—that you're trying to wring information from her, as you tried to wring it from poor Emily Whittington."

"That *was* your work," Allison said coldly.

Rinaldi shrugged. "Time grows short," he said. "I want you out of Ogoro before dawn. *Move!*" And he gestured the fully dressed Allison back to the living room.

Erika sat there under guard. The other soldier had just returned with a suitcase. "All right, my dear," said Rinaldi. "While John writes a little note, dress. Do not be troubled by considerations of modesty. We have no time for such things."

Her face was already beginning to swell from his slap. She stood up, looking at him wordlessly. With utter coolness, she threw off the negligee; beneath it, she was nude. Rinaldi made a sound in his throat. "I suppose this is the last time I shall see you so. That knowledge hurts me more than you know."

Erika's voice was surprisingly steady. "Don't worry," she said. "I'd rather be dead than have you see me like this again."

"I suppose you will be," Rinaldi said; and he hit her again, a solid slap. She only stood there, naked, and looked directly into his eyes, without fear. Then she pulled the dress over her head.

Rinaldi dictated the note, and Allison wrote it. He was surprised at how his hand trembled as he did so. Because, he thought, it might work. It might very well work. And even if it did not, that would not help him or Erika or the hundreds of people who would die with them in M'nanda. The note itself was plausible; there was no chance of any tip-off in it. Nor could Allison see any way of escape. Those soldiers with guns were well trained, alert.

By then, Erika was dressed. "Now," Rinaldi said, "we go. These men will be ruthless if you try to escape; they are part of a very large elite organization I have formed, totally loyal to me personally. You understand, John, I need such men for the work at hand . . . Out the back way."

They were herded into a service elevator; at the ground floor they wound through kitchen and laundry corridors. Behind the hotel, a Mercedes waited in the rain. There were two more soldiers in it and a Land Rover parked nearby. Rinaldi gestured them into the Mercedes with the pistol and got in with them. In the front seat by the driver, a soldier, at Rinaldi's command, drew his pistol and turned around, keeping Allison covered with it. Rinaldi chuckled. "As you see, John, any Wild West cinema tactics will only get you shot."

Allison saw it only too well. Outwardly impassive, inwardly seething with frustration at his own helplessness, he settled back on the seat. The Mercedes moved out; the Land Rover followed it.

Rinaldi's talkative streak was over now. In silence they wound through the rain-wet streets of Ogoro, struck a wide boulevard, where walled villas slept behind the glistening fronds of rain-wet palms. Presently they turned into the drive of one of these, and Rinaldi finally spoke. "My residence, John. This is where I shall take my leave of you. Do not, however, think that gives you any advantage. You will be in the charge of Lieutenant Mubaba and a detail of picked men. They have orders to shoot at the first suspicious move." He got out of the car, signaled. A lanky dark officer left the Land Rover and came to him. Rinaldi spoke to him briefly; then the lieutenant took Rinaldi's place in the Mercedes, on the jumpseat by the door.

Rinaldi leaned in, looked at Erika with a strange expression on his face. "My dear," he said, "I can only say, *Auf Wiedersehen*. When we meet again, it will be in M'nanda. Until then—" He raised and dropped a hand.

"Sandro—" Erika said, her voice trembling.

Something flickered in his eyes. "Yes? Are you going to beg?"

"No," Erika said. Her voice steadied. When she spoke, it dripped contempt. "I only wanted to tell you that you were never really a very good lover."

Rinaldi's big hand clenched. Then he relaxed. "Well, you shall have more," he said. "Perhaps an entire company of them, in M'nanda. I think you will have enough there to satisfy you at last. And I think they will be even less gentle with you than I have been." Suddenly he slammed the door, turned away, disappearing in the rain.

Then the car pulled out of the drive; the Land Rover followed. Mubaba, catlike, sat immobile, his service automatic out and trained on them. The guard in front likewise continued to keep them covered.

At this time of night, the outskirts of Ogoro were deserted, save for a few military vehicles and detachments of MP's here and there. The tires made a hissing sound on the wet pavement; the engine hummed smoothly; the windshield wipers ticked with hypnotic rhythm. At last the lieutenant spoke.

"We have a long ride before us," he said in halting, accented English. "So we shall now understand each other. At the slightest threatening move, you will be killed. Clear?"

Allison said bitterly, "Clear. Can we smoke?"

"No," Mubaba said. "The seeing conditions for the driver are very bad. We will not have smoke in his eyes."

Allison's respect for him rose. "Tell me," he said. "Why do you, a black man, serve under a white one?"

"For Acanara. For West Africa." His lips quirked. "Do not try to play the black-white game with me, Mr. Allison. I serve General Rinaldi willingly. Now, no more talk. The driver must have silence. The rain is very heavy."

Indeed, it came down as if someone had slit the belly of the sky. The headlights of the Mercedes, on low beam, played against it as if against a wall. They left the city, challenged by a roadblock of miserable-looking soldiers who inspected them closely, then waved them through. As they gathered speed again, the Land Rover moved up behind, and Allison blinked as its lights glared in the Mercedes' rear-view mirror.

Now it was like traveling on the moon. The rain curtained off all vision. Erika's hand groped, found Allison's. He took it, squeezed it. Her palm was damp. She returned the squeeze.

Allison sat calmly, his rage and frustration oddly quenched

by her touch, his head strangely cleared. She was behaving well; she was behaving magnificently. He had not expected that; he had expected hysteria, a collapse. He wondered where she had found this reservoir of courage and control that she had so suddenly tapped. It was as if, somehow, in defying Rinaldi, she had become a different woman.

But he did not think long about that. What he had to think about was escape. He had not given up, had no intention of giving up, not so long as there was one second's breath left to him. And his task now was to remain alert, wholly and totally, looking for, hoping for, the one instant's opportunity of which he could take advantage, any gamble that would have a chance of payoff.

As the car sped on, it became apparent that there would be none. Mubaba was remorselessly alert; so, also, was the guard in front. The highway was empty ahead of them; the driver increased his speed. On either side, the rain-swept jungle was a deeper blackness in the night.

And, Allison thought bitterly, the Land Rover hard on their rear was additional insurance against his making a break. Despite himself, he was threatened by hopelessness, apathy. He had to make a conscious effort to keep himself ready, clear-headed.

Then the driver increased speed again, perceptibly. Without taking his eyes from Allison, Mubaba said something cautionary in dialect. They slowed a bit. The rain still made a wall before them. The Land Rover kept its interval precisely.

Presently, as if he himself were at last yielding to boredom, Mubaba spoke. "You understand, Mr. Allison, that—" Whatever he was going to say broke off in a single shouted word of dialect, and Erika screamed.

The old bus, crammed with people, loomed up as suddenly and unexpectedly in the rain-shortened glare of headlights as if it had been dropped in their path from above. It must have broken down, been abandoned by the evening convoy; and it sat full on the pavement, with no signals out, no lights on. Through its windows Allison caught a flash of terrified black faces, of hands waving frantically. Then the driver of the Mercedes wrenched the wheel; tires screamed, and even as the sedan skidded sickeningly all the way around and the Land Rover hit it, Allison was grabbing for the pistol of the guard in front, who was thrown off balance. There was a crash as the Land Rover slammed into the sedan's rear fender, bounced off, careened by, and the big car slewed around again, whirled onto the muddy shoulder of the road, and went over.

But Allison had the gun. As the car rolled, Mubaba was thrown across the seat, full into Allison's lap, and in that split second, Allison shot him in the head. Then they were all hurled savagely against metal, wood and leather, upside down, and Erika screamed again. Allison's skull hit something and hit it hard, but it did not quite knock him out and he did not lose his grip on the pistol. They had come to rest, and he was at the bottom of a pile of flesh, with Erika atop him and Mubaba's body on her.

Frantically, still dazed, Allison struggled to get out from under. He felt a wetness that he knew was blood, but whose it was he could not tell. Burned into his brain was the knowledge that there were still two men in the front. Summoning all his strength, he pushed upward, got hand and gun-arm free. The silhouette of a head that was not Erika's reared above the sprawl of bodies on the roof of the upside-down car on which they all lay. Allison put the muzzle of the gun full up against its face and pulled the trigger. Then his groping hand found a door; he pushed and it swung open, unlatched by the impact. He squirmed free from beneath the weight on his legs. Erika screamed, "John! John, where are you?" Allison wriggled out into mud and driving rain, got shakily to his feet, the gun ready; the driver was still to be accounted for. Then Allison saw him face down in the muck, where he'd been thrown through

the open door and knew at once that he was dead. "John!"
Erika screamed again.

There was no time to answer. Up on the highway, fifty yards
away, the Land Rover's one remaining headlight was a yellow
eye trained on the wreck, its glare diffused by rain. Against
that background, he saw the two men with rifles plunging toward the Mercedes through the mud.

His hands were trembling. With the overturned car between
himself and them, he braced his right wrist on the hot under-
carriage, ignoring the burn, steadied his forearm with his left
hand. He did not hurry; he was sure they could not see him.
Carefully he took aim.

At the first crack of the pistol, one man went over backward
under the bullet's impact. The second instinctively threw himself out of the light. Allison fired, anticipating this and changing aim. There was a howl; then the bright flame of a rifle, and
bullets chugged into the car's flank. Allison fired back immediately at the muzzle-flare, a spread of three shots, left, center,
right. The gun fell silent. Then someone grabbed Allison's arm;
he whirled. Just in time he realized that it was Erika who clung
to him, almost collapsing against him.

"Are you all right?" Allison gasped.

"Yes . . . Yes, I think so."

"Wait . . ." Allison plunged back into the car, hand groping.
He found Mubaba's pistol. He seized it, thrust it into his belt.
"Let's go!" he snapped, grabbed Erika's wrist, and dragged her
around the Mercedes.

He pulled her through calf-deep mire toward that yellow
light ahead. In the first three steps, his shoes were sucked off.
Far behind—the vehicles had skidded hundreds of yards past—
he heard frightened voices at the bus. Then they were on the
pavement. Erika stumbled, Allison pushed her on.

They reached the Land Rover. Its left front was all bashed
in, but its engine was idling smoothly. "Get in!" Allison rasped

and slid behind the wheel. Half praying, half cursing, he gave it a turn, and something unclenched within him; it moved well. He put the vehicle in gear, eased it forward; nothing gave way. Its heavy-duty bumper, reinforced with a winch, had chopped the corner of the Mercedes, but the Rover was built to take punishment and keep going. Allison spun the wheel, turned it around, then stamped down on the gas, and the Rover leaped forward.

Beside him, there was a strange, gasping noise. Erika had begun to cry.

Allison took one hand off the wheel, patted her thigh. "It's all right," he said. "It's all right now. We've got a chance."

Allison blessed the downpour. The rain fell in incredible quantities, rendering the single headlight almost useless. But by the same token, it had driven the Acanaran army under shelter. There was no traffic on the road, no more checkpoints. Presently he dared stop, search the Rover. To his relief, he found what he sought in its dash compartment: a flashlight and a map.

His luck had held; the map covered the sector between Ogoro and M'nanda and south to the Acanara River. The roads and towns were clearly marked on it. The only trouble was, he thought bitterly, they meant nothing to him; none of their names offered refuge.

Erika bent over it with him, her hair a matted mess, her face bruised and muddy. Yet, the last traces of shock were gone from her; she was as cool and steady as if they were on a Sunday drive. "If we could get back to Ogoro and reach the American or German embassies. Or on to M'nanda, see General Kopapo or the consuls there . . ."

Allison laughed without humor. "Once Sandro finds out we've escaped, that's exactly what he'll hope we'll do. He'll curtain them off with his private army; the minute we surface, he'll take us. No, we've got to find some other place, even if we have to hide in the jungle. And then, somehow, I've got to get word to Buckley—" He bit his lip. "Damn it, I don't know anything about this country, I don't know the roads or—" Moving the beam of the torch, he said, "Wait. Sinawa."

"What?"

"Sinawa. The mission Sandro raided with Marc's tanks. In M'nanda, I met a priest— He was going back there. He was sympathetic to Marc and the N'terua before the raid. If he's there, and if we could find it, maybe . . . Maybe, hell. It's our only hope."

Frantically he searched the map. In the uncertain light, he found the dot, but his heart sank. It was so far, so damned far—forty, fifty kilometers along the paved road, then another fifty along what seemed to be little more than a track. It lay almost on the bank of the Acanara, in the heavy jungles of the lowlands. He sat up straight, instinctively looking at the sky.

Sixty miles of unknown roads, and dawn only a few hours away. But they had to go somewhere. And there was nowhere else to go.

"God help us," he said, "if there're government troops there. But I don't know of any other choice." He paused. "God damn it, Erika, I wish I did. For your sake."

She laid her hand on his. "Don't worry about me, John." Her voice was steady. "I'm all right. I'm fine."

Allison turned to her in the darkness. "Damned if you aren't," he said. Then, quite naturally and without premeditation, he put out a hand, cupped her chin, and kissed her briefly on the lips with great gentleness. Then he released her and put the car in gear.

Allison drove flat-out in a nightmare race against daylight. The rain was both friend and enemy, hiding them but blotting out everything ahead, the road almost invisible in the feeble glare of the single headlight. Yet there was nothing to do but plunge into that wall of water as fast as they could. He drove leaning out the window for better visibility, skidding crazily around curves that were on him before he could see them.

Somehow they held the pavement. The jungle sped by on either side, and for a while, so long as the road was level with its floor, its great black contour served as a guide to the twists and turns of the highway. Presently, though, the road climbed, on a high fill now, with a steep drop at either side, and Allison, though he begrudged it, had to slow a little, lest they go over.

Even so, he began to relax a bit as the odometer ticked off kilometers. Twenty miles to the turn—if you were on a pleasure drive, no distance at all. Less than an hour, and so far not a sign of trouble, not a trace of another vehicle on the road. If their luck only held— But, he thought, of course it would not. They had already had more than their share of miracles tonight.

Then, as if to prove him right, he saw the headlights.

They were distant, perhaps miles, at first hardly more than a wink in the blur of rain. Then the oncoming vehicle tilted enough to ray its beams upward, like spotlights, and they were plain to see. Erika gasped. "Johnny! A car."

Allison's voice was a growl. "Car nothing!" Behind the first came a second, a third, a fourth. "Those are trucks—a convoy!"

Erika looked around frantically. On either side the embankment plunged straight down for a good ten feet. "Then what shall we do, where shall we go?"

"Well, two whites in a bashed-up army Rover aren't going to get past that convoy!" Allison's decision was instantaneous. "Hang on!" He hit the brake. The Rover skidded to a halt; deftly, Allison spun it around. Then he sent it leaping back in the direction in which they'd come. "Watch for a side road, a path, anything!"

"Yes." She leaned out of the car.

Like a rabbit ahead of dogs, they raced along before the convoy. Losing ground, Allison thought bitterly, losing time,

losing precious darkness. But there was no help for it ... The
level of the road changed, the height of fill dropping. Now they
were even with the forest floor again. Then Erika clutched his
knee. "Johnny, stop! I think we just passed a path of some
kind!"

Again Allison hit the brake. Then he threw the Rover into
reverse; it squawled backward. Erika pointed, and in the
narrow beam of the single headlight Allison saw it. No road,
certainly. Perhaps not even a trail. But a break in the jungle of
some kind. Anyhow, there was no choice; it was their only
chance.

"Hold tight!" He turned the wheel, sent the Rover plunging
off the pavement.

Brush crackled; the wheels sank into mud, spun and whined.
Allison cursed, shifting into low, four-wheel drive, low range.
The Rover wallowed like a hippo, fighting through the mire,
grinding down cane and thorn, which thrashed back up behind
it.

Allison dared not go far. In fact, he could not; ahead trees
closed off the lane. He stopped, shifted into neutral, and cut off
the headlight. He did not dare turn off the engine for fear it
would not start again; he only hoped the thunder of the trucks
would drown its smooth idling—that and the drum of rain on
hoods and cabs.

They were coming now. Through the brush that screened
them, Allison could see the rain-blurred glare of headlights.
"Get down," he whispered. "If there's any shooting, run." Then
he drew Mubaba's pistol from his belt.

The trucks came on. Now they were a quarter mile away,
now an eighth. Allison wondered. Had they glimpsed his tail-
lights, seen them turn? He did not think so, he'd been too far
ahead. Still, there would be guards on the alert for ambush. If
they spotted the Rover's tracks across the verge, the smashed
brush—

Then another Rover roared by, loaded with soldiers; Allison

could see their silhouettes. It was the convoy commander's he supposed. It did not slow as it passed the entrance to their hiding place. Behind it came the trucks.

They posed more danger. Their drivers, their other occupants if any, were up higher, could command a better view of the jungle on either side. The guards who rode beside each driver and had nothing to do but watch for ambush should be scanning the jungle carefully.

But the first truck rumbled by, then the second, the third . . . Allison held his breath. The fourth passed.

Beside Allison, Erika let out a gasp of relief. "John, they didn't see us!"

"No," Allison said. Nevertheless, he did not move. There could always be a laggard. Besides, they had to be well out of sight before he dared try regain the highway. But it took all his will power to sit there idly while precious minutes dribbled past.

Presently, though, he judged enough time had elapsed. "Now," he said, "if we can only get back out of here . . ." He put the car in reverse, easing power to it gently. But its wheels had sunk deeply in the mire; now they spun. The Rover did not move.

Allison cursed. Erika asked fearfully, "Are we stuck?"

"I don't know." Allison tried again. No results; as he increased power, there was only the howl of tires. The Rover quivered like a bird with its wings clipped, but wanting to take flight.

"Damn," Allison said. "Erika, get behind the wheel."

She slid over. He got out, in mire up to his knees. "When I push on the front, give it power slowly, but feed it all its got." He slogged around to the front, leaned against the smashed hood with both hands, and shoved.

His feet sank deeper in the mud. Consciously, he summoned every ounce of strength he possessed. His teeth grated together, veins stood out in his forehead, as he put his full weight against the front of the Rover. Meanwhile, Erika followed his orders, giving it power gradually.

The car trembled, shook, but did not move. Allison's breath rasped in his nostrils; blue lights seemed to dance before his eyes. It *had* to go, it *had* to. If they were stuck here—

Then, with Allison's margin of strength almost gone, Erika reached full power. The engine roared, wheels whined. And suddenly, as Allison put everything he had into a final effort, the Rover inched back, then slid, then roared out from under him. He floundered in the mud, but he was laughing crazily with delight as he leaped up. Suction broken, the car roared back the way it had come, out onto the highway, and Allison blundered through the rain, slime and thorns after it. Erika moved as he jumped in.

It took him only seconds to whirl it around. "Okay," he wheezed. "Back toward Sinawa. Hang on; this time we don't turn around for anything—I hope." And he sent the Rover rushing forward, haunted by the knowledge of dwindling time.

This time their luck held; a half hour later, they turned off the pavement onto what they hoped was the road to Sinawa. And now Allison saw that the bog-down in the jungle had only been a foretaste of what lay ahead of them.

The road to Sinawa was not a road at all; it was, in this downpour, only a river of mud.

The moment the Rover's tires sank into it, Allison's heart sank with them. The Rover slithered and wallowed as it fought for solid bottom, for any sort of purchase, and Allison held his breath. But he had shifted into low range and four-wheel drive, and with a whine of rubber, a spin of the back wheels, the Rover grabbed, then ploughed forward.

In fact, it made a half mile before it bogged down hopelessly.

Allison did as he had done before. Erika slid behind the wheel; Allison shoved with every bit of his strength. The back tires spun, spewed him with mud. Then the front wheels found a bite; the car lurched forward, on.

That was a pattern repeated endlessly in the next ten, fifteen miles. Over and over, the vehicle bellied down. Allison spent his strength recklessly, desperately, pushing, digging with the pioneer tools or rigging the winch. He was a ludicrous, wheezing, staggering apparition by then, mud from head to toe, eyes sunken, breath a continual wheezing gasp, limbs trembling from strain. Yet, somehow, they managed to keep going. Somehow, he regained enough strength in the intervals when they moved, even though he had to fight the steering wheel remorselessly, to break free when they bogged again.

And yet, he knew it was hopeless. Dawn was only an hour away, and they had too much distance still to cover. By daylight Rinaldi would know of their escape. Then, thought Allison grimly, the helicopters would come over.

"Another half hour," he gasped to Erika during one of the intervals when the Rover wallowed forward. "Three quarters, at the most. Then we'll have to hide it in the jungle, try to make the rest of the way on foot." Then he cursed as the Rover hung again, engine roaring, wheels spinning fruitlessly. He started to get out, but Erika seized his arm. "No, John. You'll kill yourself. Let me try it this time."

He lacked strength to argue. Anyhow, before he could answer, she was out, slogging through the mud. "Now," she called from behind, voice barely audible through the rain. Allison gave the Rover power. It wallowed motionless, then swayed, slithered, as he turned the wheel a little. It caught, inched forward. Erika jumped in, panting. Allison kept up the forward momentum. Beside him, he could hear Erika gasping. "I'm stronger than I look," she managed.

They went on. It was like running in a nightmare, pursued by something frightful, and never getting anywhere. But they went on. There was no telling how far they had come; all that spinning of wheels had thrown the odometer off completely. Maybe half, maybe three-quarters of the way. Or maybe, Allison thought bitterly, head swimming with fatigue, not a tenth of that. He no longer knew.

Outside, it seemed to be getting lighter. There were only a few minutes left now before they would have to take to the jungle. Maybe, Allison thought, it would be as well. Maybe— Then he was aware of something. The angle of the road had changed; now it was tilting sharply downhill. And it had been a full ten minutes since they had last bogged . . .

Hope rose in him. They were nearing the river. The new slant of the road seemed to provide just enough drainage so that the surface layer of mud was not so deep. The Rover's wheels were biting now. It was actually picking up speed.

The forward movement was like wine to Allison; he felt despair slough away. There was a chance, just a chance . . . He gave the car more gas. It leaped forward perceptibly, slewing and slithering wildly. On each side the jungle seemed even heavier, thicker, more impenetrable. There was a turn ahead, a sharp one. Allison fought the wheel to guide the car around.

Then Erika seized his arm. "John, look!"

Allison blinked and stared. Not more than a quarter of a mile away, the wall of jungle broke on the left. In the clearing there were big pale shapes of white barely visible in the gray fag end of night. It was a moment before Allison comprehended what they were: the walls of ruined buildings.

The single word came from him in an explosion of breath. "Sinawa."

He leaned forward over the wheel. It seemed to take forever for the outlines of the mission to draw nearer, define themselves; but he could see now: he could see the compound wall, the ruined hospital, the broken gate. He drew abreast of it, fought the Rover into the opening. It was almost daylight now, but they had made it, by God, they had made it!

Then Erika gave a short-cut, startled cry. Allison hit the brake as the black shapes in helmets and ponchos, carrying rifles, loomed up in front of them, around them. Before there was time to think, much less reach for his gun, the doors were jerked open; he and Erika were yanked roughly from the car. He felt the cold steel of three different rifle muzzles gouging against him as, swaying with fatigue, he instinctively raised his hands. Well, he thought bitterly, almost too tired to care, they had gambled and they had lost. There had been a government detachment stationed here at Sinawa.

And now, after all that risk, all that labor, it was over. Rinaldi had them again. He blinked, as the beam of a flashlight shone full in his face.

Then a deep voice said in English, "Well, I'll be damned. John Allison." And as Allison's eyes focused on the man behind the light, he stared in bafflement and amazement; it was Roy Hausa.

And the shorter, wider man standing just behind him was General Marc.

CHAPTER 9

THE HELICOPTER CAME over a half hour after dawn. Until its crass, chopping roar had faded, the six people in the cellar of the hospital at Sinawa instinctively held their breaths. Then it was gone, and Roy Hausa hit Allison again, hard, with the back of his hand. "This time, you mother, I want the truth!"

O'Kerry, the tall, gaunt priest, burst out, "General, this is too much! I insist—"

General Marc turned on him. Allison, through eyes veiled with tears of pain, saw the big head shake negatively. "You stay out of this, Father. This man's betrayed me one time. I ain't going to let him do it to me again."

Erika Wolf's voice was shrill, outraged. "He's told you the truth, you beast. If you hit him any more—"

Marc said heavily, "You be quiet too, lady. I don't want to have to hurt you too."

Allison saw her spring to her feet, a pathetic, mud-splattered parody of a woman, from where she had sat huddled against the wall. "For God's sake!" she snarled. "Do you think I'm afraid of you? After what we've been through? He's told you the truth, all of it!" Her voice trembled, but not with fear, as she pointed at Hausa. "Make him stop! Do you understand? Make him stop!"

Marc stared at her. Allison, collapsed against the opposite wall, waited, groggily, without hope, for another blow.

By now he could barely remember the events of the past hour. There had been that endless moment when he had stared

171

at Hausa and at Marc and they had stared back. Then Hausa's big hands seized him. The black man's voice was savage, triumphant. "Buddy, I don't know why you came here. But you came to the wrong place this time. Oh, you came to the wrong place! You were warned!" There was, in the darkness, the snick of a switchblade, and Allison felt its point against his throat. "Now, I'm gonna carve—"

"Wait!" Marc's voice had rapped the single word. Then, "All right, Allison, what the hell you doing at Sinawa?"

Allison had tried to talk. Fatigue had him, though; it all came out a mumble. Then Marc said, "Shut up. Come with me." They were herded through the ruins, under a patch of roof still standing among the rubble. Marc knelt, fumbled, then opened a door like that of an old-fashioned storm cellar in a Midwestern house. "Down there," he ordered and pushed them down the stairs into the glow of a single lamp. The two priests there stared wide-eyed at Allison and Erika, as if they were ghosts.

There was a table, chairs. Roughly, Marc pushed Allison into one, Erika into another. He bent over Allison, his face looming huge before Allison's eyes. "I told you," he rasped, "that you had better never let yourself fall into my hands. I meant that. What are you doing here, you goddam turncoat?"

Allison remembered groping for words, finding only one. "Coffee."

It had come, in a canteen cup that burned his lips as he drank. He felt new life flow into him; he disregarded the pain. Then there was a strong Rhodesian cigarette. Allison inhaled gratefully, mind clearing.

"Now." The evil look on Marc's face had not mitigated one bit. "Now, you tell me. And you tell me straight, hear?"

Allison had gathered all his strength; and he had told Marc. Had told him everything; about the forty M-60's, about the five captured Shermans, about Rinaldi's plans for M'nanda, Kopapo's offensive ... And about their flight, escape. It was all complicated, difficult, and he was exhausted, and even as his voice droned on, faltering from time to time, he knew he was not convincing Marc.

"But that's it," he'd whispered at last, the end of his strength near. "Rinaldi's going to hit M'nanda."

Then Hausa's voice came from darkness. "For God's sake, Marc. You don't believe this crap, do you?"

Marc's lips moved. "It's wild," he whispered. "Wild." Suddenly he seized Allison's coat, half jerked him to his feet, his teeth white in a snarl. "Listen, you, I want the truth. I got to have the truth!"

Allison shook his head groggily. "I told you—"

Marc flung him down into the chair. He stood looking at Allison for a moment. Then he drew in a long breath. His voice was flat, metallic, as he said, "All right, Roy. You see if you can beat another story out of him."

That was when Hausa had begun to work on him. Hausa was thorough, experienced, ruthless. Twice, Allison lost consciousness, was revived each time. Then the helicopter had come; there had been a moment's surcease, then another blow.

Now, as Allison sat there dazed, Erika's voice went on, shrill, angry, unafraid. "What kind of swine are you? Why don't you let him alone? Why don't you work on me for a while, see what you can beat out of me?"

"My dear," O'Kerry said in a cautionary voice. Hausa cut in, straightening up. "Listen, you white bitch, I just might do that—"

Then Marc let out a long, whistling sigh. He turned. "No, Roy," he said heavily. "Knock it off."

"But, General—"

"Goddammit!" Marc roared, "I said knock it off!" He strode over to where Allison sprawled against the wall, looked down at him. "I know this man," he said. "If you haven't broke him now, you ain't going to break him." Then he said, "John. You hear me?"

Allison nodded.

"Can you stand?"

Allison mustered all his strength. Slowly, unsteadily, he got to his feet. "I can stand," he heard himself whisper.

"All right," Marc said. "Nobody's going to hit you again. I want to hear it all once more."

Slowly, carefully, speaking through puffed lips, Allison told it all again. Marc stood there, thumbs hooked in belt, head cocked, listening closely. When Allison was through, the room was silent.

Then Father Devlin said, "I think the man speaks the truth. M'nanda is crowded with white refugees."

"I know," Marc said. He began to pace, slapping his thigh with his fist. "All the same, it don't make sense. It just don't make sense! M'nanda's the key point in this whole country. No general would uncover it like that—not if he was in his right mind!"

"Maybe he's not in his right mind," O'Kerry said. "Any man who has done what I witnessed here is not. Besides, what risk to him? He thinks you're sealed off south of the Acanara, with a hundred miles of river and impassable jungle between you and M'nanda. He doesn't know you've managed to get tanks through there."

The single word penetrated Allison's consciousness. He jerked erect. *"Tanks?"*

Marc looked at him. "Yeah," he said after a moment. "Tanks. A half dozen Shermans." His mouth quirked. "I wasn't supposed to be able to do it. It's supposed to be impossible to get tanks through that terrain. But I did it anyhow."

Allison lurched forward, stumbled, braced himself on the table. "Listen," he rasped, "I want some more coffee."

"Who the hell are you to give orders?" Hausa flared. But Marc, staring at Allison, raised his hand. "Father, bring him a cup, will you?"

Devlin brought it; Allison drank again. When he set down

the cup, he was no longer swaying. He dragged his hand across his eyes, and then he was all right. No, not all right, but he would do, he told himself; he could think now, talk. He said, "Then you've got a chance to beat Rinaldi to M'nanda." He pointed a finger. "If you've got tanks here at Sinawa, you've got a chance to do it."

Marc's voice was impatient. "Man, you think I don't know that? I can't fight Kopapo's Centurions—but you say Kopapo's pulled his Centurions out. That would only leave Rinaldi's five Shermans—against my six."

He began to pace. "A white mercenary sold me out, let Rinaldi take those five tanks without a fight. And he's used 'em to ruin me in the eyes of the world, make an outlaw out of me! I came north of the Acanara to find those tanks and destroy 'em." He flung out an arm in a southward gesture. "They thought I couldn't cross that hundred miles of jungle, those two rivers they had me penned up behind. But they didn't know I had Roy Hausa. He engineered me a way through there, through places a crocodile wouldn't travel." He hit his thigh again. "My spies tell me the tanks are at a secret base in the jungle, south of the Ogoro-M'nanda highway, place called Ruala. That's where I was headed for—until I met up with you. Now . . . Now, I don't know."

"Dammit, General," Hausa said pleadingly, "forget M'nanda. I tell you, it's a trap, and these two honkies are nothing but the bait to pull you into it! It's too far to M'nanda. We can strike Ruala like we planned, wipe out those Shermans, then hightail for home and get into position before Kopapo hits. If we don't, if we go off in the other direction, Kopapo'll take Edwardville before we can get back to stop him. And if Edwardville goes, the whole country goes. Besides"—he looked at Marc—"Maria's at Edwardville."

Marc was silent a moment. Then he said, "You're a damned good engineer, Roy, but you're no general. If I took M'nanda, I'd have Kopapo's supply line cut. He'd *have* to turn back on me, away from our flank down south." He went on pacing. "If we could get there before Rinaldi, meet his tanks ... that would be an even fight. I'm not afraid of that; I can fight rings around Rinaldi with tanks any day. We could beat him, take the city, make Kopapo swing around—"

"And rub us out with his Centurions!" Hausa grated.

"Maybe not," said Allison. "Maybe if you had the city, Kopapo would stop and talk to you."

"Talk?" said Hausa in a voice strangled with incredulity.

But Marc had already seized Allison's thought. "Either we'll have beat Rinaldi by then or we won't have. And if we have, it'll be plain to Kopapo what Rinaldi was trying to pull on him. There just might be a possibility that—"

"He'd come over to you?" asked Allison.

"Well, he couldn't stay with Rinaldi after that, could he? He'd have to, or be a third force, and he doesn't have the political base for that; he's a soldier, not a politician. He'd *have* to talk—"

"General, it's still too wild a gamble!" Hausa snapped.

"Is it?" Marc was excited now. "Look, Roy, down south people are starving to death, women and children, the hope of Southern Acanara's future. Every day that passes, that hope dies a little more—and so do hundreds of kids. If I've got a chance to win this war by one wild gamble, win it quick, I owe it to them to take it. And I'll never have a chance like this at M'nanda again." He broke off. "It all boils down to two things. Can I trust Allison and can I get there in time?"

"Listen," Allison said. "If you don't trust me, put me in your tank with you. Then, any time you want me, I'll be where you can lay your hands on me."

Marc looked back at him coldly. "Don't worry, friend. That's exactly where you'll be." Then he said, in a voice like the ring of iron against iron, "All right. We're going for broke. We're gonna try it."

CHAPTER 10

ALLISON AWAKENED in the darkness of the cellar. His watch's luminescent dial told him he'd had only five hours sleep. But he came awake refreshed and alert, though his face was very sore from Hausa's beating. A nameless excitement, a strange eagerness, combined in an exhilaration that took the place of rest.

After Marc's decision, he'd given out very quickly this morning. He'd barely had strength enough left to wash the mud off himself, force down a little bread and meat, and then fall onto one of the mattresses reclaimed from the hospital, with which the cellar was stacked. Now he found cigarettes and matches that O'Kerry had given him and lit one.

At the match's flare, Erika's whisper came from nearby. "John?"

"You're awake? How do you feel?"

"Much, much better. You?"

"Okay. Where is everybody?"

"I don't know. Upstairs. Out. You have cigarettes? Light me one, please."

"Yes." Allison did so. He heard the soft rustle of movement. In the match flare, he saw her bending over him, wrapped in a blanket. Allison threw back his own cover. "Come here," he said, passed her the cigarette and took her hand, pulling her down.

She came willingly, easily, to lie beside him on the mattress. Part of his awakening mood was a physical desire that was

177

irresistibly powerful. He had felt it like this before; it had something to do with the knowledge that he was going into danger. He slipped his arm under her, held her tightly, began to caress her with his other hand.

She shivered, but not with cold. He heard the rasping of her breath, its warmth was on his face. Her thigh crossed over his body and she rubbed herself against him. They lay like that for a moment, as the cigarettes burned down.

"I feel strange," she said.

"Strange, how?"

"I don't know. I feel changed, different, somehow."

"You are," he said. "You changed last night. You changed when you realized you couldn't be Rinaldi's woman."

"I think I knew all along I couldn't be. And yet ... He was strong. Until now, I have always seemed to need somebody strong. Perhaps I still do, but not in the same way."

"What do you mean?"

"I don't know. It's only as if I have been in a dark tunnel for years and now I have come out into daylight. I— When I learned about my father, it was something I didn't have strength to bear. I just ... let go. Depended on other people to give me strength. Perhaps I lost my self-respect. If I did, I found some of it again last night. Anyway, I feel different. As if ... as if I am ready to take responsibility for myself again. As if I had ... paid off a debt that was ruining me."

She was silent for a moment. Then she said, "I think that is it. I assumed my father's debt. It was one that seemed to me beyond my ability to pay. But I see now that it can be paid. Not completely, not ever. But I can pay enough on it so that I may hold my head up again. So that I won't have to hide from the world any more with people like Sandro." Then her cigarette had burned down, and she crushed it out. "I know who I am now. I am not only my father's daughter. I am myself."

Allison extinguished his own cigarette. "You sure as hell are," he whispered, and then his mouth bore down on hers.

Later, she whispered, "Are you really going with Marc?"

"I have to. I'm his hostage."

"Then I want to go too."

"No," said Allison. "You can't. You stay here with O'Kerry. I'm insisting on that."

"But—"

"Listen," he said, "you don't know what a tank battle is like. You don't even know how to get in and out of a tank. You've seen enough, had enough. You stay here."

"But I shall worry about you."

"Don't. I'll be all right."

She was silent for a moment. "Nevertheless, I shall. Do you know, it seems very strange to worry about someone beside myself. It has been a long time since I have done that." Then her fingers gripped his tightly, gouging into his flesh. "For God's sake, John, be careful."

"I tell you—" he began. Then the trapdoor above opened. A dim ray of oyster-colored light fell into the cellar. A voice from above called, "Allison!" It was Marc's.

Allison's mouth brushed Erika's again. Then he threw aside the blanket, reached for his clothes.

The tanks were hidden in the jungle, camouflaged, yet in position to cover the road to Sinawa with their guns. The two hundred men were in bivouac there too, fireless, in the rain. Inside one of the ruined buildings of the mission compound, Marc, Hausa, Allison and four tank commanders bent over a map.

"Here's Ruala," Marc said. "About fifty miles from M'nanda, just outside Kopapo's military district. Rinaldi's got a straight shot down the highway; he can start about midnight tonight and hit M'nanda at dawn without working up a heavy sweat."

"Right," Allison said.

"And Sinawa." It was at the apex of an inverted triangle, far to the south between Ruala and M'nanda. "It's only about fifty miles from here to M'nanda too. But there's one big difference.

We're going to have to go cross-country. We won't be able to make a fifth of the time Rinaldi can. Not, anyhow, until we come out of the jungle and hit the high plain—and we've got thirty, thirty-five miles of jungle before we do that."

Hausa made a sound of protest. "We can go straight up this road from Sinawa to the highway, turn right and go straight to M'nanda on the paving."

"Sure," Marc said caustically. "We can send Rinaldi a telegram and let him know we're coming too. Then he can change his plans. He can send out Centurions from Ogoro. Shermans we can fight, Centurions we can't. Those high-velocity 105 guns'll eat us alive. No, we don't dare take a chance of spoiling our surprise."

"Then we got to start early, before darkness," Hausa said.

Marc shook his head. "Can't do that, either. Same problem. Besides, we don't dare get there early. Rinaldi knows his timing. He's set this thing for the ideal moment when Kopapo will be so far away he won't be able to get back. We tip our hand, Kopapo wheels back too soon, we're in big trouble, with Rinaldi coming at us from one side, Kopapo from the other. No, we got to follow Rinaldi's schedule, travel under cover of darkness, make it there by daylight—ahead of Rinaldi. That plain outside of M'nanda's an ideal place for tank fighting; if we can take him by surprise, knock out his tanks, then take the city, we're in like Flynn."

Hausa was silent for a moment. Then he said, "Suppose Rinaldi changes his plans. He knows Allison's got away by now. And he knows Allison knows what he's up to."

"I've thought about that," Marc said. "But what difference could it make? He knows Allison don't dare surface in Ogoro or M'nanda, that this man's loose in strange country where he knows nobody. He's counting on running Allison down in time. Meanwhile, he's got Kopapo moved out—and so far as Rinaldi knows, I hope, we're a hundred miles south of the river and in no position to do anything. It's all still wide-open; I think he'll go. I only hope he leads the attack in person."

"He won't dare do that," Hausa said. "A white man in a fight like that?"

"And suppose he plans never to show himself? Suppose he commands from inside a tank? Knowing him—"

"Listen," Allison said. "One of the last things he told us was that he'd see us in M'nanda."

"That's what I mean!" Marc struck the table with his fist. "I been fighting that man long enough to know him! On an operation like this, I'll bet you he'll be in the lead tank himself! And I hope to God he is! I hope to God I get the chance to fight him man to man, tank to tank!" He turned to Hausa. "Now. We've got guides who know this country. I want you to take most of the infantry, head out right now, start making us a trail straight through the jungle. Move as fast as you can, keep under cover, stir up no fuss, get as much as you can done before we come up behind you. We'll be moving out ourselves at first dark."

Hausa hesitated, sullen, looking from Marc to Allison. "Dammit, General, one last time. You can't risk the whole war on this white man's say-so."

Marc looked back at him for a moment. His face softened; he clapped Hausa on the shoulder. "All right, Roy, I know how you feel. I'm not risking it on his say-so. I'm risking it on mine."

Their eyes met. Finally Hausa nodded, and his face relaxed into something almost like a smile. "Yes, sir," he said, his voice quiet, almost submissive. "Just watch him, that's all I ask. Just watch him." He put on his helmet. "Now, I'll get this show on the road."

When he was gone, Marc dismissed the tank commanders. He and Allison stood alone in the ruins. Marc took out a cigarette and lit it, staring out at the rain. Presently he said, "I guess I owe you an apology."

"For what?"

"You know for what. For last night. But there wasn't any way I could know how that deal with those M-60's came about.

Not until you explained it. And I still had to think about it, sleep on it . . . If I owe you an apology, you've got it."

"Let's wait and see how the M'nanda thing comes out."

"Yeah." Marc let out a gusty breath. "I don't know. Am I a fool, risking everything on one dice roll? There are so many ifs, so many things that could go wrong. And yet—I've got to move before those M-60's are in service. I've got to do something. We're penned in like sheep down yonder, John. Every day, they bury more kids." He laughed raspingly. "Kids! They look like little skeletons, like the skeletons of little old men. Well, I got to try. Like they used to say, an amputation's better than a weeping wound." He dropped his cigarette, ground it out. "And you— you're a problem."

"I know," Allison said.

"I got to have you with me. I got to have you where I can watch you. I owe Roy that much. We wouldn't be here today, in position to strike, if it weren't for him. But there's no room in a tank in combat for a deadhead." He turned to Allison. "How long since you fired a tank cannon?"

"What?" Allison stared at him. "Why, hell . . . fifteen years."

Marc nodded. "Fifteen years ago, you were the best tank gunner I ever saw. You were raw handling men, not too good at judging terrain, but you could drive and shoot rings around anybody I ever saw. A natural . . . But, hell, you always were a natural with any kind of gun." He took the cigarette from his mouth, dropped it and stamped it out with a muddy boot. "We've got no ammunition to waste and couldn't fire it if we had. But we've got a day of waiting ahead of us. You go out there and get in one of those tanks. Re-familiarize yourself. Dry fire and go through drill. Then come back to me and tell me if you feel qualified to ride as my gunner."

"No," said Allison quickly. "No. I can't do that. You need a trained man."

"It'll either come back to you or it won't. If it doesn't, we'll cram you in somewhere. If it does, I won't have any better gunner than you." He looked at Allison. "But it's your decision."

Allison looked back at the bulky black man, standing there with lines of fatigue grooving his face, his hair graying. He was moved. Slowly, he nodded. "All right, I'll try it. But I won't do it unless I'm sure I can."

"It'll come back," Marc said in a voice of certainty. "Don't worry. It'll come back. Hell, you never forgot it in the first place." Then he slapped Allison on the back. "I've got a half hour. Come on, let's get you a helmet and a sidearm. Then I'll show you my tank."

CHAPTER 11

TWICE MORE DURING the day, there were helicopters. At their first distant chatter, the alarm was given, and like chickens before the threat of a hawk, those men left around the mission scattered. Always the choppers passed without incident; Marc had given the order that they were not to be fired upon. Allison, remembering the impenetrable wool of jungle he had seen from the airplane, was not surprised that their surveillance was fruitless, especially since Marc was a master at the art of camouflage. Eventually, he supposed, a patrol would reach Sinawa. When it came, though, it would be too late.

He had already said goodbye to Erika.

The priests had come to Sinawa upstream on the Acanara by motor launch. But now it was impossible for them to remain here; if they were discovered amid the spoor of all Marc's tanks, and sheltering Erika, there was no doubt about what Rinaldi would do to them. Marc's orders had been firm. They were to abandon Sinawa. At dusk they were to go up the river twenty miles, cross through flooded jungle, strike the Laramba, go downstream, and anchor at one of his outposts where they would be received and taken to the rebel capital of Edwardville. Marc provided guides, and at twilight they embarked.

Before they did, Erika clung to Allison almost desperately.

"John," she whispered, "please be careful."

"Don't worry about me."

It was banal, he thought, holding her; yet, it was the only

184

thing men and women had found to say to each other for cen-
turies when men went off to battle.

"But I will. Where will we meet again?"

"In Ogoro," he said. "Or M'nanda. Or, if not there, the
Hofbrauhaus in Munich. Or the Algonquin in New York.
Somewhere."

"Yes," she said. "Somewhere." Her face turned upward; he
kissed her. Then she pulled away. "John, don't let Sandro kill
you." Her voice was a rasp in the darkness. "If you get the
chance, kill him, but don't let him kill you."

Allison said nothing, only raised a hand. The launch's engine
fractured the quiet of evening over the river. It swung out from
the bank, pulled away. Allison waved; in the dusk Erika waved
back. Then they were gone. Allison watched them until they
were out of sight, his hand still up. Then he dropped it, and in
the rain turned and walked back from the river toward the
ruined mission.

Slogging up that muddy bank in the downpour, he felt a
curious sense of unreality. More that fifteen years ago he had
been intensively trained to fight tanks. And yet, after all this
time, he would only now know the reality of his first tank
battle. It was curious; he felt dislocated, as if time had somehow warped and caught him in a seam.

Fifteen years, he thought. And yet, this morning, when he
had dropped through the hatch of Marc's Sherman, they had
peeled away like dry skin. Marc was right; he had never really
forgotten it. The moment he had settled in the gunner's seat, it
had all come back to him, everything he had ever learned and
known about using a tank gun—and that had been a great
deal. All that remained was practice, to reestablish the coordina-
tion, the linkage of mind and hand. Hour after hour of un-
remitting drill had brought that to him again. There was no
way of knowing until the test of battle, of course. But deep
within himself he was confident he could outshoot any of

Marc's men except Marc himself—and, more importantly, Rinaldi's gunners too. So it was settled: he would ride with Marc.

He reached the top of a rise. From here he could see the broad swirling bosom of the Acanara through a silver pattern of rain. The jungle on the opposite side was dark. The boat was a speck on the river. It was a totally exotic scene. But somehow he felt at home in it, now.

Then a noise like thunder—louder, coarser than thunder—brought him around. It came from the mission: the deep voice of a tank engine firing into life. It was joined by another, and yet another, until the whole twilight shook with that chorused roar. Allison hurried up the hill, to where, in the gathering darkness, the tanks were getting ready to move out.

In the jungle they had formed up into line, their commanders standing high in their dome-shaped turrets. Their outlines were huge, massive, dwarfing Allison as he ran past them toward the lead Sherman. Their cleated treads sloughed huge gobbets of mud as they jockeyed into position, tracks clanking and squeaking as they traveled endlessly, pulled by sprockets at the front, across the big idlers at the back. The long, tapering tubes of their guns pointed straight ahead. As their engines heated, they filled the rain-washed air with the rankness of exhaust fumes, the smell of oil, and of water turning to steam on hot engine grilles. Allison drew in a deep breath: it was a smell with the bite of iron in it, a smell of raw, sheer power. Everything in him that was masculine, violent, primitive, responded instinctively to all the leashed, kinetic potency of these man-made brutes, greater than any natural ones that ever walked the earth of Africa.

Marc was waiting, checking as that small remnant of infantry that had remained behind climbed aboard the Shermans, seeking any handhold. The long, whiplike radio aerials were tied down to avoid breakage by the jungle foliage; in any event, Marc had decreed radio silence. Allison mounted up over the final drive, the rounded front of the hull, climbed the turret and dropped through the hatch into the gunner's seat. Then Marc got in behind him, booted feet braced on the commander's seat just above Allison's head.

The turret's interior was small, painted white, divided by the breech of the cannon riding on two hydraulic recoil tubes. The loader sat to the left, with rounds of gleaming shells in the ready rack at his feet, more stored in the sponson, the tank's wall. There were also belts for the thirty-caliber machine gun aligned with the cannon, which could be fired in concert with it. On a shelf at the rear was the radio.

Allison, on the right of the breech, was confronted with a maze of equipment. The elevating and traversing handwheels, periscope and telescope sights, the pistol grip of the power traverse, which could spin the turret—and the gun—in a whole circle in seconds. A trigger on the power traverse grip fired the machine gun; a solenoid switch near his left foot fired the cannon. Another switch, on the big gun's breechblock, could be used to shoot it manually if there were no power in the tank. He switched on the gyro-stabilizer, which would keep the gun fairly level even when the hull of the Sherman bucked up and down cross-country.

The lower half of the turret was separated from the driver's and assistant driver's compartments by a partial basketwork of metal. The driver was settled behind the twin steering levers that, by braking the individual tracks, turned the tank. His hand was on the huge gearshift—five speeds forward, one reverse. The assistant driver—"Bog" he was called, short for "bow gunner"—was behind a dual set of levers and controls, with another thirty-caliber machine gun's grip protruding from a ball socket.

Allison pushed the plug trailing from the earphones in his helmet into the little box on his right, making sure the switch was on *Intercom*. There was a *Radio* setting too, but only the commander used that; otherwise everything said in their tank was broadcast and conversations from other tanks were confus-

ingly received. Then he adjusted his throat mike and he was
ready, settling back in the stiflingly hot turret, pulling off his
shirt stowing it behind his seat.

Above him, Marc turned, hand raised. Down the line, as he
was ready, each commander raised his hand in turn. Then
Marc's voice crackled in the interphone as he swept his arm
forward and down in the ancient signal inherited from horse
cavalry— "Driver, move out!"

The mammoth steel animal stirred itself, lurched forward.
The roar of its V-8 engine swelled to crescendo, thunderous in
the turret. Slowly, like a dinosaur too massive for its own
weight, it began to waddle through the jungle. They were
rolling; they were on their way to M'nanda. Allison felt a
strange thrill of excitement mixed with fear. Then both
emotions vanished, swallowed up by hatred as he thought of
what lay ahead. Marc was not the only one who wanted to
meet Rinaldi tank to tank, gun to gun.

It was like riding a ship in a storm or a roller-coaster at
carnival. Allison, like a sailor returned to the sea, quickly
caught the rolling, bucking rhythm as the Sherman plowed
through the jungle.

There was nothing for it but to use the headlights; in their
beams, Allison, through his periscope, saw the road Hausa had
laid out and marveled. With a fine, intimate perception of the
capabilities, the limitations, of the tanks, he had found solid
ground wherever it existed; and where there was none, he had
made it, with a corduroying of logs, Not one moment had he
wasted hacking down trees or vines the Sherman itself could
crush, nor moving logs or spanning gaps over which it could
buck or thrust. But the bigger trees had been felled, the wider
gaps spanned. Now Allison understood how Marc had
traversed the supposedly impossible terrain to the south. The
old tankman's axiom flashed through his mind: *It's all good
tank country. Some of it's just better than the rest.* With Marc in
the turret and Hausa out ahead, that was true.

Still, it was rough, treacherous, tortuous going. The driver fought constantly with levers and gearshift; Marc's voice, giving instructions, guiding him over, around obstacles, was almost constant in the earphones. Allison made a mental computation: Thirty-five miles of jungle before they struck open country; at best, they were making six miles an hour. Then another fifteen miles up onto the plain, maybe faster going, maybe not. It was going to be close, damned close.

Closer than he realized. Suddenly Marc rasped a command; the tank halted. Questioningly, Allison came up through the turret as Marc's legs withdrew. Marc cursed. "Number six has thrown a goddam track!"

Allison sat behind the fifty-caliber atop the turret as Marc jumped down, strode to the end of the long column. For the next three-quarters of an hour, impatience gnawed at him more fiercely than the insects that swarmed around his naked torso, biting, stinging. The big idler wheel at the right rear of number six had not been properly adjusted; too slack, the right track had peeled off as the tank slewed while bucking over a huge log at a crazy angle. Now, thousands of pounds of steel, it lay almost buried in mud.

Marc and his men worked like madmen to repair it. It had to be unbolted in the middle; with the help of the next tank in line, the heavy track was horsed by cable back onto the sprocket, across the idler. Men sweated, grunted with exertion as they guided it; finally it was on, rebolted. Then, with the huge wrench that was part of each Sherman's equipment, the idler wheel was adjusted, tightening the track to proper tension. Marc was panting, streaming sweat, and sickly furious at the delay when he returned to his own tank.

"One more like that," he husked, "and we lose M'nanda." He gave the signal to move out. The Shermans ground on, like careless, browsing elephants, bearing over, crushing to earth everything in their path.

It was airless, sticky, inside the turret; Allison gasped for breath, drank sparingly from his canteen. They came to a swamp, a vast expanse of dead water, stretching endlessly on either side. Hausa had staked a path through it, left a man behind to guide them. Nevertheless, Marc dismounted. In the headlight glare, he waded into the stinking, scum-topped mess, probing with a pole, beckoning the lead tank on slowly, occasionally halting it. Allison saw snakes festooned from limbs overhead; once, he saw the vee of one swimming not far from Marc.

The water came up to Marc's knees, his thighs. It swirled about the Sherman's volute springs, climbed almost midway up the running gear, dangerously close to the engine compartment. If it climbed higher— But Hausa's judgment, Marc's leadership, were sound. As the track blocks fought for purchase on the muddy, silted bottom, the level stayed constant. The tanks plowed on, at last lumbered up onto higher ground on the far side. Marc stood there muddy and panting, burning leeches off his naked legs with a cigarette. There were some still clinging when he regained the turret. Allison lit a cigarette of his own, burned them away as the tank rolled on, then quickly put out the thing. A compartment full of fumes and laden with high-explosive ammunition was no place to smoke.

An hour passed, another. At Ruala, Allison thought, five more Shermans would be forming into line. But no heartbreaking jungle journey for them. A sweep, according to Marc's map, up a dirt road, then high speed along the highway... Allison leaned forward, as if urging on his own vehicle. But it took every ounce of the big tank's power to pull its way through the deep, clinging duff and clay of the sodden forest floor. There was no way it could increase its speed.

All around them, their enemy, the jungle, towered over them. Their more deadly enemy, the rain, fell remorselessly. And their worst enemy of all, time, haunted them with its swiftness of passage.

Then, despite all of Hausa's and Marc's judgment, the tanks began to bog. Hausa could not corduroy every foot of the way, and the character of the soil changed, more sodden, muddier, than before. The first two or three Shermans in line usually made it; but their passage churned such a mire that, inevitably, one of the following vehicles would sink to its belly, its tracks useless. Then cables had to be passed, one by one the tanks at the tail of the column towed through. It was hard work, maddeningly time-consuming. And what was worse, it ate gas.

They had gas; each tank was laden with extra jerrycans of it, strapped and crammed everywhere there was room. But Marc had counted on a fast, clean sweep to Ruala, perhaps even had calculated on finding more fuel there. Now it was going to be a close thing, a damned close thing, just to get them to M'nanda. Maybe they would arrive there with enough gas to fight; certainly, unless they took the city, there would not be enough to retreat.

As they refueled, as he watched the vital fluid poured into the hungry engines, Allison's heart sank. He had thought he'd realized the magnitude of the gamble Marc was taking. Now he understood that he had far underestimated it, And he could perceive how agonizing had been the decision that Marc had had to make. With Kopapo hammering at his flank to the south, Rinaldi's Judas Shermans threatening from the east, his tanks short of gas, his infantry a rag-tag of men armed with any sort of rifle that would fire—Allison had seen Garands, old Lee-Enfields, even ancient trade muskets, single-shot, of the sort still manufactured in Europe for use by primitive West African hunters—the risk must have seemed overwhelming. And yet, Marc had dared—

Now he was everywhere at once along the column, in and out of his own tank, haranguing, encouraging, working with shovel and crowbar when he had to. Fighting against time, fighting against daylight— And he moved the tanks. That,

Allison thought, was the incredible thing. Somehow he moved the tanks. He was a master tankman, the most superb one Allison had ever seen. And if they had any edge, any hope at all of success, that was it. Everything rode on Marc's skill and leadership.

Once, they halted. A soldier from Hausa's force lay beside the path, in terrible agony. A Gaboon viper's bite is like that of a cobra, and there was no hope for him, he had to be abandoned. He watched them file past with stoic, pain-filled eyes. "We ought to have put him out of his misery," Marc said bitterly. "But there's one chance in a hundred, maybe two, that he might beat it. He'll have to fight it out for himself, though. We can't help." And they rolled on.

Now Allison felt himself caught up in a nightmare that would never end. This jungle was going on forever. They were Flying Dutchmen, lost in it, doomed to traverse it for eternity. He put his eyes to his periscope. It was still there, the great dark barrier. Then he stiffened. Men swarmed in the lights of the tank—armed men. Instinctively he reached for the machine-gun trigger on the power traverse. Then he took his hand away as he recognized a tall, half-naked figure lurching wearily toward them. They had caught up with Hausa and the infantry. That meant there was no more road ahead—only raw jungle, to be navigated foot by foot. Despair gripped Allison, black and total. Hell, they were finished! So was Allison Trading Company. So were the refugees in M'nanda. He seemed to hear O'Kerry's voice again, in the hotel suite there: *Two of them ... bound together, petrol poured over them ... a match thrown.* That was only a sample of what would be happening in the city in a few more hours.

As if it took the last of his strength, Hausa mounted the tank. He and Marc conferred a moment ot two. Then Marc snapped a command. The bow gunner climbed out of his compartment, handed his helmet to Hausa. Hausa dropped into the seat behind the machine gun, slumped there, a picture of utter exhaustion, discouragement. Then Marc's voice rasped in the intercom. "All right, driver, move out! And give this bitch all she's got! Tear right on through!" He dropped down into the turret. "Let's go!"

The tank lurched forward. It confronted the black, solid wall of jungle. Hungrily, it tore into it, bucking and heaving as its bow slammed against all that tangled growth. Trees crunched, toppled. Like a maddened animal, the tank threw itself against the jungle again and again, with all the power of its great engine. Steel against wood, and wood gave, vines popped, the tracks clawed. Allison watched the gun, swinging it frantically, keeping it clear. The tank hammered deeper and deeper into that fantastic, impenetrable foliage. It struck trees, bounced off, struck them again; they went down, crashing, and the tank waddled over their carcasses. Marc was using the tank as a sledgehammer now, a sledgehammer to drive through, knock down, tear up, make a way. Within the turret Allison and the loader were thrown around like peas; yet Allison watched the gun; he watched the gun.

The driver fought his gears, his levers; Marc kept up a stream of rapid-fire directions, urgings, pleadings, cursing. The infantry aboard had long since dropped off, out of harm's way. Then ahead, through the periscope, Allison saw their way blocked by a tree it seemed impossible for the tank to hurt. Nevertheless, Marc threw the Sherman against it, and it shivered. The whole tank rang and vibrated with the impact. Marc screamed for the driver to back up, charge again. He did. Again the tree shivered, but it did not go down. A third time the Sherman charged, slamming hard into the massive trunk; then the tank bucked, rolled, almost turned turtle as the tree crashed down, its whole enormous root structure coming up under the belly of its destroyer. Allison was thrown hard against the turret wall; only his crash helmet saved him from concussion. Then the tank came down, hard and level, waddled on, and suddenly Allison let out a shout that was drowned in the engine sound.

Marc's voice crowed on the interphone, "That's right! We made it! We're in the clear!"

And through his periscope, Allison saw for the first time that night a horizon, as the great tank ripped out of the jungle and into the open, with the beginning of the high plain of M'nanda rising before it.

Then Marc's voice again. "Headlights off. Wait for the infantry to load up. Then we go flat-out."

CHAPTER 12

SITTING BEHIND THE GUN, John Allison no longer felt fatigue. He was still sweating, but not from the heat; he felt curiously cold. Now they were on the last leg of it; they were going into battle. An hour from now, two, he might be dead. If he died, it would not likely be in any neat or easy fashion; tankers did not die that way. Not with all that gasoline and high explosive around them.

And yet, that was not what chilled him. What nagged at him now was the possibility that Marc had put too much trust in him, too much faith. *Machiavelli was an Italian too . . .* Suppose, all along, this had been some elaborate trick, suppose it were a trap that Rinaldi had somehow set. Suppose, instead of speeding to possible victory, Marc were speeding to disaster—and he was the one responsible?

There was that to occupy him as the tanks roared through the night, climbing, always climbing. And there was this too: Suppose he were inadequate? He was a gunner, yes; he felt at home behind the cannon. But after all these years, this would be his first real combat in armor. And the real thing was very different from simulation. A moment's hesitation, miscalculation, could mean the difference between life and death. And, damn it, it had been so long—

In the glow of the turret's travel light, he looked at his watch. Four o'clock. Another half hour would see them outside M'nanda. His hand sweated on the power traverse. He bent to the periscope; already, it seemed to him, the sky was lightening.

They were on a road now, had struck it a half hour after leaving the jungle. Marc had held to it; miserable though it was, it would lead toward the north-south highway running into M'nanda; any minute now they should come to that. Meanwhile, they swept through an area where, not long before, combat must have raged. It was scabbed with deserted villages, half their houses leveled by artillery, their pitiful crops trampled in the mud; twice, gaunt stray dogs ran across their path, and once a goat; they saw no other life. Then Marc's voice exploded in the intercom. "Allison! Switch your box to radio!"

Allison's hand hit the toggle. Immediately his ears were full of gibberish, some native dialect, distorted by distance and static. Then he heard it—a deep, familiar voice, dominating the conversation. The sound of it was like a blow in the pit of the stomach. All at once Allison's doubts vanished. He sat up straight, knocked the switch back to intercom.

"You've heard his voice since I have!" Marc's tone was excited. "Is it him?"

"Yes," Allison said. "It's Rinaldi."

"Hot damn! I thought I recognized that accent! He's speaking N'terua; no radio silence, he wants everybody to be damned sure it's me! And he's on his way—in person!"

"How far?"

"I don't know, but we're in a horse-race now. The highway's not more than five minutes ahead. Everybody button up. If there's a roadblock, we don't stop, we shoot straight through."

"All right," Allison said. "I'm loading a round of shot."

"Roger," said Marc in the old radio lingo to which he still clung. The breech slammed closed as the loader shoved in the big shell with the heel of his hand. Allison's foot inched closer to the firing solenoid. At any moment now they might be in action. At any moment now the test would come—

Hausa and the driver dropped their seats, slammed down hatches. The tank slowed; poorer visibility. Only Marc remained exposed, high in the turret, watching, observing . . .

Then it came, a strange vibration—bullets bouncing off of armor. Marc's fire command was instantaneous. "Gunner, BOG, doughs, those woods right front, machine-gun!" Allison twisted the power traverse handle, picked up a dark bulk that was a grove. It sparkled with the muzzle flashes of many rifles. Allison pulled the trigger. He could not hear the machine gun as it fired, but he could see the tracers arcing toward those flashes. Another stream of them sprayed from Hausa's gun, from the guns of the tank behind. Then Marc's voice came again. "Driver, hard right! Pull hard right! We're coming to the pavement." They were past the grove now; the whole movement of the tank changed suddenly; they were on the pavement.

Then Marc's voice cried out again: "Gunner! Armored car!" But Allison already saw it, a Saladin, there in the middle of the road. Allison whipped down the gun to point-blank range, swinging the turret simultaneously. Before Marc could finish the command, his foot stamped the solenoid. He could not even hear himself yell into his intercom, *On the way!* He saw the red tracer of the projectile hurl itself squarely at that squat, low shape. It smashed through the Saladin like steel through butter, knocked it sideways off the road. Bright flame ballooned, then was gone as the tank sped past. The breech clanged as the loader slugged in another round. Allison sucked in a heavy breath. *First blood,* he thought. But it would be different, very different, when they met tanks.

Now the highway was open before them. Allison shrugged on his shirt; if they caught fire, it would be some protection from the flames. Outside, the light was metamorphosing into a leaden gray. Not long now, not long . . . Then he saw them, far ahead, through the rain: the lights of M'nanda, like a scattering of jewels on the great plain. And his hand gripped the elevating wheel in a clutch like iron. Before the city, bright tongues of flame winked back and forth in two directions— cannon fire!

Marc's groan was audible in the intercom. "It's Rinaldi! He's beat us there! He's clobbering what defenses Kopapo left! But he'll beat us in, goddammit, he'll beat us in!"

Allison struck the steel of the turret in frustration. He knew what that meant. If Rinaldi charged into the town before they could stop him, he held the whole city hostage. In a superior defensive position, he could hold them off, call up Centurions from bases toward the east. If Rinaldi got into M'nanda first, they had lost, they were ruined.

And he was going to make it. Through the telescope, Allison saw the hellish fire laid down on the defenders, the diminishment of their own firing. Kopapo had left nothing but a screen; Rinaldi was chewing it up fast. He had to be made to turn, to fight Marc first. But that was impossible. The moment he knew they were coming, he'd charge on in— Allison began to curse. So close, so damned close, and yet so far, so late . . . Then, with sudden decision, he sat up straight. "Marc! What frequency's he on?"

"Radio? Same as ours! But—"

"Then I'm going on radio!" Allison hit the switch before Marc could answer. "Hello," he said. "This is John Allison. This is John Allison calling Sandro Rinaldi, before M'nanda. Come in, Sandro Rinaldi. This is Allison. I'm still alive!"

Marc said something incoherent. Allison's earphones crackled as he strained to listen, caught only the confused battle commands of Rinaldi's column, in dialect. "Come in, Sandro Rinaldi!" he yelled. "I'm with Marc, we're hitting you on the flank! Come in, Rinaldi! Marc's here with me! This is your chance to kill him and end the war!"

Hausa's voice cut in fiercely. "You goddam traitor! I'll shoot—" He was struggling around in the bow compartment, pistol in hand, trying to bring it to bear. Marc's voice overrode his. "No, Roy, wait—"

There was silence in the earphones now, dead, total. Then, loud and clear, Rinaldi was there, in English. "Hello, John Allison. This is Sandro Rinaldi. Where are you broadcasting from?"

"From a tank, five thousand yards on your right."

"Impossible! Marc cannot get tanks north of the Acanara!"

"Watch my muzzle blast, watch my tracer!" Allison snapped. He elevated the gun, fired. The tracer in the base of the projectile made a high arc. "See that, Rinaldi? I'm alive. We're here. Come and fight."

"No," said Rinaldi promptly. "The way into the city is clear. I'm going in." He laughed. "Sorry, Allison. Sorry, Marc. You'll be able to commit no atrocities in M'nanda."

"No atrocities," Allison said. He fought to keep the desperation out of his voice, make it scathing. "I see. Well, I was wrong, wasn't I? I thought you were a Roman, suckled by a wolf. But it wasn't a wolf, was it, Sandro? It was a mongrel bitch. I thought you were one Italian soldier who would fight. But I was wrong. You don't fight any better than you make love. Remember what Erika said? Remember that, Rinaldi? She said you were no good at—"

Rinaldi's voice cut in, utterly cool. "Marc, are you there? Over."

"I'm here, Rinaldi," said Marc. "Over."

"Then Allison didn't lie. Very well. Then come. We shall settle this war here and now, between the two of us. John Allison. John Allison? Over."

"Here, Sandro. Over."

"I shall show you something, John Allison." Rinaldi's voice was hard. "I shall show you that it was indeed a wolf. Over and out." Then the radio went dead.

Marc let out a whistling breath. "John. By God, John, you did it! Get ready for combat. Rinaldi's tanks are changing front."

In the rain-streaked dawn, Allison saw them do it. Slowly, ponderously, like enormous beetles at that distance, they wheeled and formed a line. Against the smudge of sky, black palls of smoke arose from the knocked-out armored cars that had been part of Kopapo's overmatched screen before the city.

Meanwhile, Marc gave orders of his own. The rebel Shermans also left the highway, formed a wide-spaced rank across the plain, with Marc's tank in the center. The infantry dismounted, scattered through the waist-high grass.

Meanwhile, day came swiftly. Allison's view of the field through the telescope improved. Across the nearly three miles that separated the armies, the plain was open, shelterless, except for— Then he tensed. Except for a gentle roll of ground, thousands of yards distant from their own line, but very close to Rinaldi's and running parallel with it. As Rinaldi's tanks deployed, he held his breath.

But Rinaldi was no fool. He had seen that swell in the terrain too, and now the great, dun beetles that were his tanks took advantage of it. As Marc's line remained poised, motionless, Rinaldi's tanks lumbered into the shelter that low ridge offered and did not reappear. Spread out behind it, they went into defilade, their hulls protected, only the turrets and the guns clear. Allison's mouth went dry; his hands sweated on the elevating wheel and the power traverse. Whatever advantage in numbers Marc had, that cover negated.

Marc knew that too. Standing high in the turret, he scanned the plain with binoculars, and Allison heard him curse softly into the intercom. This was the penalty for keeping Rinaldi out of the better shelter of M'nanda, the penalty for losing the edge of surprise. Now they would have to charge without cover for miles across the open, full into the fire of those hidden guns. They would have to race, weave and dodge, and they would not dare stop to fire and make targets of themselves until they had closed. Like cavalry! Allison thought suddenly. Like cavalry charging artillery! This was not going to be a tank battle— it would be a cavalry charge!

Marc's voice in the intercom verified that. "Driver, listen to

me. When I give the signal to move out, you give her every bit
of speed she's got. We're going to zig-zag, but I want you to
bear for the center of their line. You hear me? The center of
the line."

Allison's pulses hammered. Yes, the center. Rinaldi would be
there ... Then Marc's voice came to him. "Gunner, hold your
fire until my order. You'll have to fire while moving, with the
gyro. We don't have the ammo to make an artillery duel out of
this. We'll go in fast as hell; after I give the order, you can take
any target of opportunity."

"Roger," Allison said.

The big Sherman, poised, trembled like a warhorse on a tight
rein. The driver and Hausa closed their hatches. Marc dropped
the seat on which he stood a little lower, but he did not come
down into the turret. His head and shoulders still protruded,
exposed, vulnerable.

And so now ... Allison thought. Now, after fifteen years ...
By the standards of modern warfare, this was a small, an insig-
nificant action; a handful of tanks, that was all. And yet, the
lives of hundreds of people in M'nanda hung on its outcome, of
thousands, millions, in the rest of Acanara ... and even of
more thousands, perhaps, all unknowing, now at rest half a
world away in America.

He waited for Marc to give the order. When it came, it was
not the usual, "Driver, move out." Instead, Marc's voice was
an excited blare in the intercom as he swept down his hand.
"Charge!" he yelled.

The line of tanks rolled forward, slowly at first, in low gear.
Then, quickly, it picked up speed. Now, through the telescope,
the grassy plain flowed swiftly toward Allison, then seemed to
hurtle at him. The tank rose and fell and bucked; it was indeed
like riding a galloping horse. Now he quit thinking, feeling; all
emotion, all being, concentrated, focused, through the lenses of

his sight, his hands unconsciously fighting the gun, keeping it lined and ready.

Five hundred yards gone, a thousand— They were in high gear now, and within maximum effective range. The tank zig-zagged right, left, and Allison whirled the turret to compensate, never taking his sight off the center of that rise ahead. Rinaldi was there; he wanted Rinaldi; Marc wanted Rinaldi—

He brought the gun down, checking off the yardage in the gunsight's reticle. Three thousand yards and closing... Still, not a shot had been fired. Rinaldi's guns were as silent as theirs, waiting, tracking... Twenty-five hundred yards... The tank's engine roared, it seemed to throw itself at the ridge. Why didn't Marc give the order, why didn't he—? Two thousand yards—

Then, suddenly, terrifyingly, the plain ahead erupted in smoke and flame. Rinaldi's tanks had opened fire, and a curtain of death came down before Marc's line, a barrage like a wall. Allison's view was blanked by thundering high explosive; his foot reached for the solenoid. Marc had to give the word, he had to!

And now they were in the midst of that hell; he heard shrapnel and machine-gun fire ring on the turret as if men with hammers sledged it. The tank slewed, skittered, and as Allison swung the turret, he saw a chilling thing. One of Marc's tanks halted suddenly, as if it had hit some great, invisible wall. Instantly it was enveloped in a balloon of fire, a terrible orange ball of flame. Allison saw the commander's figure disappear, engulfed by that fireball. Then it was past; Marc's Sherman hurtled on. And now, ringing in Allison's ears came Marc's command. *"Fire!"*

Allison caught the muzzle flare of a Judas Sherman behind the ridge, crushed the solenoid. He saw the tracer flare of the round of shot in the scope, lost it, knew that he had missed. The empty shell rang on the floor, the breech clanged as a new one was rammed home. Allison fired again.

It was like shooting from a galloping horse; again he had no idea whether he had hit or missed, and Marc was too busy coordinating the attack to give him directions. Smoke swirled; the other tanks began to fire; the top of the rise erupted in mud and flame. In the gray light, the long spurting muzzle flares of the enemy tanks were clearly visible. So, too, was the oily black smoke that boiled up suddenly from the right of their line.

Now they were climbing, full into the fire of the enemy guns. *This time—* Allison thought and waited. White smoke veiled his sight, then blew. He saw the mushroom shape of a tank turret, its gun swinging toward him. Despite the menace of that long, snouted weapon taking aim, he did not hurry. He depressed the gun, took up slack, traversed it, lined that steel mushroom precisely in the sight, hit the solenoid. Marc was already yelling a frantic fire order, but Allison did not hear it. The gun slammed back, then forward into battery. The turret of the enemy tank jerked convulsively, strange for so heavy, rigid a dome of steel. At almost point-blank range, the round of armor-piercing had smashed through its armor; in the next instant the force of an explosion within blew open its hatches, bulged out its metal. Then they were over the ridge and among the enemy.

After that, it was all a blur. Allison could see only patches, fragments of the world through his sights as the tank bucked, lurched, in a swirl of smoke. Sky, earth, the dark steel of armor, the flash of flame: it was a jigsaw vision. When he saw a target, he fired. Only once was he sure of another hit. Meanwhile, blow after blow rang on the turret, and once there was a great one, a stunning one, as a round of shot hit obliquely and glanced off.

Then Allison heard Marc screaming something to the driver in the intercom. "Turn right, turn right! There! After the sonofabitch!" Instinctively, Allison traversed the gun. Then as Marc's tank skidded, straightened and rocketed on, he saw it, clear of the battle—another Sherman, three hundred, four hundred yards distant—and rocketing at top speed straight for the city, fleeing the melee. Allison formed a single, excited, soundless word: *Rinaldi!* Then Marc's tank was pursuing.

Rinaldi's cannon was swung to the rear; it fired as Rinaldi fled. Allison saw the tongue of flame, the flicker of the co-axial machine gun. But the round missed and now Marc's own tank was clear of the battle and on level ground. "Driver, stop!" The Sherman halted. Then Marc's first formal fire command sounded in John Allison's ears. "Gunner, moving tank, shot—" Marc was still exposed in the turret, crouching low, lining up the fleeing tank with the blade sight there. "Traverse right, steady . . . on. Five hundred . . . Lead five—" Then Marc gave a strange sigh. "Fire . . ."

Mechanically, Allison's hands whipped through the adjustments, swung the gun to cover the fleeing tank. Then, just as he moved his foot down on the solenoid, something from above fell on him, knocked him forward. His hand jerked the elevating wheel as he was crushed by the weight of Marc's body. As the gun fired, it bounced up, the shot going wild. Allison twisted. Marc lay sprawled across him, eyes wide, lips moving, torso red with blood. Allison struggled to get free, to find the sight. Hausa gave a frantic cry in the intercom: "Goddammit, shoot!" But there was no chance to fire again.

All at once the tank was smashed sideways, as if by the impact of an enormous hand. There was a deafening sound, indescribable, of heavy metal smashing. Allison, Marc and loader were all thrown together and suddenly the air was rank with the fumes of gas. There was no more thunder of engine, but a strange roar from somewhere.

Hit, on fire . . . Panic surged in Allison. He struggled upward, saw Marc draped crazily across the gun. Somehow, he got purchase, got his feet beneath him. He seized Marc's body; it was slippery with blood and sweat. Marc gave a cry of pain as Allison jerked him erect.

Then there were hands reaching through the canted turret hatch—Roy Hausa's! "Lemme have 'im! This mother's on fire!" Hausa seized Marc, dragged him with enormous strength straight up through the hatch. As Marc's booted feet disappeared, Allison surged after them. Flame gusted close as he tumbled down the side of the tank, into the rain-wet grass. He landed hard and the loader fell on top of him.

Allison rolled free, got to his knees. Five hundred yards away, Rinaldi's tank had stopped. Nearby, Hausa was dragging Marc well away from the burning tank. The loader ran past Allison, vanished into the grass.

Hausa screamed at Allison, "Gimme a hand! Gotta get to cover!"

Allison, crouched low, ran toward them through the grass. Then he fell flat as machine-gun fire chopped the air. Hausa threw himself atop Marc, crushing him to the ground, shielding him with his own body. Then the whine of lead ceased. Allison got to his knees. Suddenly he was aware of another sound—a tank's accelerating roar. His head jerked around, and he froze. Rinaldi's tank was fleeing no longer. It had turned, was changing direction. Its turret swung forward again, the gun like the snout of a great animal testing the air. Then it began to roll forward, picking up speed. Allison swallowed hard as he realized its intent. It was headed straight for Marc and Hausa!

Hausa jumped to his feet, grabbed Marc beneath the arms, began to run, dragging the general's body. Allison saw his eyes flashing white in terror, his chest heaving with the strain of the burden. The hatch of Rinaldi's tank turret opened; a figure emerged from it, helmeted, goggled. Then it shoved back the goggles; Allison saw the handsome face, the wide mouth, the triumphant grin that twisted it, as Rinaldi gave his driver instructions to run them down and crush them.

Hausa changed direction, so did the oncoming tank. Hausa changed again, then stumbled, fell. The tank was only a couple of hundred yards away now. Hausa scrambled to his feet, tried to get another grip on Marc—

Allison jumped to his feet too, reaching for his pistol. If he could knock that tall figure out of the turret— But the gun was gone, lost in his fall. He turned, looking desperately, saw Marc's tank fifty yards away, canted, flame billowing from its back deck. For perhaps a second, he stood poised, staring. Then there was no more time to hesitate, no more time to think. He ran toward the burning tank.

Like a monkey, he went up over the bow; but he cringed back when a searing blast of heat hit him from the burning engine. The turret was not engulfed in the flames yet, but it might be at any minute. Allison hesitated, turned.

Hausa had fallen again over the dead weight of Marc. Rinaldi's tank roared straight at him.

Allison sucked in a long breath. Then he dropped into the turret.

It was like dropping into hell. Already, low flames were playing brightly across the floor, dancing around the brass cylinders that were armor-piercing and high-explosive shells in the ready rack. Allison fought back a terror almost paralyzing. There would, if he were lucky, be time for one shot before the whole thing blew.

He scooped up a round of high explosive. He shoved it into the breech, and the block slammed closed. Then he seized the elevating and manual traversing wheels and cranked the turret of the tank.

It moved smoothly on its ring. Allison disregarded the searing pain on ankles and calves as he bent into the sight. He searched desperately through that narrow aperture—

Then he had it, the high flank of Rinaldi's speeding tank. He aimed slowly, carefully. One round, high explosive. If it missed, they were through. Then he crunched the solenoid.

Nothing happened. There was no power in the tank.

Allison cursed. He aimed again, saw Hausa's terrified face, then, fifty yards back, Rinaldi's triumphant grin, high in the turret. He triggered the manual switch on the breechblock.

The gun slammed back, then forward, as the round fired.

And there was no time to see if he had won or lost; flame was all around him. He scrabbled up through the hatch, burning. Still not drawing breath, he came out of that steel inferno, launched himself through gusting flame, searing air, and hit the ground hard. Rain poured on him, blessed, cooling. He rolled through wet grass, putting out the flaming cloth about his legs. Then he came up on his knees, staring through the driving rain at Rinaldi's tank, fifty yards away, half that distance short of Hausa crouched over Marc's body, eyes white and enormous in his coppery face.

The round of high explosive had caught Rinaldi's Sherman in the engine compartment. Its terrific force, dead-on, had ripped away the track, canted the tank as a slewed, crazy angle. And even as Allison watched, there was a dull *whuff* like the puff of breath from some enormous dying animal; in that instant, a bright, orange billow of flame roiled up from behind the turret, a huge, abrupt mushroom of it, topped by a twist of black, oily smoke, as the gasoline went. In one second more, the great metal monster was at the core of a roaring inferno.

Rinaldi! Allison tried to rise, fumbling for a pistol that wasn't there, as, in the midst of that swirl of fire, the head and shoulders of a man appeared in the turret hatch. He caught a glimpse of a white agonized face beneath a crash helmet, of a mouth gaped wide in a soundless scream. Then Allison sank back strengthlessly, as the figure vanished as quickly as it had come, dropping back inside the turret. Flame roared up, obscured all: black smoke billowed over the pyre from which no one had escaped.

Allison sat there with the rain falling on him, suddenly totally empty, drained. Marc's tank burned not far behind him with a gusting sound; he could feel the blast of heat on his back, knew vaguely that it was urgent that he move, get away before the ammo went. For the moment, he was unable to; he only sat there in the rain.

Then, in front of Rinaldi's incandescent tomb, Roy Hausa

scrambled unsteadily to his feet. Bare-headed, naked torso gleaming in the downpour, he looked around, as if dazed at his deliverance. His eyes went from one burning tank to the other, and to Allison, sitting between them. Then Hausa bent, got his hands under Marc's armpits, and dragged Marc a long way off, through the grass. He put Marc down tenderly; and then he shambled stiffly, limping a bit, to where Allison sat.

He stood over Allison, looking down at him. "End of Rinaldi," he said dully, voice barely audible above the roar of the burning tanks. Rain streamed down his face like tears; his eyes were opaque, strange. "It's over. The war."

Allison's lips soundlessly formed the word: "Yes."

Then Hausa drew his pistol from its holster. He stood there with it dangling at his side. "And now I got to kill you," he said.

John Allison only looked at him blankly, not comprehending. "What?" he whispered.

"Goddam," Hausa said. "It's funny. I ought to want to do it. But I don't. Still, I can't help it. You ruined 'em—all my plans. There ain't but one way to save 'em now."

"Hausa," Allison said. "You're in shock. You're crazy."

"No, I ain't," Hausa said. The gun still dangled at his side. "Marc's still alive and he's won the war. So I got to kill you and I got to kill him. Out here now, where there's nobody watching."

Allison's dazed brain tried to make sense of this. "You didn't want Marc to win the war?" he whispered.

"He had to lose it. But not until Rinaldi got American equipment. I had to keep him alive until then, so that when he died, it was the United States that killed him. Then what I have been workin' for so long, so hard, would have happened. We'd have had the martyr we needed—"

Suddenly Allison understood. "The Black Liberators," he said.

"Not only them. Everybody at home who worshipped Marc.

Rising up in their anger—" Hausa's voice mounted now, oddly like that of a preacher delivering a sermon. "Rising up in their anger at last. Overthrowing the whole rotten system. Because it was American tanks and American planes that killed Marc. But you've ruined that now." His eyes had come alive; Allison saw the gleam of fanaticism in them. "And I've still got to make it work somehow."

"Hausa," Allison said hoarsely, "you're crazy. It won't work now."

"Maybe it will. If Marc's dead and you're dead and I'm the only survivor. If I'm the witness to how the American secret agent killed him in cold blood at the time of his victory. As soon as we're in M'nanda, I spread the story." His eyes glittered. "Once it's made known, it'll be like fire, you can't stamp it out. It'll hit the States, people will come out in the streets—" His voice was harsh. "He'd won, and you Fascist bastards couldn't let him win. So you shot him. And they'll rise up, oh, they'll rise up, believe me." His face worked. "I don't want to do it," he said. "Christ, I don't. I love that man. But I got to, you see? I got to." And he raised the pistol, lined it on Allison.

Allison's paralysis broke. Despairingly, he threw himself aside, face down in the grass. At that instant the whole world seemed to explode. The earth shook; overhead, there was a ripping, roaring rush, as if a freight train thundered over him. A blast and then another blast as he hugged the ground, while the ammunition in the burning tank blew and blew again.

Then it was over. Except for the sound of falling rain, the earth was silent. Allison lay there, not sure he was still alive. And yet he was. He moved a hand to prove it. Then he sat up, fearfully, until his dazed eyes came to rest on the crumpled, bloody thing in the grass before him. As the armor-piercing shells in the tank had exploded, Hausa had taken the full blast of all that outward ripping steel.

Allison just sat and looked at the thing in the grass for a moment; then he turned his gaze away. Except for the gusty sound of the burning tanks, the rattle of rifle fire in the distance, the plain was unearthly quiet. And it seemed to Allison that there was no one left alive on earth except himself. He sat there foolishly in the rain, feeling that. Then a rasping groan from the grass where Marc lay brought him to reality.

Shakily and with effort, he got to his feet. His legs hurt where they had been seared as he tottered forward. "Marc—"

The general lay on his back, the blood clotted in the bullet wound in his shoulder. His eyes were closed. His lips, ashen, moved. "Where's Roy?"

After a moment Allison said, "He's dead."

"Killed in action," Marc whispered.

"Yes," Allison said. He dropped to his knees beside Marc.

Marc lay there. It was hard to tell whether it was rain or tears on his cheeks. Then he said, "The poor son of a bitch. Oh, the poor son of a bitch."

"Yes," Allison said. Then he said, "Rinaldi's dead too. We've won."

Marc's eyes opened. "Then I got to get into M'nanda. John, you got to get me into M'nanda."

"I will," said Allison. He raised his head, looked around. He saw black palls of smoke rising from the plain. Amid them, only two tanks moved, both rebels, crawling toward the highway. He stood up and waved his arms frantically. The tanks did not see him. Allison kept on waving. Then one of the iron monsters changed direction, waddled toward him. Allison waited there beside the wounded general until the Sherman roared up and men dismounted to help him.

CHAPTER 13

FROM THE OFFICE of the president of Acanara, the docks of Ogoro were visible, and Allison could see, in the bright, hot sunlight, the big gantry cranes unloading tank after tank from the ship tied up there. American M-60's, forty of them . . .

Too little and too late, he thought. At least for Rinaldi, for Victor Nadunda. Then he turned his attention back to Calvin Buckley.

"Of course," Buckley was saying, "we're delighted with the prospect of a coalition government. While I don't think you can count on any more military aid, I'm sure all serious consideration will be given to credits to restore and repair your economy."

Behind the president's desk, Peter Baunda nodded. A very dark, bony man with iron-gray hair, his voice was soft and cultivated. "I think the first favor we would ask, Mr. Buckley, would be the recall of Ambassador Middleton." His eyes shuttled to his personal military adviser, Gil Markham, then to the new defense minister of Acanara, General Lewis Kopapo. "I assume you gentlemen agree."

"Definitely," Kopapo said at once. "Hell, yes," grunted Marc.

Buckley smiled. "I think it's safe to say that's already in the works."

"And one other thing," Baunda said. "I trust your government will take due recognition of Mr. Allison's services to us."

"Oh, yes; yes, indeed." Buckley's answer was quick. "You

211

understand, of course, Mr. Allison has always worked closely with us."

"Of course," said Baunda dryly. He was silent for a moment. "Well, Mr. Buckley, we shall look forward to receiving your new ambassador."

"Yes," Buckley said uncomfortably. "I think you'll find him very sympathetic. Well, thank you very much, Mr. President, for this interview. Consider those tanks out there yours, and don't worry about the terms. We'll make appropriate arrangements with Mr. Allison." He turned to Allison. "John, can I give you a lift back to the hotel?"

Allison arose, a little stiffly because of the bandages still on his ankles, though the burns were minor. "Why not? General Marc will ride with us, if you don't mind."

"Delighted," Buckley said. They shook hands with Lewis Kopapo and Peter Baunda and went out.

In the embassy car, Buckley looked at Marc. "General, I didn't care to mention it before the president, but there's something else. If you care to return to the United States, I think there'd be no trouble about any of those old charges against you."

"And I'd be where you could keep me under surveillance." Marc's voice was a rasp, his eyes hard. "No, thanks, Mr. Buckley. Besides, you don't want me in the United States at this stage of the game. My flash point's too low and, after all, I'm married to a white woman. If I went home, no telling what kind of rebellion I'd be mixed up in next, and I'm getting too old for any more fighting."

Buckley bit his lower lip. "As you please. Anyhow, the charges will be taken care of; you may come and go as your duties require. And, unless you renounce it, you'll still have your citizenship."

Allison watched Marc's face. For one instant, then, the hard façade broke. "I didn't expect— That's no small thing."

"No," Buckley said. "It isn't. Now, please, may I ask you

both—what do you think of the real viability of this coalition government? I mean, apart from Middleton's gibberish."

"It'll stand," Marc said promptly. "What happened was this. We took M'nanda—"

"Yes," Buckley said.

"And I got on the radio to Kopapo. That swung him back from his assault on our territory. He didn't know the slenderness of our forces then, and rather than attack the city, cause a lot of civilian casualties, he agreed to a parley. Then, when I convinced him that Rinaldi had planned to have him shot— Well, he didn't like Rinaldi anyhow, couldn't understand why Rinaldi wouldn't turn him loose to run down those Judas tanks. Anyhow, I had enough proof so it all fell into place ... And besides, he thinks blacks should be governed by blacks. We negotiated, and ... well, being defense minister of Acanara is a lot better than being stood up against a wall and shot. So we agreed to use his Centurions to mount a joint assault on Ogoro. Nadunda had no guts, Rinaldi was his guts. When he heard our column was on the way, he bugged out. He's in Liberia now with just about all the hard currency that was in the treasury, and instead of coming back, he'll probably screw himself to death. Anyhow, we took Ogoro without twenty shots being fired. Oh, Kopapo's a strong man, and powerful, but I'm strong and powerful too. I think we can get along. I'll watch him and he'll watch me, and neither one of us will be able to mount a coup."

"Hopefully," said Buckley.

"Listen," Marc said. "You come back in ten years, and if this isn't the most prosperous, peaceful country in Africa, I'll eat your hat."

"I hope it will be," Buckley said.

Maria and Erika waited in the hotel dining room, and of the two, it was hard to say which was more striking. Maria had gained weight, lost that haunted look; wearing the smartest clothes Ogoro shops could provide, she was stately, almost regal in her bearing. On the other hand, what Erika had been through had stripped away every bit of immaturity; what Allison saw now was a self-confident and lovely woman, with all illusion and uncertainty burned away. The very sight of her struck a sudden, surprising chord in Allison.

Marc was ebullient at lunch. He drank too much, praised Allison too highly. "All right," he bellowed. "So you leave tomorrow. Well, by God, any time you want a job, you can be general of the Acanaran Armored Force—and I'll supply the burnt cork!"

Maria laid a hand on his. "Not so loud, darling." The smile she gave him was radiant.

"Listen, woman, you're talking to an American citizen! You know what that means? An American citizen! I can take you to New York, Fifth Avenue, a lot of places—" Then some of his euphoria drained away. "But not everywhere," he said almost dully. He turned to Allison. "Johnny, you really got to leave?"

"I'm long overdue in London and then I've got to go back to the States," Allison said.

Marc turned to Erika. "You're going with him?"

Allison looked at her. Something rose, poised itself within him. Then it dropped as she said, "No. Not right away."

He felt a sudden loneliness. "Couldn't you get an assignment in New York?"

Erika's eyes met his. "I don't want one. Not yet. First I have to go home and talk to my brother."

"Oh," Marc said, sensing something here he didn't understand. "Yeah. Of course." Then he turned to Allison. "Anyhow, Johnny, we'll give you a send-off at the airport. Jesus, will we give you a send-off! You'd better figure on two days in London to sober up!"

Maria arose. "Of course, darling. But now it's time for your nap." She plucked at Marc's sleeve.

Marc stood up. "You see how it is, eh, Johnny?"

"Come," Maria said firmly, and she led the general away.

"Well, I've got work to do," Buckley said, and he also arose. "Johnny. Erika. See you later." He went out, leaving the two of them alone at the table.

Allison looked at Erika. "I had hoped you'd come back to the States. Or London."

She looked down at her coffee. "Maybe I will, soon. Meanwhile, don't you come often to Germany?"

"Yes," he said.

"Then we shall see each other. But I must have time to think."

"Think about what?"

She met his gaze. Something within him moved at the beauty of her. "Very frankly," she said, "about what you do. My father sold gas tubing. You sell guns, tanks, airplanes. I must think about that." Her eyes pleaded with him. "You understand?"

"I understand," Allison said.

"For a while, at least, I must remain myself. I have just learned how to be myself again. That is more important even than love. If I approve of anything someone does simply because I love him— Well, then, I am lost again. And I do not want to be lost again."

"All right," said Allison. "Take your time." But he felt a curious sadness, and he said, "Let's have another drink."

Erika looked at him. "What time does your airplane leave?"

"Not until late this afternoon."

Her hand moved across the table, touched his. "Then perhaps we could have it in my room." Her voice was soft. "And say a proper goodbye."

"Why not?" Allison said. He stood up.

Marc had already taken care of the check. As they walked across the lobby, Allison savored the brush of Erika's hip against his. But he was thinking too, almost against his will, of the cable from London, and the man waiting there to buy fifteen thousand M-1 American rifles.

As they got into the lift and Erika leaned against him, he reminded himself that his signature was needed on the contract within three days if the deal were to go through.

ABOUT THE AUTHOR

RICHARD MEADE is the alter ego of an American who has traveled widely and whose novels under his own name have been major book club selections in the United States, Germany and Scandinavia, as well as having been translated into many other languages.

Mr. Meade, a Southerner, is married and the father of three sons. He has always been interested in weaponry and boasts the distinction of being the only American member in the history of the four-hundred-year-old Klosterneuburg, Austria, Shooting Society.